SOMEONE IS WATCHING

Fascinated by the photo of the child known as Amy Bennett, the dark-haired man carried it into his bedroom, where he propped it up against the clock radio on the nightstand next to his bed. Looking at the little girl's smiling face made him feel good, and he hadn't felt really good in a long, long time.

His glance fell upon the binoculars he'd bought that afternoon. He picked them up and walked over to his bedroom window. Pushing back the drapes, he peered through the high-powered lenses across the courtyard and pool area toward the windows of Jennifer Bennett's apartment. Her drapes were drawn and her lights were turned off. But that didn't matter so much right now. He had her on tape, and he had the child captured in the photograph. Yawning, he set his binoculars down on the windowsill, where they would be handy when he resumed his surveillance tomorrow.

As he pulled back the bedcovers and crawled into bed, the little girl's image smiled at him from the nightstand. It was the last thing he saw before he fell into a deep, dream-filled sleep.

Books by Nancy Baker Jacobs

*Daddy's Gone A-Hunting**
*Cradle and All**
See Mommy Run
The Silver Scalpel
A Slash of Scarlet
The Turquoise Tattoo
Deadly Companion

*Published by HarperPaperbacks

DADDY'S GONE A-HUNTING

Nancy Baker Jacobs

HarperPaperbacks
A Division of HarperCollins Publishers

This is a work of fiction. The characters, incidents, and dialogues are products of the author's imagination and are not to be construed as real. Any resemblance to actual events or persons, living or dead, is entirely coincidental.

HarperPaperbacks *A Division of* HarperCollins*Publishers*
10 East 53rd Street, New York, N.Y. 10022

Copyright © 1995 by Nancy Baker Jacobs
All rights reserved. No part of this book may be used or reproduced in any manner whatsoever without written permission of the publisher, except in the case of brief quotations embodied in critical articles and reviews. For information address HarperCollins*Publishers,*
10 East 53rd Street, New York, N.Y. 10022.

Cover illustration by Donna Diamond

First printing: October 1995

Printed in the United States of America

HarperPaperbacks and colophon are trademarks of HarperCollins*Publishers*

❖ 10 9 8 7 6 5 4 3 2 1

For
Jocelyn, Brian, and Amanda
and
Rebecca, Jim, and Lisa
with love

Daddy's Gone A-Hunting

Chapter

1

Jennifer Bennett held up a Raggedy Ann doll, its gingham dress torn and soiled and a clump of its red yarn hair missing. "What about Annie here? Which box do you want her to go in?"

Seven-year-old Amy frowned. "The apartment box."

"That one's getting pretty full, hon. Looks like you'll have to take out something else to make room for Annie." On this night before they were scheduled to move out of their Pacific Palisades house, Jennifer had set up three large boxes for her daughter's toys. The first was for those they would move to their temporary apartment, the second for things that would go into storage. The third was destined for charity. So far, only one item, a toy stove that Amy had never liked—she was more tomboy than aspiring cook—was in the box headed for storage. The charity box was completely empty.

Amy twisted one of her light auburn curls around a finger. "How come I can't take all my stuff, Mom? I wanna keep everything."

Don't we all? Jennifer thought, frowning. "We talked about this, Amy. You know we won't have room at the new apartment for all your things, and we're going to be moving all over again in just a few weeks. I thought you understood that."

The child flounced onto the yellow eyelet cover on her bed and stuck out her lower lip. "But I don't *wanna* move, Mommy. I don't see why we havta. I wanna stay here. Puh-leeze."

Jennifer sighed. Truth was, she didn't want to move, either, but it couldn't be helped. She'd been out of work for three months now, and her cash supply was dwindling fast. The lease on this house would expire tomorrow and, the way things looked, when Jennifer found a new job, it wasn't likely to be here in Los Angeles. She'd been trying her best to find a job locally, ever since KNLA had canceled her morning TV talk show, but she wasn't having any luck. "I understand how you feel, sweetie," she said, trying to be patient. "I know you don't want to leave. But sometimes people just have to do things they don't want to."

The truth was, Amy had already had to do plenty of things she hadn't wanted to do; moving away from here was just one more entry on a very long list.

Tears welled up in Amy's blue eyes and her chin began to quiver. "Will I still get to go to my same school after we move?"

"While we're at the apartment you can, sure. But maybe, when I get a new job, you'll go to a new school in a new town. You can make lots of brand-new friends there. Won't that be great?" Jennifer's forced enthusiasm sounded phony even to her own ears; no wonder she wasn't convincing Amy that this move was going to be great fun.

"But I wanna stay here and be with Joey and Patty, Mom. Maybe me and you could live at their house. Patty's got bunk beds in her room. I could sleep with her and we could ride to school together and—"

"*No*, Amy, we're not going to live at Joey and Patty's. We're going to have another house that's all our own, just as soon as I get a new job." Jennifer's frustration level began to soar; it was becoming almost as high as the layer of guilt that weighed so heavily on her shoulders.

Maybe, she thought, she'd made a mistake in letting Amy choose what to do with her toys. It would have been so much easier to sort through them herself while her daughter was in school; that's what her own mother would have done. But that didn't seem fair, and Jennifer had always tried to treat Amy with fairness and consideration— the way she wished her mother had treated her.

It was at times like this that Jennifer wished she were married, that there were a husband and father around to help her raise Amy, to help the child understand why they had no choice about leaving this place. But then, if Jennifer were married, she and Amy might not have to move at all. Then there would be a second salary coming in to help pay the bills that seemed to mount up so quickly. She sighed audibly. "We've only got tonight, Amy." Her tone was much sharper now. "The movers will be here in the morn- ing, so you're just going to have to choose which toys you're taking and which ones are going into storage. Otherwise I'll have to do it for you."

Amy's small shoulders slumped and she stared at her knees in silence. She picked at an emerging hole in her jeans with a fingernail for a long moment, then clasped both her hands over her face and burst into sobs.

Jennifer sank down on the bed next to her daughter and pulled the child toward her. Slowly, Amy's arms crept around her mother's neck and she held on tight, as though she were afraid of losing her, too, if she ever let go.

Jennifer's heart melted as she felt Amy's small but sturdy body trembling with grief and loss. As hard as these past few months had been on her, she knew they'd been even harder on Amy. This truly was a wonderful house; it had a big yard for Amy to play in and an ocean view Jennifer never tired of seeing and more than enough room for the two of them. The fact that she'd been able to afford the lease had been a visible symbol of her success in a difficult business in a difficult town, too. She had loved every minute of living here.

But for Amy, this place meant even more. It had been the only place she'd ever felt safe, the only real home the child had ever had. They'd now lived here for more than half of Amy's seven years. When they first moved in, she'd been a very disturbed little girl, still caught up in the difficult process of adjusting to her new adoptive mother. Back then, three-year-old Amy had been a hyperactive whirlwind who communicated her emotional distress mainly through unintelligible half words and temper tantrums. Now she was a wonderfully normal second grader, a budding athlete, and the light of Jennifer's life.

Jennifer's greatest fear now was not that she wouldn't find work again; she was a good broadcast journalist and she felt confident she would find a new job eventually. What struck her with terror was the chance that, in disrupting Amy's home and school life, she would somehow cause the child to backslide into that deep emotional abyss she'd been living in when Jennifer adopted her.

"It's going to be okay, baby," she cooed as she stroked Amy's hair and kissed the top of her head. "I wish we didn't have to move, too, but we'll find someplace else and love it just as much. And no matter what happens, you and I will always be together. I promise. You'll always have me and I'll always have you."

"Cross your heart and hope to die?" Amy's round, wet face was buried against her mother's chest and her question came out muffled.

"Cross my heart and hope to die, sweetheart. I'll never ever let you go."

Amy sniffled for a while longer, then loosened her grip on her mother's neck. She wiped her tears away with the backs of her fists and slid off the bed. Without saying another word, she crawled across the floor and lifted the toy stove out of the storage box, then transferred it into the box destined for charity. Her tear-streaked face now a study in stoic acceptance, the child took first one toy, then another, from the apartment-destined box and shifted them into the ones headed for storage and charity as her mother watched.

Chapter

2

The movers were an hour late the next morning and Jennifer was nearly a nervous wreck by the time they arrived. She'd taken Amy to school promptly at eight o'clock and the rest of her day was very tightly scheduled. The moving van had to be loaded and gone before Amy had to be picked up again, and the entire house had to be completely cleared out by the end of the day. If it wasn't, her landlord would deduct an extra day's rent from her lease deposit. That would cost her more than a hundred dollars and, these days, every dollar counted.

But it wasn't the movers' tardiness alone that was pushing Jennifer's nerves close to the edge. It was what she found on her front doorstep after delivering Amy to school. She parked across the street so the movers would have access to the driveway and crossed the lawn to the front door, leaving shallow footprints in the damp, spongy grass. She was half a dozen feet from the door when she spotted it—an innocuous-looking brown paper bag with Safeway's markings. Her fingernails pressing hard into her palms, she stopped in her tracks.

A woman who'd never been in the public eye might think nothing of finding a paper bag on her front steps. But it frightened Jennifer, particularly because this was the second Safeway bag she'd found there in the past week. She quickly spun around and looked up and down the street, but it was deserted and silent in the bright morning sunlight. There was nobody in sight, not one unfamiliar vehicle parked nearby, and the only footprints on the dew-soaked lawn were her own.

The bag had probably been delivered sometime during the night, she realized, her sense of violation growing stronger. She and Amy had left the house by way of the attached garage that morning. Since she canceled her *Times* delivery, she no longer had a reason to open the front door first thing every day. All she knew for sure was that the bag hadn't been on the steps when she'd locked up the house last night.

Her pulse quickening, Jennifer walked up to the bag, leaned over, and jerked it open. Inside was a brand-new rubbery baby doll wrapped in a small fuzzy pink blanket. There was no note or sales receipt with it. Jennifer quickly thrust the toy back inside the bag and carried the unwanted package over to the already bulging trash can. She added it to the pile of castoffs already inside the can and forced the lid back on.

Shuddering, Jennifer went inside to wait for the movers. What kind of weirdo was leaving children's toys on her doorstep? This was a first for her. During her years as a television show host she'd had her share of devoted "admirers"—a couple of them downright terrifying—but none had ever tried to woo her with toys. Just thinking about the doll made her skin crawl.

No female celebrity could really feel safe in this town anymore, not since actress Theresa Saldana had been stabbed nearly to death right in front of her own home, and then Rebecca Schaeffer had been murdered when she answered her doorbell—both by obsessed fans. Not that

Jennifer considered herself either a great beauty or anywhere near as famous as those two actresses. She was simply a local TV talk show host. Actually, she reminded herself, she was currently nothing more than a *former* talk show host.

Jennifer knew she was considered a fairly attractive woman in a fresh-faced, outdoorsy sort of way, even by Hollywood's strict standards. Her looks were a combination of what she'd been born with and the self-improvement tricks she'd acquired during the years she'd spent in front of the television cameras. Her naturally mousy hair was now tinted a flattering golden blond, and her knack for applying makeup helped her slightly square-jawed face sprout what passed for cheekbones. She worked hard to keep her figure trim, too, although now that she was nearing forty, the battle to keep off that extra ten pounds was becoming more and more difficult.

Although she wouldn't give Michelle Pfeiffer much trouble in a beauty contest and she was no more than locally well known, Jennifer knew that there was no accounting for the tastes of fanatics. Nuts who became fixated on women working in the public eye followed no particular rules of logic.

Nowadays obsessed fans went with the territory in the profession Jennifer had chosen, of course, but she'd never been able to get used to them; they still frightened her. She'd received lots of gifts from all kinds of admirers over the years she'd been working here in L.A., everything from bouquets of flowers and homemade cakes on her birthday to obscenely graphic sex novels and photos. One particularly persistent man had sent her a pair of black lace panties from Frederick's of Hollywood every week for an entire year. After the first two or three weeks, Jennifer hadn't bothered opening his packages anymore; doing so made her feel both dirty and frightened. She'd had her secretary turn his packages over to the police; what the authorities had done with them, Jennifer didn't know, but eventually the gifts stopped arriving at KNLA-TV's studios. Maybe the guy had simply shifted his bizarre obsession to some other unfortunate woman.

A few years ago, undesired attention from fans had spurred Jennifer to take a self-defense class, where she earned a permit to carry mace. But as soon as she got her canister, she hid it on the highest shelf in her bedroom closet; she didn't want to take a chance that curious little Amy might find it and hurt herself. For the same reason, buying a gun was completely out of the question. Instead, to diminish her feeling of helplessness, Jennifer had spent hundreds of dollars installing alarm systems in her car and her home.

Still, the offerings of the past few days had upset her in a new, even more terrifying way. Today's baby doll and the earlier package, which had contained a child's makeup kit, had been delivered directly to the doorstep of her own home. This latest guy—whoever he was—obviously not only knew where Jennifer lived, he knew she had a young daughter as well. What terrified her most was the possibility that someone was trying to get to her by using Amy.

Now, almost five hours after she'd found the doll, Jennifer watched the movers loading the last piece of furniture into the moving van. It was already after one o'clock; in an hour and a half, she was due to pick up Amy at school, and she still had to load the station wagon.

"Want us to do somethin' with them boxes you got in the little girl's room?" the younger of the two moving men asked her. His bare arms were darkly tanned and totally covered with blue tattoos that reminded Jennifer of varicose veins. With unkempt shoulder-length blond hair, he looked like a cross between a surfer and someone who would feel at home straddling a Harley-Davidson.

"Don't worry about them," Jennifer told him, trying not to stare at his tattoos. "That stuff's going to the apartment with me. Just take what's already loaded and put it into storage, like we discussed."

"You're the boss." Squinting under the hot California sun, the mover thrust a clipboard at her. "Just sign here, give us the check, and we're ready to roll. Comes to nine-ninety-six with the tax for the move. Company'll bill you monthly for the storage charges."

Jennifer signed the form attached to the clipboard without taking the time to read it and made out a check for the specified amount—another big dent in her dwindling cash reserves, but it couldn't be helped. It was time for her and her daughter to move on—to their temporary housing at Santa Monica's Edgewater Apartment Hotel until she found a new job. After that, Jennifer only wished she knew.

As the moving van pulled away from the curb, Jennifer saw the driver hesitate briefly, braking and swerving slightly to the right to allow a late model Ford to pass by on the narrow street. Her neck muscles tightened involuntarily. The dark Ford seemed familiar somehow; she felt sure she'd seen it somewhere before, probably sometime in the past few days, yet it certainly didn't belong to anyone living on this street. Seaview Ridge was a private lane, high in the hills above Sunset Boulevard. There was no reason for anyone who didn't have business here to be on this street. That was one of the reasons Jennifer had originally been attracted to the place—here, she hadn't had to worry about Amy running out into a road filled with traffic.

Jennifer shaded her eyes against the sun and stared openly at the car as it passed by, but she couldn't get a good look at the driver. A dark-haired man was at the wheel—she could tell that much—but his face was hidden in shadow.

Relax, she told herself, maybe the guy's just thinking about leasing this house. Or he could be a real estate agent canvassing the neighborhood for sales prospects. Yet his presence still made her nervous; he might be the man who'd left the toys on the doorstep.

As the Ford disappeared around a curve in the road and didn't return, however, Jennifer's initial impulse to call the police faded. What could she tell them—that a man in a dark Ford had driven past her house? There was no law against that. She had no proof that he was the same guy who'd left the toys, either. Besides, she reassured herself, after today, this house wouldn't be her home anymore. Whoever her pursuer was, within just a few hours, he wouldn't know where to find her.

She turned and went back inside the house, pausing for a long moment in front of the living room's glass rear wall. With the room empty of furniture, the panoramic ocean view seemed even more dramatic. The sea was a particularly vibrant shade of teal today, with just the tiniest line of brown smog visible along the horizon. Jennifer felt a wave of nostalgia for this house—where she'd watched Amy's emotional wounds slowly healing, and where the two of them had slowly become cemented into a real family.

Still, Jennifer was now beginning to feel more than a little relieved that the two of them were moving away. If some weirdo really *was* beginning to stalk her, this move should put him off her trail once and for all.

As she loaded her boxes into the station wagon, Jennifer kept an eye on the street, but the dark Ford didn't reappear and she was soon too busy to worry about it. She shifted Amy's box of toys forward and spread a clean bedsheet over a space where she could lay a stack of clothing on hangers.

Luckily, she and Amy wouldn't need much to live at the Edgewater Apartment Hotel. They'd stayed there once before, for the first month after they moved to Southern California. The Edgewater's apartments were fully furnished, down to dishes and bed linens. The building was a

U-shaped high-rise; not at the water's edge at all, it was actually a good three miles from the seashore. The complex catered to relocating executives and tourists willing to pay a minimum of a month's rent to avoid traditional hotel living. Although it would never feel like a real home—its transient population worked against that—the Edgewater would be perfectly adequate for this period of limbo.

Jennifer had spent the past two weeks separating those things she and Amy would need while she looked for work from what she was sending into storage. The items she'd kept behind included only the essentials—mainly clothes, Amy's box of favorite toys, personal things she didn't want to risk losing, like photo albums, plus anything necessary to Jennifer's job search. This last included a laptop computer and a small laser printer, a stack of audition tapes, padded mailers, paper, stamps, and other office supplies. The thought of that elusive new and better job was what kept Jennifer going. That, and little Amy, of course.

Jennifer took half a dozen silk suits from her closet and carried them on their hangers out to the car. Purchased to wear on her TV show, these outfits were simple, figure-slimming designs in varying shades that complemented her fair complexion and blue eyes—aqua, beige, coral, bright green, and orangey red. During her hours at home with her daughter, she preferred more comfortable jeans and T-shirts. Laying the suits flat on the sheet in the back of the station wagon, Jennifer wondered when she would ever wear them again.

No! she ordered herself. *Think positive.* If she allowed herself to feel desperate, she knew the media vultures would sense that in her. They would begin circling, and then she would never find a new job. If she wanted to succeed in this cutthroat business, she would have to look as though she had plenty of offers and was simply taking her time choosing among them. As far as anyone else could be allowed to know, this move to the Edgewater Apartment Hotel was simply designed to make her expected move from Los Angeles to greener pastures easier; it couldn't be interpreted as an admission that she could no longer afford the rent on this house.

As she loaded the last box of food from the refrigerator into the car, Jennifer realized it was already after two o'clock. There was no way she could get all this stuff delivered to the Edgewater before picking up Amy from school. She would have to get the child while the car was still packed up.

But maybe that was okay. If Amy helped carry her own things into the Edgewater, she might be less upset about moving. She might begin to feel more a part of this inevitable change. Little kids were flexible, weren't they? Certainly, in the past, Amy had shown she could adapt to changes . . . eventually, anyway. She would be able to do it again. And no matter what happened, the two of them always had each other; nobody could change that.

Wherever Jennifer went from here, she knew that at least she would be with Amy. Wonderful little Amy, who'd made her whole life worthwhile.

Jennifer turned the key in the ignition, put the car into gear, and backed out of the driveway. As she drove downhill, then turned right and headed toward Sunset Boulevard, she never looked back.

3

As the rich garlicky smell of pizza baking reached her nostrils, Jennifer realized she was famished. She hadn't eaten since breakfast, and she'd been doing the hard physical work of moving all day long. She and Amy had unloaded the car and made a good start on putting their things away at the Edgewater. Now, too exhausted to cook, she was taking her daughter to a nearby pizza parlor for dinner.

"I'm not having any of those yucky mushrooms on mine, Mom," Amy declared as she slid into a booth at Bardolino's Restaurant. "Just cheese and tomatoes and hamburger."

The place was crowded and they'd had to wait a few minutes before being seated.

"Nobody's going to make you eat mushrooms, Amy." Jennifer noticed that the two women in the adjoining booth were staring openly in her direction. She averted her gaze and, pretending to be unaware of their scrutiny, smiled at her daughter. "Tell you what—how 'bout we get half hamburger and half mushroom? I'll eat the mushroom half and you can have the hamburger half all for yourself."

"Only if no mushrooms leak onto *my* half. I really, really *hate* 'em." From the look of exaggerated disgust on Amy's freckled face, a bystander might have thought Jennifer had suggested her daughter order strychnine on her pizza.

A woman's voice drifted over from the next booth. "Nah! I tell you it's not Stephanie Edwards. She's a redhead."

"Well, I tell you, it ain't Meredith MacRae," answered her companion. "She don't look a bit—"

Turning back to Amy, Jennifer shut out the women's conversation. "You find any mushrooms on your part, kiddo, I'll pick off every last one and eat it myself, 'cause I really, really love them. Deal?"

As Amy nodded her agreement, a portly, gray-haired waitress approached their table. "What're you two ladies gonna have tonight?" she asked, smiling and winking at Amy. Many families with children were eating in the restaurant and the waitress obviously enjoyed catering to them. With a flourish, she pulled a green order pad from the pocket of her apron and a pencil from behind her ear and stood poised to write.

Jennifer gave the waitress their order, requesting two house salads, a glass of milk, and a glass of Chianti in addition to the large pizza.

"And make sure nobody puts any mushrooms on *my* half," Amy told the waitress.

"Say please, Amy," Jennifer insisted.

"*Please* make sure nobody puts any mushrooms on my half." Smiling sheepishly at the waitress, Amy twisted a curl of reddish hair around her finger.

"I'll be sure to tell the cook, little lady. Your salads and drinks'll be right out." The waitress bustled off in the direction of the kitchen.

Amy was generally a good eater, but she had strong opinions about the handful of foods she disliked. Chief among these were mushrooms, any kind of peppers, and what she called "tough meat," which encompassed anything from pot roast to overcooked ham. On the other hand, Amy considered raw broccoli a snack food prefer-able to potato chips, so Jennifer had no problem with indulging her daughter's tastes when it came to their family dining habits. She did, however, insist that the child learn and practice good manners.

"Oh, Mom! I almost forgot," Amy said when the wait-ress had brought their first course. "I gotta bring that six dollars to school tomorrow or I don't get to go on the field trip." She shoved a forkful of romaine lettuce into her mouth and began to chew it. "My 'mission 'lip, too."

"Amy, please swallow before you speak. You know I can't understand you when your mouth's full."

Amy chewed some more, then swallowed hard and wiped her mouth with her napkin. "Six dollars, Mom, plus the per-mission slip. Ms. Butterfield said." A piece of lettuce was wedged between her two front teeth. "I was s'posed to bring it to school last week, but you forgot, and if I don't have it by tomorrow, I have to stay in the principal's office while everybody else gets to go to see *The Secret Garden*." Amy was clearly stricken by the prospect of being left behind.

"Oh, *The Secret Garden*." Jennifer felt a twist of guilt. "Now I remember. Sorry, hon, I guess it slipped my mind. Tell you what. I'll put the money and the note in an envelope by the front door of the apartment before I go to bed tonight. That way, we won't forget tomorrow morning."

She'd been so overwhelmed by her job worries and packing for the move that she'd completely forgotten about this school field trip that was so important to Amy. That Brinton Academy was taking the entire second grade to see the film version of *The Secret Garden* was an example of what Jennifer most appreciated about the school, too.

She knew that the school had stringent rules about field trips, as it did about almost everything else. If a child's parental permission slip wasn't on file, that child wasn't allowed to leave the school grounds. No exceptions. In general, Jennifer appreciated that strictness, found it to be reassuring, but it left no room for the errors of a stressed-out, forgetful mother. "Don't worry, sweetie," she promised, "you'll get to go to the movie."

"We been reading the book about it, Mom, and it's really, really great!" Amy wiggled in her seat with barely suppressed excitement as she talked and her blue eyes widened. "There's this girl, see, and her momma and daddy both get killed, so she hasta go live with her old uncle in this great big mansion over in England. But the uncle's real weird, see, and he's never, ever home, and the housekeeper's real mean to the girl. But then she finds out there's a boy hidden away in the house and—"

Jennifer broke into delighted laughter as Amy continued her interpretation of the classic children's book, complete with wild hand gestures. Typical of the seven-year-old, her enthusiasm for her subject overshadowed her occasional poor grammar and sometimes less-than-accurate rehash of the plot. "Hey, I remember that story, sweetie. It's great. But don't you think you'd better eat your salad? Our pizza'll be here any minute."

"Hey, you're somebody, aren't you?" asked a loud woman's voice.

Jennifer glanced up to find one of the women from the next booth standing next to her table. The woman was fiftyish, tall and very thin, with a narrow, lantern-jawed face. Jennifer swallowed her mouthful of romaine. "You talking to me?"

"Yeah. I said I just know you're somebody."

"Everybody's somebody." Christ, Jennifer thought, now her so-called fans couldn't even remember her name. And she'd been off TV only three short months.

"No, no, I mean somebody *famous*."

As people at the surrounding tables began to turn and stare, Jennifer felt her face redden.

"My mom's Jennifer Bennett," Amy announced, her round face beaming with pride. "She's on TV."

Jennifer looked down and smirked into her lap. Leave it to Amy to be so open with total strangers. But she was secretly pleased to observe her daughter's obvious pride.

"Jennifer Bennett. Whaddid I tell ya, Trudy? I knew she wasn't Meredith MacRae." The shorter of the two women elbowed her way in front of her companion. "You're on that shopping channel, right?"

"No, ma'am. I used to be host of *Only in L.A.* on KNLA."

The woman's eyebrows knitted together and she shook her head. "No, that's not it."

Jennifer was beginning to find the two women's near-recognition of her less and less flattering. "I should know," she said.

"Oh, for godsake, Helen, don't be stupid. Miss Bennett here knows what TV show she's on." The taller woman thrust a folded paper napkin at Jennifer. "Can I have your autograph? Just write, 'To Trudy'—that's Trudy with a *y*, not an *i*—'to Trudy, my biggest fan, love, Jennifer Bennett.'"

Jennifer fumbled in her purse for a pen. She'd always believed it was easier and more appropriate simply to give a fan her autograph than to get into an argument about not wanting her family outing interrupted. This situation, however, was trying what little patience she had left after her long, tiring day. "To Trudy . . ." she wrote.

"Me, too," said Helen, grabbing a clean paper napkin off an empty table nearby and shoving it at Jennifer. "My name's Helen. Say, when's your show on, anyway?"

"It's not, anymore."

"How come?"

"The station canceled it." Jennifer's time slot was now filled with reruns of old network sitcoms. A cost-cutting move, her boss had told her, nothing that she should take personally. Right, she thought. As though there were nothing personal about being deprived of her entire livelihood.

"Well, can we write a letter or something? I always thought you were a lot better than that Joan Lunden."

"Thank you, Trudy, but I think it's a little late for that. My show's already been off the air for three months."

"Oh. You got a new show comin' up?"

Don't I wish, Jennifer thought. "I'm considering several offers; haven't made up my mind yet." She handed the second autographed napkin to the shorter woman. "Well, our pizza will be here any minute. It's been nice meeting you both." She turned away and resumed eating her salad.

The women's eager smiles faded and they exchanged a glance that seemed to say Jennifer was not all that friendly, considering she was really just a show business has-been. They mumbled something that resembled thanks and retreated to their own booth.

"Mom," Amy asked, leaning across the table, her eyes wide. "Did you get a job?"

"Huh? No, not yet, hon. But I will soon, I'm sure I—"

"But you told those ladies . . ."

Jennifer wilted. Caught in a lie by her own daughter. "I—I just didn't want to tell them that I don't have anything yet, Amy. It's none of their business. Wait till you're grown up, then you'll understand about these things."

"But you always tell *me* not to lie, ever. You said fibbing is real, real bad. How come you—"

"Here comes our pizza, Amy." Saved by the bell, Jennifer thought, as the waitress delivered a savory-looking pie to their table and placed it between them. "Look at that—not one mushroom on your side!"

"Yippee! Hey, thanks." The child grinned up at the waitress.

"You're very welcome, my dear."

Jennifer reached over and grabbed a slice of pizza,

grateful that the delivery of their food had distracted Amy from her uncomfortable line of questioning. Exhausted, Jennifer would be lucky if she could summon enough energy to eat her dinner and make it back to the apartment to bed. She certainly didn't have enough left over to tackle explaining situational ethics to a seven-year-old.

Chapter

4

The dark-haired man parked his rented Ford around the corner from Seaview Ridge and walked. It was after midnight, but there was a nearly full moon tonight and he had no trouble finding the right house. He'd been up to its front door on two occasions earlier in the week, and he'd driven by the place at least a dozen times. He didn't even need to use his flashlight.

What he'd seen there during this afternoon's drive-by had upset him—a moving van had been pulling away from the curb just as he approached the place. He was worried about where the woman and child were going. If they were leaving L.A., it could take him days, maybe even weeks, to locate them again.

After he'd spotted the moving van, he realized he had a choice. He could follow the van, or he could wait and follow Jennifer Bennett. He chose the latter, parking around the corner and waiting for the woman to leave in her station wagon.

He'd thought it would be easy simply to follow her wherever she was heading. Then he'd know where the two of them had moved. But some bastard in a red Jaguar had cut him off and forced him to wait to make the left at the Temescal Canyon stoplight. By the time he was able to follow her into the heavy southbound traffic on Pacific Coast Highway, she was nowhere in sight. Now he would have to try another tactic.

A dog in the next block began to bark, but the man ignored it. He was dressed all in black, and he knew how to move silently, how to keep from being detected by the enemy. The army had taught him that and he'd never forgotten the lesson.

The house was completely dark tonight. He crept around the perimeter and peered through each window that wasn't covered with draperies. Nothing. From what little he could see of the interior, the place seemed completely empty. Between the moving van and the station wagon, they seemed to have moved everything out. They weren't coming back.

His gaze fell upon the trash can at the edge of the concrete driveway. Sometimes people's trash could tell you all kinds of things about them, maybe even where they were moving.

He stole over to can and dragged it slowly and quietly around the side of the house, where the beam from his flashlight wouldn't be seen by the people living across the street. The last thing he needed was some nosy neighbor calling the police and reporting a burglar. Hell, he was no burglar; he was just trying to find somebody, somebody he had every right to find. But just try explaining that to the cops.

Once out of view of the street, the intruder upended the trash can and let its contents spill onto the grass. He turned on his flashlight and cast the beam over his find. Most of it was useless to him—old newspapers, two empty rolls of packaging tape, a broken clock, an empty Tampax carton, a half-full box of stale Saltines, a crumpled, handwritten list of items labeled, "For the Apartment," and the like.

As he picked his way through the refuse spread over the ground, he found several envelopes addressed to Jennifer Bennett. Most were clearly junk mail—advertising flyers, solicitations for credit cards, a computer-generated letter hyping a "free" Las Vegas vacation. But one could be useful—a tear-off receipt from one of Jennifer Bennett's credit card bills that included her card's number. He shoved it deep into a pocket of his black pants, along with two letters with return addresses of TV stations in San Francisco and San Diego.

After ten more minutes of searching, he had found nothing to lead him to Jennifer's current destination. He had only three brown paper bags left to check. The first two contained wet garbage that couldn't go into a garbage disposal—four corncobs and their husks, a pile of artichoke leaves, and a few wilted stalks of celery.

But the last piece of trash looked disturbingly familiar. The man's anger began to rise even before he ripped open the brown Safeway bag. Inside, he found exactly what he'd suspected he would. The baby doll he'd spent more than an hour selecting at Toy World gazed uncomprehendingly at him with its flat blue plastic eyes.

That fucking bitch! Who the hell did she think she was, throwing away the gift he'd so carefully chosen! He would show her, he would make her pay.

Angrily the dark-haired man switched off his flashlight and stuffed it into his back pocket. Gripping the doll under his arm, he made his way silently back to his car.

Chapter

5

Jennifer pulled the station wagon into the circular drive in front of Brinton Academy and parked. Traffic on Santa Monica's San Vicente Boulevard near the school was heavy today, as it was every morning when the caravan of parents and nannies arrived to drop off the children.

Until she lost her job, Jennifer almost never drove Amy to school. Her workday at KNLA had started at five-thirty, so her housekeeper, Maria, had been responsible for Amy's school transportation. But in these past three months, Jennifer had discovered that she liked doing the driving herself; it gave her extra time with her daughter, plus it got her up and moving early—even on days when she felt like pulling the covers over her head and hiding rather than facing another day of searching for a new job.

"Here's your six dollars and your permission slip, sweetie," Jennifer said, handing Amy a sealed white envelope. "Give it to Ms. Butterfield right away, okay?"

"Sure, Mom. I won't forget." Amy unzipped her backpack, grabbed the envelope, and shoved it inside. In anticipation of the school outing, she was more dressed up today than usual, wearing her favorite blue-and-green plaid jumper and a bright green blouse. "Hey, there's Patty!" The child pushed her thumb hard against the button that released her seatbelt and shoved the car door open. "Patty, wait up!"

"Hold on just a minute here, miss. Think you forgot something."

Amy swiveled around toward her mother, her round, freckled face inquisitive. Jennifer arched an eyebrow and tilted her face upward. Amy giggled. "Sorry, Mommy. I love you." The child leaned across the seat and planted a wet kiss on her mother's waiting cheek.

"I love you, too." Jennifer gave the child a brief hug and returned the kiss. "Have a great day, sugar. I hope you love the movie. Pick you up at three."

"'Bye, Mom." Amy scurried out of the car, a strap of her backpack clutched in one hand. "Hey, Patty, wait for me!" In a flash, she caught up with her best friend and the two were quickly engrossed in girlish chatter.

Jennifer watched until the two children had safely entered the two-story beige stucco building, then waved a greeting to Catherine Chesterton, the teacher on "door duty" this morning, as she restarted her car.

As she pulled out of the circular drive and back onto San Vicente Boulevard, Jennifer observed the oncoming traffic and mentally checked her list of errands for the day. She didn't even notice the beige Toyota with the Alamo rental car sticker on its rear bumper as it pulled away from the curb and began following her at a discreet distance.

On her way back to the Edgewater, Jennifer stopped at the Lucky Market at Lincoln and Ocean Park boulevards to stock up on groceries. She hadn't been grocery shopping, except for milk and bread, in a couple of weeks now. She and Amy had done their best to deplete the food in their pantry and refrigerator so there would be less to move. But now it was time to restock their larder.

An hour later, when she wheeled her overloaded cart to her car, Jennifer had put more than a hundred dollars' worth of food and toiletries on her already-stessed credit card. As she loaded the heavy brown paper bags into the back of her station wagon, the dark-haired man behind the wheel of the beige Toyota observed her, his eyes hidden by an oversized pair of sunglasses.

The man started the Toyota as Jennifer loaded the last bag of groceries into the station wagon and returned her cart to the holding area. He wasn't far behind as she made the right turn onto Ocean Park Boulevard and headed eastward up the hill. She drove past the branch library, the dark glass building that housed the west side offices of the *Times*, and the recent outcropping of minimalls whose restaurants, dry cleaners, and drugstores serviced the hundreds of workers from the industrial park across the street. By the time she turned left onto Centinela Avenue, then took a second quick left into the underground parking structure of the Edgewater Apartment Hotel, the Toyota was half a block distant.

U-turning at the corner past the Edgewater and heading back south on Centinela, the dark-haired man in the sunglasses smiled to himself. It had been a smart move to dump the Ford last night and exchange it for a different, equally nondescript rental car. Even if Jennifer Bennett hadn't suspected anything when she saw him driving the Ford near her Seaview Ridge house, there was no reason to take unnecessary chances. If she was on the lookout for any car that might be following her this morning, it obviously wasn't a beige Toyota.

Pulling to a stop against the red curb of a bus zone, he gave her five minutes to unpack the groceries from her car. Then he drove down the ramp into the parking garage, ignoring the sign that announced, Cars Without Parking

Permits Will Be Towed at Owner's Expense. He pulled into an empty space three cars away from Jennifer Bennett's station wagon and headed for the elevator.

The lighted display above the gray metal doors announced that the elevator was currently stopped on the third floor, but the man quickly realized he couldn't follow the Bennett woman there. A key was required to gain entrance to the elevator from the garage level. It was just as well, he told himself. He didn't want to be spotted someplace he had no right to be, certainly not at this stage in the game. There was an easier, more foolproof way.

Leaving his car where it was, the man headed up the parking ramp to the street on foot. He climbed the steps at the front of the building, pushed open the tall, glass door to the apartment complex, and headed across the lobby toward the registration desk.

Chapter

6

<hr/>

"Hey, Mom. Mommy! Look at me!"

Jennifer looked up from her magazine to see Amy standing at the side of the Edgewater's swimming pool. Water dripped from her light red hair and her firm, strong little body shivered in the late afternoon shade, but the child didn't seem to notice the cold.

"Watch me, Mom!"

"I'm watching." Amy performed an imperfect swan dive, her arms in correct position, but her legs sprawling. As she surfaced, she took care not to disturb the pool's only other occupant, a man who was swimming laps along the far edge. Like Amy, he'd been at the pool every afternoon for the past few days. Each time, he spent no less than forty-five minutes methodically breast-stroking in one direction, then flipping over at the end of the pool and backstroking in the other.

When Amy surfaced at poolside after her dive, Jennifer called to her, "Great dive, kiddo. But it looks like you're getting pretty cold." Jennifer herself wore a lightweight long-sleeved shirt, jeans, and a wide-brimmed hat to protect her thirty-nine-year-old face from the sun's damaging rays—a necessity for a woman whose career was spent in front of television cameras. Now, as the sun traveled west, leaving the pool area completely shaded, she was beginning to feel chilly despite her clothes. Amy had to be freezing.

The child climbed out of the pool and ran over to where her mother was reclining on a blue-and-white plastic chaise lounge. "I'm not cold, Mom, honest." Her lips had a bluish tinge. "Please, I wanna swim some more."

Jennifer was reluctant to pull Amy away from the pool until it was absolutely necessary; swimming was the one thing the child seemed to thoroughly enjoy here at the Edgewater. They'd been living here a week now, and Amy had spent every afternoon after school in the water. She was a strong swimmer for a seven-year-old—the net result of the two years of swimming lessons Jennifer had insisted she take. She had also sent the child to ballet lessons for a few months, but Amy hadn't done very well there—she hated wearing the ballet slippers, and the dainty movements dance required of her were beyond her physical capabilities. So Jennifer had switched her to judo and karate, which were much more her style. The two of them had even taken a mother-daughter self-defense class together last year. Amy had scored better in her age group than her mother had in hers. Jennifer sometimes thought her daughter might grow up to be an Olympic athlete, but Amy certainly was not destined to be a prima ballerina.

Jennifer compromised. "Five more minutes, then it's time to come out." Amy immediately dived off the pool's edge, swam to the bottom of the shallow end, and did a handstand, her legs flailing just above the surface of the water. Jennifer returned her attention to her magazine.

"She's a strong little swimmer."

Jennifer looked up to find the man who had been swimming laps standing next to her. Draped over his shoulders was a white towel with the words, "Edgewater Apartment Hotel," in blue lettering across it. "What?"

"Your daughter—I assume she is your daughter? She really takes to the water."

Jennifer smiled. The man was tall and fairly slender, but, like most serious swimmers, he was well-muscled through the arms and shoulders. His curly, dark brown hair was just beginning to show the first signs of graying at the temples, and Jennifer guessed him to be about her own age. "Yes," she replied. "She's a real little water bug."

The man sat down on the chaise lounge next to Jennifer's and thrust his right hand out. "Hi. I'm Forrest Hathaway."

Jennifer shook it. "Jennifer Bennett."

"I've noticed you and your daughter—what's her name?"

"Amy."

"Amy. I've noticed you and Amy here at the pool the last couple of days. You new to L.A., too?"

"No," Jennifer said. "We've lived here for four years."

"At the Edgewater?" Forrest Hathaway's face registered a combination of amazement and amusement.

Jennifer laughed. "No, not here specifically. I mean we've lived in L.A. for four years. We've only been at the Edgewater for the past week." She saw no need to volunteer any more information about her personal situation. This man was attractive and friendly, but she had no idea who he was.

"What about your husband? He here with you?"

"I don't have a husband," Jennifer said, her suspicion that Forrest Hathaway was trying to pick her up growing stronger.

"Well, *that's* a relief."

"Really? I'm not so sure." Jennifer's voice held a touch of indignation.

Forrest grinned broadly and Jennifer found herself smiling back at him despite herself. "Hey, I'm just being brutally honest," he said. "It's a failing of mine—and among the reasons my wife divorced me." He rubbed his wet hair with one end of his towel. "Say, Jennifer Bennett, you must know a lot about L.A. after four years. Maybe you could give me some advice about where to look for a more permanent place to live."

"Well, I don't know a—"

"Don't say no. Not yet, anyway. It's only fair that you get to know me a lot better before you decide you hate me, right?"

Jennifer unsuccessfully tried to stifle a laugh. "Well . . . I guess parting with a little advice won't kill me. But right now I've got to get my little fish out of that pool before she's frozen solid. It'll have to be some other time."

"How about tonight? Nothing fancy, maybe just a glass of wine before dinner. We could talk."

"Look, Mr. Hath—"

"Forrest."

"The thing is, Forrest, I don't have a babysitter and I don't take my daughter to bars, so I don't think—"

"My place, then? I'm just around the corner from you, in three-eighteen."

The fact that Forrest Hathaway knew which apartment they lived in made Jennifer a touch nervous. She and Amy were in apartment 3-12—as the man said, just around the corner from 3-18. If he'd noticed her, why hadn't she noticed him? But, then, Jennifer told herself, unlike Mr. Hathaway, she hadn't exactly been looking. With the move and searching for a new job, finding a new man had been the last thing on her mind. "Hey, look, I can be brutally honest, too," she told him, "and the truth is, I don't even know you. There's no way I'm going to go to your apartment with you, so—"

Forrest held up a hand. "Hey, sorry, Jennifer. I didn't mean to suggest anything . . . uh, 'improper.' I don't know what's the matter with me. Of course, you wouldn't want to go to some strange guy's apartment." He stopped rubbing his head and grabbed a white terrycloth robe from a nearby table. His still-damp hair was unruly now, badly in need of taming; it gave him a vulnerable look, reminiscent of a small boy emerging from his bath. "Tell you what. Give me a chance to shower and make myself presentable and I'll meet you down here by the pool." He gestured around the shaded poolside area, with its half dozen glass-top tables and plastic chairs. "Should be safe enough here, right? I'll bring a bottle of wine and a couple of glasses. What'll it be—white or red?"

He looked so eager that Jennifer didn't want to disappoint him. "White," she said, "if it's dry. But just one glass. Then I have to go back upstairs and make dinner and help Amy with her homework." She looked at her watch, then called out, "Amy, your five minutes are up. Time to get out."

"One hour, then." A grin on his face, Forrest Hathaway tied his robe tightly around his waist and sprinted for the elevator.

Jennifer watched his retreat, unsure whether the butterflies in her stomach were a sign of excitement or of apprehension.

*Jennifer watched the steam rising from the surface of the swim-*ming pool and pulled her periwinkle blue cardigan more tightly around her shoulders. The early evening air was growing cooler now, as the fog began to roll in off the ocean. "So exactly where will you have to go to work?" she asked.

"The production company that bought my screenplay is in Culver City," Forrest Hathaway told her, "but this is only my first sale . . . at least I *hope* it's only the first. With luck, I'll sell Hollywood more than one script." He patted his stomach. "It's either that or starve. Could be my next one'll sell to Universal or Disney or who knows where."

"So you could end up working anywhere from the west side to Burbank."

"Right, although most of my work will probably be done at home. Mainly, I'll just have to go to a few meetings at the studios, unless I take a staff writing job somewhere."

Jennifer took a sip of her wine and glanced over at Amy, who was sitting at the next table, poring over an illustrated book of *The Secret Garden* that Jennifer had checked out of the library that afternoon. Dressed warmly in a bright orange sweat suit, the child looked content and oblivious to the adults' conversation. "What I'd do if I were you, Forrest," Jennifer said, "is pick the part of town I liked best, rent something there, and deal with whatever commute I might be facing later. If you're going to be a real Southern Californian, you'll have to get used to killer commutes."

Forrest raised his eyebrows. "You make it sound so attractive."

Jennifer grinned. "It's not so bad, really. The trick is to get yourself a nice air-conditioned car with a really good radio and tape player, maybe even a CD player, if you're into music in a big way. I know people who listen to whole books on tape while they drive the freeways in this town. And one friend of mine keeps a collection of these zen meditation tapes in his glove compartment—says listening to them helps him relax, claims it quashes these strong urges he gets when he's driving."

"Urges?"

"Yeah, to get himself a fifty-two Magnum and use it to blast all the bad drivers on the road to kingdom come."

"You make me wonder if I ever should've left Minneapolis."

"All depends on what kind of life you want to live," she told him, turning serious. "One thing about living here in L.A.—it's seldom boring." Her voice became wistful now, and she felt her throat begin to tighten. Despite Los Angeles's smog, crowds, crime, fires, earthquakes—the city's seemingly constant engulfment in the "disaster of the week"—she really did not want to leave it.

"Not boring, eh? Probably a good place for an adrenaline junky like me after all." Forrest picked up the wine bottle and motioned to add more wine to Jennifer's glass, but she quickly placed her hand over it and shook her head no. He shrugged and refilled his own glass. "So, in your opinion, where's the best place to live around here?"

Jennifer explained that she'd always preferred the west side's neighborhoods—Santa Monica, Pacific Palisades, Brentwood. "Here we've got a whole lot less smog than farther east, less crime, more moderate temperatures, not to mention the beach. But sometimes you have to put up with a lot of yuppie 'attitude' on this side of town. And it does cost more to live here." She described the house she and Amy had just left. "The rent was awfully expensive, but it was just perfect for Amy and me."

"So how come you left it?"

Swirling around the half ounce of wine she had left in her long-stemmed glass, Jennifer considered her options. She could feed Forrest Hathaway a line of typical Hollywood double-talk and try to save face, or she could tell him the truth. She realized that the choice she made now would surely color their future relationship—*if* they were to have any future relationship. Oh, what the hell, she thought. She was tired of lying to people, tired of pretending she wasn't feeling completely poleaxed by her chosen profession. Besides, Amy was nearby and Jennifer had no desire to explain another lie to her straitlaced young daughter. "My TV talk show was canceled three months ago," she said, finally, "and I haven't been able to find another job around here."

Forrest listened as Jennifer gave him an abbreviated version of her career in broadcasting, starting with her first reporting job after college and ending with the disappointing past few months.

"That really stinks," Forrest agreed. "Real tough business you've picked. Me, too, I suppose." He told Jennifer he'd been an advertising and public relations man in the Twin Cities since graduating from the University of Minnesota's Journalism School. "But I was always a frustrated filmmaker at heart. I've probably seen every American film ever made and at least half of the foreign ones. Whenever I wasn't watching movies or working, I spent my spare time writing screenplays and sending them off to agents on the West Coast, waiting for that lucky break."

"And you finally got it."

Forrest nodded. "Right. Now I'm what Hollywood calls an overnight success."

"After how many years of writing scripts?"

"Roughly . . ." His eyes crinkling around the edges as he grinned, he counted on his long fingers. "Fifteen, sixteen, thereabouts. I've started some pretty good-sized fires with a dozen or more of my rejected screenplays. Can't even count how many of my treatments have bitten the dust. But this last one finally hit." He glanced over at Amy and lowered his voice. "Throw enough you-know-what at the wall and I figure something's gotta stick."

"I sure have to give you credit for perseverance," Jennifer said. "Guts, too. Giving up your job, moving out here, all on the strength of one sale."

"Like I said, I'm an adrenaline junky. Truth is, I'm having the time of my life right now. I love the excitement, the ups and downs. And I figured, if I didn't go for it now, well— I'm thirty-seven years old, Jennifer, not getting any younger. Unfortunately, my wife didn't share my enthusiasm."

Jennifer listened as Forrest told her about his divorce a year earlier, which he admitted had been precipitated by his spending so much of his free time at the word processor. "Lucy wasn't into fade-ins, so I faded out. Luckily, there weren't any kids in our marriage's script . . . although there was a time I wanted them pretty bad." He drained his glass. "She's living with somebody else now, planning another wedding. Guy's a nice, dull computer engineer." He added more wine to his glass and smiled impishly. "He's got no ambition to be something he's not already, so they'll probably be very happy together. What about you? You divorced?"

Jennifer shook her head. "No, never been married.

Wedded bliss didn't seem to be in the cards for me, but I really wanted a child. So I adopted my daughter on my own about five years ago." She did not tell Forrest Hathaway about her penchant for picking the wrong men. Right up to now, she admitted to herself as she thought about her recent breakup with Howard Whittaker. Howard was a perfectly nice forty-eight-year-old airline pilot, a smart and sexy man. But he had one fatal flaw—an intense dislike of children, including his own three, who lived with his ex-wife in Dallas. Jennifer had wasted an entire year dating him.

"That took guts, too."

"What?"

"Adopting Amy all by yourself."

"Yes, well, I guess it did. But, no guts, no glory, as they say. Speaking of Amy—" The child's head popped up from her book as she heard her mother say her name. "It's dinnertime and she needs to be fed." Jennifer drained her glass and stood up. "Can I help you carry this stuff back upstairs, Forrest?"

"No, thanks. I can manage." Getting to his feet, Forrest took Jennifer's empty glass and put it back on the tray he'd used to bring the wine bottle and glasses down to the pool area. His own glass was still half full. "Think I'll just sit here a while longer, finish my wine. Maybe I'll start writing the sequel to *Citizen Kane* in my head," he said.

"Hey, thanks for the drink, Forrest. It's been nice getting to know you."

"We've only just begun. How about we continue this real soon?" He smiled at Jennifer, meeting her eyes directly. His face, although not technically handsome, had an open, friendly quality, and his green eyes crinkled at the corners.

Jennifer returned his smile, basking for a moment in its warmth. "I'd love to," she said. "But the next drink's on me, okay?"

"Fine with me. I'm liberated."

"Come on, Amy, let's go. Time for supper."

Amy closed her book and glanced shyly at Forrest Hathaway. She tended to be bashful around adult males, a byproduct of her being reared without a father. There were no male teachers in the lower grades at Brinton Academy, either, so the child had had little exposure to men.

"Nice to meet you, Amy," Forrest said with a slight bow and a wink. "I hope I'll see you again soon, too."

The little girl nodded and a smile began to creep over her face. "He looks like the man in the movie," she whispered to her mother.

"What man?"

"The uncle."

"Oh," Jennifer said with a laugh. "Well, Mr. Hathaway is in the movies, in a way, but he's not an actor. He writes down the stories that they make into movies."

Amy held up her book. "Did you write this story, Mr. Hathaway?"

"No, young lady, I'm afraid not. Wish I had. But I'm certainly glad to hear you like movies."

"Going to movies is one of my very most favorite things," she told him solemnly. "It's almost as good as swimming and playing kickball at school and eating pizza and watching TV and . . ." Her shyness quickly evaporating under Forrest's good-natured encouragement, Amy listed half a dozen more of her favorite things.

Finally, Jennifer took hold of her daughter's free hand and spun her around toward the elevator. "Come on, sweetie, we'll see Mr. Hathaway again. Right now, we have to go eat and get your homework done before bedtime."

As they entered the elevator and Amy pressed the button for the third floor, Jennifer saw Forrest Hathaway still looking in their direction. As the door began to close on them, he lifted his glass in a toast and smiled.

Chapter

8

Jennifer was stacking the dinner dishes in the dishwasher when the phone rang. She grabbed a towel, quickly dried her hands, and picked up the receiver.

"Jen? Hi, it's Sal." Sally Donovan was a good friend from KNLA, one of the producers of the six o'clock news. A woman more than a decade older than Jennifer, Sally was a plump, chain-smoking, hard-drinking newswoman from the old school.

"Hi, Sally, what's up?"

"Got a hot rumor for you."

Jennifer's pulse quickened. Most of the jobs in broadcast journalism were filled through word of mouth, not through ads in professional publications or even by talent agents. Sally loved to gossip and she often was one of the first to know about a job opening—sometimes even before the person currently holding the job had been informed. More than one of Sally's "hot rumors" had resulted in a new employment opportunity for someone Jennifer knew.

"Shoot," Jennifer said, feeling a spurt of hope for the first time in days.

"Word is that Christie McNally's leaving KXXT up in Santa Barbara."

"She's the anchorwoman?"

"On the six o'clock news, not the eleven o'clock. You remember her, she's the redhead—a real fashion-model type and not too bright. KXXT's supposed to be a decent place to work, and I hear the news director's looking for considerably more brains in the anchors he hires from here on out."

"I've seen Christie around, I think, maybe at the Golden Mikes dinner last year. Where's she going?"

"Moving up to one of the network affiliates in Atlanta, from what my sources tell me. Anyway, thought you might want to send your tape up there before the word gets out . . . if you're interested, that is."

Jennifer sighed. Santa Barbara would be a big step down in market size for her, undoubtedly in salary as well as prestige, but working there would allow her to stay in Southern California, and Santa Barbara was certainly a nice enough town. "I—I guess I'm interested. Thanks for the tip, Sal."

The sound of Sally exhaling smoke came across the wire. "Hey, Jen," she said, "I know it's a bitch. But just wait till you're my age, if you think things are bad now."

"What?"

"Ageism, my dear. Look around you. Women like Christie McNally are moving up—red hair, firm tits, and all. Women like us are moving down. At least if they want to work in front of the cameras, they are."

"But I'm not even forty yet, Sally. My age can't be making *that* much difference, not yet."

"Want to bet? Why do you think they hired Anna Sanchez instead of you for that spot at Channel Ten?"

"I don't know, maybe because she's Hispanic."

"Maybe that, too. But Anna's also twenty-five, my dear. I overheard the news director at Ten saying Anna's got at least a dozen good years left before her face starts looking like a road map."

"Road map!" Still holding the telephone receiver against her ear, Jennifer leaned over and peered into the shiny chrome surface of the refrigerator's handle. The reflection of her face was long and skinny; it was like looking into a fun-house mirror. "Hell, Sally, I've hardly got any wrinkles you could notice, certainly nothing makeup can't hide. I take care of myself, I stay out of the sun. Besides, I'm a helluva good reporter and interviewer."

"Well, whatever. I wish you luck, my dear. But, if I were you, I wouldn't set my heart on an on-camera position in a top-five market. Not at thirty-nine."

Jennifer's heart plummeted toward her shoes as Sal's comments confirmed what she already knew, but didn't want to acknowledge. Hell, it wasn't fair. She was thirty-nine, not eighty-nine! "What would *you* do, Sal?" she asked. Sally had always been a good friend, someone she could trust, and the woman certainly wasn't shy about speaking her mind. Of the many people Jennifer knew in television, Sally was one of the few who still called her regularly, too. Most of the others were acting like rats deserting a sinking ship, as if they were afraid her job loss might be contagious.

"One of two things, Jen. Either I'd start getting my tapes out to the smaller markets, like Santa Barbara, or I'd do exactly what I did at about your age—I'd move over to the production side."

"You really think I'm finished on-camera?"

"Who the hell knows? Barbara Walters is still going strong, but she's the exception everybody likes to point to. Listen, sweetheart, I've seen some of the tapes that come in here and I hear what the powers that be say about them. One poor woman last week—Jesus Christ, Jen, she's a good reporter, and reasonably attractive, but she's about forty-five and looks every day of it. Know what the general manager had to say about her?"

Jennifer wasn't sure she wanted to hear, but she asked anyway.

"Laughed right out loud and said, 'Maybe we should take up a collection and buy the old broad a rocking chair.' And that bastard's over fifty himself! I can't tell you how many times I've heard these assholes make cute comments like that—'Somebody ought to blow the dust off that old girl!' or 'If her tits sag any lower, she can use 'em to sweep the floor.' They're under the impression that they're incredibly witty."

"You're really cheering me up, Sal. Got to hand it to you." Jennifer felt close to tears.

"'The truth shall set you free,' or whatever the hell the saying is. Hey, Jen, I'm sorry. I didn't mean to depress—"

"You didn't. I was *already* depressed."

"Anyway, you gotta know what you're dealing with, hon. Might keep you from wasting too much time chasing the impossible dream."

"You know the news director's name at KXXT?"

"Yeah, fellow by the name of Bob Harris. He's got a good reputation as a straight shooter, runs a quality operation."

"I'll send him a tape tomorrow."

"Good move."

"Thanks for the tip. And, Sal?"

"Yeah?"

"Keep your eyes and ears open for production jobs I could handle, too, would you?"

"Sure thing, Jen. Listen, you've got great news judgment, you're good with people, and you're one of the most organized people I know. I think you'd be damned good at what I do. And there are some real advantages to being on the other side of the camera."

"Like what?"

"Like that's the fastest route to management, my dear. Management—translated real power. Plus I can eat anything

I want and nobody's going to give me any shit about an extra twenty-five pounds. And if my face wants to sag, let it. Believe me, kid, once gravity starts to take over, you can't fight it anyway. I am what I am, that's my motto."

Jennifer thanked Sally again for the tip and the advice and rang off. After she finished loading the dishwasher, she went straight to her computer and wrote a letter to Bob Harris, applying for Christie McNally's job. She coupled the letter with a copy of her résumé and one of her audition videocassettes and put them all into a padded mailer.

As she licked stamps for the package, Jennifer's eye fell upon the envelope of photographic proofs that Amy had brought home from school today and her black mood began to improve. She opened the envelope and laid out the proofs across the surface of the desk. Amy looked sort of goofy in two of them, with her eyes half closed and an unnatural, forced smile on her lips, and in one her two front teeth looked enormous. But the other three were all appealing. Jennifer's favorite was one where the photographer had added a blue bow to the little girl's curly auburn hair, giving her a perky, feminine look. She jotted down the number of that proof on the outside of the envelope.

Jennifer grabbed a second mailer from her supply drawer and addressed it to her mother in Spokane. One more attempt to turn Hilda Bennett into a real grandmother couldn't hurt, could it? Maybe, Jennifer hoped, her efforts might actually pay off someday. Maybe someday her mother would grow into the role of Amy's only grandparent, a part the older woman had refused to play during the past five years. Sure, Jennifer thought, and maybe Bill Clinton would resign the presidency to become anchor of the *CBS Evening News*. Still, she felt compelled to try once more; Sally Donovan was right—Jennifer was an incurable optimist.

Jennifer scrawled a quick note asking her mother to choose which of the enclosed proofs she wanted made up into an eight-by-ten. Matted and framed, she suggested in her note, the photo would look wonderful on Hilda's bedroom dresser. She stuffed the note and the proofs into the second mailer, stapled it shut, and pasted the last of the stamps on the outside.

Before going down to the lobby to mail her packages, Jennifer crept quietly into Amy's room. The child's eyes were tightly closed and she was breathing evenly, clutching Raggedy Ann close to her chest. The library book had slid off the bed covers onto the floor. Jennifer picked it up and placed it on top of the chest of drawers, then bent down to kiss her sleeping daughter's forehead.

"I'll be right back, sweetie," she whispered, but Amy didn't stir.

Jennifer locked the dead bolt on the door to the hall behind her and took the elevator down to the main floor. The lobby of the Edgewater Apartment Hotel was empty at this hour, except for the desk clerk, an elderly man whose nose was buried in a copy of the *National Enquirer*. She dropped her two packages in the large wire basket marked Outgoing Mail and checked her mailbox once again. It was just as empty as it had been when she'd checked it earlier in the day.

With a shrug, she told herself to look on the bright side—at least no bills had caught up with her today. Feeling suddenly exhausted, Jennifer took the elevator back up to the third floor.

Less than an hour after Jennifer had left the lobby, the dark-haired man approached the mail basket, clutching a long tan envelope in his hand. He glanced over at the desk clerk, who paid no attention to him, then began searching surreptitiously through the pile of outgoing mail. The man had been here at the Edgewater for several days now—registered under a false name, of course, and paying his bill in cash. In that time, he'd learned that the late evening hours were best time to check the outgoing mail. There was seldom anybody in the lobby that late. Of course, in early morning, just before the mail delivery, the basket was fuller than it was now. But there was much more foot traffic here in the mornings; the risk of being caught rifling through the outgoing mail became too great.

This time the man got lucky. Really lucky. Two small brown packages near the top of the pile bore Jennifer Bennett's return address. Placing his own letter—a contest entry—at the bottom of the stack in the basket, he quickly slid Jennifer's packages under his sweater and hurried across the lobby toward the elevator. When the doors opened, he punched the button for the third floor.

The desk clerk's eyes never left his newspaper.

• • •

In his apartment at the Edgewater, the man carefully removed the staples from the thicker of the two padded mailers and spilled its contents onto his desk. This package was the same size as several others he'd spotted in the outgoing mail basket earlier in the week. Then, however, there'd been two nosy old women hovering near his elbow and he hadn't been able to make off with any of Jennifer's packages before the mailman arrived.

He grinned broadly as he saw what this mailer contained: the Bennett woman's résumé, chronicling her years in television since her graduation from the University of Washington; a letter applying for a job at a TV station in Santa Barbara; and the real prize—a videocassette.

He got another beer from the refrigerator, then plugged the tape into the VCR, pressed the play button, and sat back to watch. The tape was about twenty minutes long and it featured short clips from Jennifer Bennett's recent TV career. As he watched her work on camera, he could see how her appearance had changed since that newspaper photo of her that he'd seen was taken. She looked older on the tape, but more attractive in some ways. He figured the Hollywood makeup people had gotten to her, taught her a few things. Her on-camera style wasn't too bad, he decided, if you preferred intelligence to glamour. In his opinion, she was getting a little long in the tooth for glamour.

The bulk of the tape featured segments from *Only in L.A.*—including portions of Jennifer Bennett's interviews with people ranging from California's two female senators to a married team of astronauts to the attorney for a famous singer accused of child abuse. He could see that the tone of her interviews was far more serious than what he'd seen on many morning TV talk shows—no four-hundred-pound women whining that they couldn't get respect here, no husbands whose wives had hacked off their dicks. *Only in L.A.* was more likely to include a spot on rebuilding the inner city or a discussion of *Schlindler's List* with Stephen Spielberg and a few local rabbis.

Maybe, the dark-haired man thought, that was why Jennifer Bennett's show had been canceled. Who really wanted to watch this kind of newsy, intellectual bullshit during breakfast, anyway? It was like this Bennett broad was trying to be morning TV's answer to McNeil and Lehrer. Who needed it?

When the tape ended, the man rewound it, but left it in the VCR. He wanted it handy, so he could play it over and over in the days to come, so he could study it to see what it might teach him about this woman who had suddenly become so important in his life. Judging by the similarity of this package to the others he'd seen downstairs, she had sent out plenty of these tapes to TV stations. If one if them failed to arrive at its destination, she would never know the difference.

Feeling pleased with his find, the man returned to his desk and finished his beer. He tossed the empty bottle into a wastebasket that was already overflowing. It bounced out and landed on the floor without breaking. Hell, he was paying extra for once-a-week maid service. The goddamned maids could empty the wastebaskets; he sure wasn't going to do it.

The second package was considerably thinner than the first. He could tell it was too thin to contain another videocassette. Pulling out the staples with care, he dumped out the mailer's contents and caught his breath. Holy shit! This *was* his lucky day.

The man read the letter twice, forcing his eyes away from the photos that held so much interest for him. He kept the pictures for last, so he could savor the anticipation— the way he always looked forward to a rich, sweet dessert after a mediocre dinner. The letter was of little interest to him, except that it was obviously addressed to Jennifer Bennett's mother and its tone revealed the older woman to be a piss-poor grandmother for the little girl called Amy. No surprise there. The dark-haired man could have predicted that.

Finally, he turned to the photos, examining them one by one. The photographer's lighting highlighted the kid's reddish hair, the dusting of freckles across her nose, her two permanent front teeth still too big for her pert seven-year-old face. She was a friendly-looking kid, destined to be a real looker when she grew up. He could have predicted that, too.

There were six different pictures in all, each with the word, *proof* written across the bottom in pale blue letters. The reluctant grandmother in Idaho sure as hell didn't need all six of them; he'd bet the old bitch didn't really want any of them. He was tempted to keep them all, but, reminding himself that there was no percentage in being stupid, he stifled that urge. If none of these photos ever arrived in Twin Falls, Jennifer Bennett would surely notice. And if she knew some of her mail was missing, she might begin to suspect something was amiss at the Edgewater. He didn't want her to move out of here, not until he was ready for her.

Staring longingly at the photos, the man decided to compromise. He picked out the proof he liked best—the one where the kid's head was tilted to the side and a big blue bow was clipped in her hair—and stuffed the others back into the mailer, along with the letter. He restapled the package and set it on the small oak table next to his front door. First thing in the morning, he would bring it back downstairs and send it on its way to Idaho.

Fascinated by the sixth photo of the child known as Amy Bennett, the dark-haired man carried it into his bedroom, where he propped it up against the clock radio on the nightstand next to his bed. Looking at the little girl's smiling face made him feel good, and he hadn't felt really good in a long, long time.

His glance fell upon the binoculars he'd bought that afternoon. He picked them up and walked over to his bedroom window. Pushing back the drapes, he peered through the high-powered lenses across the courtyard and pool area toward the windows of Jennifer Bennett's apartment. Her drapes were drawn and her lights turned off. But that didn't matter so much right now. He had her on tape, and he had the child captured in the photograph. Yawning, he set his binoculars down on the windowsill, where they would be handy when he resumed his surveillance tomorrow. Right now, what he needed was a good night's rest.

As he pulled back the bedcovers and crawled into bed, the little girl's image smiled at him from the nightstand. It was the last thing he saw before he fell into a deep, dream-filled sleep.

Chapter

10

Brushing an invisible spec of lint off his jacket, Forrest Hathaway rapped three times on the door of Jennifer's apartment. A middle-aged Hispanic woman opened it. "Oh, hello," he said. "I'm here for Ms. Bennett."

The woman grinned. "So you're the boyfriend."

Forrest's eyebrows rose. "Sounds like I've been promoted."

Amy sprinted toward the front door from the rear of the apartment, skidding to a stop just behind her baby-sitter. "Hi, Mr. Hathaway," she said. "My mom's on the phone."

"Hello there, Amy. Okay if I come in and wait for her?"

"Gotta ask Maria." The little girl yanked on her baby-sitter's sleeve.

Her hands resting on her ample hips, Maria stepped away from the doorway. "Come on in and sit down, Mr. Hathaway. Jennifer probably won't be long." Her dark eyes boldly checked out her employer's male visitor, beginning with his shoes and ending with his blow-dried hair.

"What's the verdict?" Forrest asked her. "Do I pass muster?"

"Far as I'm concerned, you do, but that one"—Maria cocked her head toward Jennifer's bedroom—"she's way too picky, you ask my opinion. I tell her, get yourself a husband while—I mean, a woman her age ought to be married a long time ago. A woman needs a husband, a child needs a father. But she's so stub—"

"Maria, please!" Jennifer came into the living room, holding her purse in her hand. Her face was quickly reddening. "Hello, Forrest."

Noting Jennifer's obvious embarrassment, Forrest burst into good-natured laughter. "Looks like Maria here has a few opinions about your love life," he said.

"Maria has a few opinions about everything."

Maria had a smug look on her face, but she held her tongue.

"Nice place you have here, Jennifer," Forrest said, surveying the room. "Impeccable taste."

"Right, the fifties motel look. Just like yours, huh?"

"Precisely. Except mine's a little smaller and I have a really exquisite Formica coffee table—vintage plastic. Very chic."

Despite her embarrassment, Jennifer's mood began to lift and she laughed.

"Ready to go?" Forrest asked her.

"In just a minute." She turned to Maria. "That call was about a job interview—next Monday. I have to go to Seattle. Can you come and stay with Amy from Sunday afternoon until late Monday night?"

The darker woman bit her lip and shook her head slowly. "Sorry, Jennifer. I'd really like to, but Armando says no more overnights. Since the plant laid him off, he says he's been stuck taking care of our kids too much— calls it woman's work. If I'm not home to sleep at night, he gets real mad. You know how it is."

"You're sure Armando won't make an exception, just this once?"

"Sorry. I don't even like to ask him anymore, he gets so—" Maria's gaze fell upon Amy, who was listening to the adults' conversation intently, and she cut herself off in midsentence. "Take my word for it, it's just not worth it."

Jennifer sighed. Armando Rodriguez was a puzzle. The man had been angry and possessive when Jennifer first employed Maria full-time as her housekeeper; although he was quick to spend the money his wife earned working for the Bennett family, he'd resented the time she spent taking care of anybody other than him and their own four children.

Armando had become even more hostile since Jennifer lost her job and was forced to let Maria go. Jennifer's guess was that the man was far more than a social drinker, perhaps a full-blown alcoholic, and she wouldn't be surprised if he were both verbally and physically abusive to his wife whenever she did something he didn't like.

Jennifer never had been able to figure out why Maria was such an advocate of marriage. Maybe it was a cultural thing, or maybe Maria subconsciously wanted other women to be as trapped as she was. "Don't worry about it, Maria," Jennifer said. She certainly didn't want to be responsible for bringing more conflict into Maria's home life. "I'll find somebody else."

"I could stay with Patty and Joey, Mom." Amy seemed eager for the opportunity to spend the night with her school friends.

"Maybe, sweetheart. I'll call their mother and ask her after I get home." Jennifer glanced at her watch and turned to Forrest. "If I take time to do that now, we'll be late for our reservation."

"Whatever's comfortable for you, Jennifer. I could call the restaurant and tell them we're running late."

"No, we can still make it if we leave now." Jennifer bent over and gave Amy a brief hug and kiss. "You be a good girl for Maria, sweetie. If you take your bath right away, she'll put on that *Black Stallion* movie we rented."

"Will you, Maria, will you?"

"Sure, Amy, long as you wash behind your ears and clean up the bathroom real good when you're done."

"Yippee!" The child raced out of the room, her curls bouncing.

"The tape's already in the VCR, Maria. You just have to turn it on. And see that Amy goes to bed as soon as it's over, will you? Tomorrow's a school day."

Maria rolled her eyes. "How long've I been taking care of Amy now, Jennifer? You think I don't know what's a school day and what's not?"

"Sorry, Maria, guess I'm a little nervous lately. I'll be back about ten, ten-thirty at the latest."

"Just have a good time, Jennifer. Relax for once, have some fun with this good-looking gentleman." Maria winked at Forrest, who smiled and winked back at her.

As he helped Jennifer into her coat, Forrest whispered into her ear, "Sounds like pretty good advice to me."

"Hey, listen, Jennifer, if you can't get anybody to stay with Amy Sunday night, I'd be happy to do it," Forrest said as he sipped his coffee. "It's only the one night, right? And I do live just down the hall."

Jennifer stiffened. "I couldn't do that—leave my daughter with somebody she hardly knows." Jennifer and Forrest were finishing their desserts at Ocean Avenue Seafood. The noisy, trendy restaurant across the street from Santa Monica's Palisades Park was packed with young, affluent patrons enjoying all varieties of the freshest fish and seafood.

Jennifer knew she didn't need the calories, but she couldn't resist having a small crème caramel. There was something about the creamy custard that she always found soothing. Maybe it was because it reminded her of the egg custards her grandmother used to make for her when she was a small child. "Thanks for the offer, Forrest," she said, "but I'm sure Amy will be able to stay with one of her friends."

"Whatever. Let me know if you change your mind. I'm pretty good with kids and I work cheap." Forrest reached across the table and patted Jennifer's hand briefly, as if to reassure her.

At Forrest's touch, Jennifer felt a jolt of electricity course through her body. Had he felt it, too? His smile was friendly as always, with perhaps just a hint of teasing behind it. He showed no sign of having felt the sexual charge Jennifer did. She told herself that the man had probably meant to display nothing more than kindness to a neighbor who was going through a difficult time.

Forrest Hathaway seemed to be a compassionate man and Jennifer could see why he had become a writer—he obviously was interested in other people and what made them tick. And he had a good sense of humor, too; Forrest could even laugh at himself, which, in Jennifer's experience, was a rare and valuable quality.

Certain superficial things about this man who lived down the hall reminded her of Howard, her most recent romantic interest—both men were tall, trim, and dark-haired. If she didn't look too hard, they resembled each other physically. But Howard was much more full of himself, far less interested in others, including Jennifer and particularly Amy. Children bored Howard. Come to think of it, almost everyone bored Howard, except Howard.

"Amy's not very used to men," Jennifer explained. "Even if I knew you better, Forrest, I'm afraid she'd be scared to death if I left her alone overnight with you. If none of her friends' moms can take care of her, I'll figure out some way to take her to Seattle with me. Or else I just won't go."

"Do you want this job?"

Jennifer let the last bite of custard melt on her tongue while she gathered her thoughts. She swallowed and washed it down with a sip of tea before she spoke. "The truth? I honestly don't know, Forrest." Two weeks ago, she would have been thrilled to get an offer from this Seattle station. Seattle was a good market, smaller than L.A., of course, but growing fast, and housing was still relatively inexpensive there—at least by Southern California standards. If she went to work in Seattle, particularly at a network affiliate station like this one, she knew she'd probably be able to afford a small house of her own. Still, right now she was feeling more aware of all she would have to leave behind.

"I'm not anxious to leave Los Angeles . . . if I don't have to," she admitted. "A good friend of mine says I should go into the production end of the news business, forget about the on-camera stuff. Maybe if I did that I could stay here."

Forrest signaled the waiter to refill his coffee cup. "How do you feel about that?"

Jennifer had finished her tea, but she refused the waiter's offer to bring her more hot water. When he had left, she said to Forrest, "I thought you said you studied journalism, not psychology."

He shrugged. "I minored in psych. Plus, I'm just interested. I don't think you can be a good writer without knowing something about psychology, how people feel, why they do what they do. And you know us advertising sharks—we have to figure out how to manipulate people's most basic urges to sell them all that stuff they don't really need." He reached across the table once more and, this time, his hand remained cupped over Jennifer's. "But, hey," he told her, "I don't mean to give you the third degree here. If you don't want to answer, just tell me to buzz off. You won't be the first."

"I'm not going to tell you to buzz off." Jennifer felt warmth radiate through her entire body. This feeling was both exciting and very, very frightening. Was Forrest Hathaway becoming one of the reasons she wanted to stay here in L.A.? But that was obviously both premature and very foolish, given her current circumstances. She couldn't afford to fall for this man. Not now. That would only make leaving here that much more difficult. She pulled her hand away and planted it safely in her lap. "You've asked me a fair question," she told him. "Only thing is, I don't know whether I've got the answer. See, when I got into broadcasting, I think a big part of its appeal for me was that I wanted to be famous. Or at least well known, special in some way. I wanted to be noticed, I wanted to count for something." She watched Forrest's face for any signs that he found her admission foolish, but she detected none.

"Let me guess." He cradled his coffee cup with his hands, as though to warm them. "When you were a kid, you never felt special at home."

"Bingo, Mr. Freud. I always did with my dad, I guess, whenever he was around. But he died when I was just a kid. My mother . . . Well, I think she has what psychologists call a narcissistic personality."

"You mean she's only interested in herself."

"Basically, yes. My relative importance to my mother has always depended completely upon what I could do for her. Still does."

With a sudden flash of insight, Jennifer realized that Howard Whittaker's personality was amazingly like her mother's. Could that be why she'd been so attracted to the man for so long? Was it the challenge of trying to reform Howard, to make him capable of loving her, that had appealed to her so strongly?

. She felt a chill of recognition crawl down her spine. If she'd been able to reform Howard's basic self-centeredness, to transform him into a loving person, Jennifer thought, then . . . Then what? Her desire to change Howard felt somehow connected to the attempts she'd made to do the same with her mother. But how?

This was all too complicated, particularly this late at night, after two glasses of chardonnay. Still, the similarity between her mother and Howard—and between her mother and Howard's many equally self-obsessed predecessors— was something Jennifer realized she would have to examine more carefully. Later, in one of her many nighttime reveries.

The waiter brought the check and Forrest looked it over, quickly verifying the total.

"Why don't we split that?" Jennifer offered. "I did promise to buy you a drink, remember?"

Forrest shook his head. "Not tonight. You can invite me over to your place for a glass of wine or a cup of coffee anytime. But this is my treat."

Jennifer was relieved that her offer wasn't accepted. Putting another fifty bucks on her credit card would definitely pinch.

"So," Forrest asked, tossing his Visa card on top of the bill, "how much would it bother you to give up stardom?"

"Stardom?" Jennifer closed her eyes and shook her head. "I never got stardom, not even close. Some local recognition, maybe. A sense of achievement, for sure. Even attracted a few nut cases, but that kind of attention I definitely don't need. Let's not get into that, though." She refolded her napkin and placed it on the tablecloth. "Hey, I'm a journalist, Forrest and, like a lot of journalists, I guess I tried to find something in my work that I didn't have in my personal life."

"Like public notoriety as a substitute for love."

Jennifer felt her throat tighten. "Amy's helped," she said in a small voice, feeling lonelier than she had in months. "A lot."

"Amy's a great kid," Forrest said, signing the credit card receipt that the waiter presented to him. "Wish I had one like her. But kids grow up, don't they, Jennifer? The catch is, if you do your job as a parent right, in the end, your children just up and leave you."

Sighing, Jennifer folded her napkin and put it on the table. This was beginning to feel too much like psychotherapy. It was getting too personal, making her feel far too vulnerable. "It's getting close to ten," she said, sliding her chair away from the table. "I'd better get back." She slipped her arms into her coat, which was draped over the back of her chair, and stood up.

Forrest put his arm around her shoulders as they left the restaurant. "Don't beat yourself up," he said, pulling her closer. "Everybody wants love. We all just have to learn to look for it in the right places."

As they walked toward Forrest's car, Jennifer wondered if she would ever really discover where those right places were.

Jennifer laid her garment bag flat in the back of the car and reached for Amy's overnight bag and backpack. "Did you remember your toothbrush?" she asked her daughter, stowing the small bags in the back of the station wagon and closing the rear door.

"*And* my brush and comb and my school clothes for tomorrow and my—"

"Okay, okay, let's go, then, sweetheart." Jennifer opened the passenger's side door and watched as Amy climbed in and fastened her seat belt. "Remember to be extra specially good at the Averys', won't you?" she said as she slid behind the steering wheel and backed the car out of her parking space in the Edgewater's garage. "Mrs. Avery says Patty and Joey both don't feel good, so you'll probably have to stay away from them as much as you can."

"We can stay inside and play. I don't mind. They got a brand-new puppy!"

"Just do whatever Mrs. Avery tells you and be a real good girl." Jennifer was bone tired. She'd had a nearly sleepless night, lying awake and feeling increasingly uneasy about this trip to Seattle. A big part of her anxiety was because of Lauren Avery's obvious reluctance to keep Amy overnight. Although both Patty and Joey had been fine at school on Friday, Lauren claimed her children both were coming down with something, and warned that Amy might catch it if she stayed overnight with them. Jennifer couldn't tell whether that was true or just an excuse.

But this was an emergency. If Lauren couldn't or wouldn't keep Amy, Jennifer knew she would have to cancel her job interview, and she couldn't afford to do that. So, in the end, she had practically begged Lauren to let Amy stay over for just tonight, and the other mother had reluctantly agreed. Jennifer had promised to pick up her daughter on her way home from the airport tomorrow, even though her plane wasn't due in until nine-thirty at night—well after the children's bedtime.

If only Maria had been able to stay with Amy at the apartment, things would have been so much easier. Next time, Jennifer thought, she would just have to figure out a way to take Amy along with her. If there was a next time. It was abundantly clear that she could no longer impose on her friends.

As Jennifer left Amy off at the Averys' front door, the little girl stretched her arms upward to give her mother a final hug. "Promise you'll come back and get me tomorrow, Mom?" The child's voice was wistful now, sad.

Jennifer bent down and put her arms around her daughter's waist. "I already told you I would, Amy. You'll probably already be asleep by the time I get here, but I'll come for you just as soon as my plane gets in."

"Cross your heart and hope to die?" Amy's forehead was deeply creased and, now that she saw her mother about to leave her behind, she looked worried. Her earlier enthusiasm over spending the night with her school friends was quickly waning.

"Cross my heart and hope to die," Jennifer said, holding

Amy close and breathing in the clean smell of the little girl's freshly shampooed hair. "Nothing's going to keep me away from you, Amy."

"I'm really gonna miss you, Mom."

"I'm really going to miss you, too, sweetie." She stood up again. "Wish me luck on my interview, okay?"

Amy nodded her head solemnly. "But who's gonna tuck me in tonight, Mom?"

Jennifer swallowed hard. "Tell you what. At bedtime, I'll be thinking about you real, real hard. If you think about me real hard, it'll be almost like we're together. Okay?"

"Okay, Mom. I love you." Amy kissed her mother good-bye and went inside the Spanish-style stucco house to find Patty and Joey and the new puppy, while Jennifer gave Lauren Avery her itinerary and a phone number where she could be reached in an emergency.

As she drove toward the airport, Jennifer felt a strong pang of guilt—the "bad mother" guilt that so often plagued her these days. If she was truly a good mother, she felt in her heart, she wouldn't be heading for Seattle today, out of work, and very nearly out of money. If she was a good mother, she would be home with her daughter, where she belonged. The corollary to this kind of thinking was that, if she wasn't a good mother, she must—by definition—be a bad mother.

Six hours later, Jennifer was lying in a strange bed, listening to the rain pelting against her hotel room's windows, and trying unsuccessfully to fall asleep. Damn! she thought. If she didn't manage to get some rest tonight, she knew she would look far older than her thirty-nine years at her interview tomorrow. She wouldn't have the sharp mental edge she knew she needed to impress the station's news director, either.

As she tossed and turned, she tried imagining Santa Monica Beach and counting the waves as they hit the shore—her version of counting sheep. But tonight this old trick wasn't working. She kept seeing Amy instead, worrying about whether her little girl was really okay, and wishing she were home with her daughter instead of here in Seattle, waiting to interview for a job she didn't even know if she wanted. Had Amy gotten to sleep without her mother to tuck her into bed for the night? The two of them were so accustomed to spending half an hour or so together at the end of the day, lying close together in Amy's bed while Jennifer read her a story.

Of course Amy's all right, Jennifer told herself sharply. One night apart wouldn't hurt either of them. Lauren Avery might not have been happy about having an extra child stay at her house tonight, but she would never let any harm come to Amy. And Amy had clearly been enthusiastic about spending the night with Patty and Joey, at least until it was time for Jennifer to leave for the airport. She was probably just fine again as soon as her mother was out of sight. The Avery children hadn't looked particularly ill when Jennifer left Amy off at their place, either. But even if they were, the truth was that Amy would already have been exposed to whatever illness they had at school on Friday. Spending the night at the Avery house probably wouldn't make things much worse than they already were.

Everything was fine in Los Angeles, Jennifer reassured herself. She had to make herself believe that.

At midnight, she got up and took two aspirin for her tension headache, washing them down with a glass of tap water. Her face, reflected in the bathroom mirror, looked haggard. Might as well forget this whole thing, she told herself. If she ever anchored the evening news looking the way she did right now, she would scare away viewers, not attract them. The lines around her mouth seemed deeper, there were dark bags under her eyes, and her skin had taken on a dull, grayish tone. She looked at least fifty.

Maybe Sally Donovan was right, Jennifer thought. Maybe it was time she started thinking about working behind the scenes. Suddenly that prospect didn't seem as terrible as it had a few days ago. Jennifer had frequently contributed programming ideas to *Only in L.A.*, and her suggestions invariably improved the show. She knew all about staff scheduling, formating shows, arranging for talent, and dealing with the brass and the consultants. Sally knew what she was talking about, all right—Jennifer could be a truly outstanding producer, if only she set her mind to it. And, at nearly forty, wasn't it about time she gave up her foolish childhood dream of becoming a star?

By the time Jennifer crawled back between the hotel sheets that smelled faintly of chlorine bleach, she'd made up her mind. If this interview tomorrow didn't result in a job offer, she could live with that. Even if it did, she would not accept the job unless she was really convinced it was right for both her and Amy. For the first time, Jennifer began to believe that there were other options opening up to her, options that might even let her stay in Los Angeles.

Pulling the blanket up under her chin and nestling her head against the pillows, Jennifer felt her shoulders and neck muscles gradually begin to lose their tension. Now, her mind more at ease, conjuring up a mental picture of the beach finally began to help her relax. As she drifted toward sleep, a man wearing a blue bathing suit jogged along the sand of her imaginary Southern California seashore. He was tall, thin and dark-haired, with just a touch of gray at his temples. A moment later, she saw herself—young, healthy and beautiful once more—racing across the sand toward the jogger, calling for him to wait for her.

As she caught up with him, Forrest Hathaway turned and held out his arms to welcome her.

Chapter

12

~

The dark-haired man picked up his binoculars and focused them once more on the windows of Jennifer Bennett's apartment. Her drapes were still drawn and her place was completely dark. Where the hell were the two of them? It was almost midnight and he'd been checking those windows across the courtyard periodically since midafternoon. This was a school night, wasn't it? That bitch had no right to keep the kid out this late on a school night. What kind of mother was she?

But maybe they were home after all, he thought. Maybe somehow he'd missed them. After all, he hadn't been watching the windows constantly. Nobody could. He'd taken some time out to eat the pizza delivered by that restaurant down the street, and he'd watched a little television, off and on.

He knew one way to find out. He slipped his shoes on and padded down the hall toward the elevator. When he arrived at the basement level, he found the apartment building's underground garage completely quiet. His own car—he'd taken the beige Toyota back to Alamo and traded it for the same model in red a few days ago—was right where he'd left it, parked next to the garage entrance. His nose wrinkling in distaste as he breathed in the foul odor of stale exhaust fumes, he walked slowly up and down all the aisles, checking out every parked car. But Jennifer Bennett's station wagon was nowhere to be found.

Shit! Could she have moved out of the Edgewater? His pulse sped up. Could she have taken the kid right out from under his nose and moved out of this place? Damn that fucking bitch! His body now shaking with rage, the dark-haired man took the elevator back upstairs to his apartment.

As he got ready for bed, he set his alarm clock for six o'clock in the morning. There was only one thing left for him to do—he would check the garage again early in the morning. If the station wagon hadn't returned by then, he would find the Bennett broad and the kid the same way he'd found them last time.

The next morning, the dark-haired man was parked just past the circular driveway in front of Brinton Academy, watching in his rearview mirror as the children were dropped off at the school entrance by their parents and nannies. He watched as one child arrived in a chauffeured limousine and two others were dropped off by a taxicab. Spoiled, pampered little brats!

But he saw no sign of either the Bennett woman's station wagon or the little girl. The man's grip on his steering wheel tightened and he could feel his sweaty hands starting to slip on the rough plastic surface. What if they'd moved out of town? What if the kid wasn't coming back to this school, ever? Shit! It could take him weeks to find them again, not to mention more money wasted on another money-grubbing private eye.

It was almost eight o'clock now, time for school to begin, and he'd been sitting here, watching the front of the building for more than an hour. Usually, he knew, the Bennett car arrived at Brinton Academy by fifteen or twenty minutes before eight. At a minute before eight, the heavy traffic in the circular driveway was down to only a few stragglers, the chronic late arrivers. But still the man wasn't ready to give up.

At precisely eight o'clock, two cars pulled into the circular driveway, a gold Volvo station wagon and a bronze Mercedes sedan. He watched as two small boys emerged from the Volvo and a little girl got out of the Mercedes. Wait just a minute! The girl was about the right height. Her hair looked redder than that of the child he was looking for, but maybe that was just a trick of the bright morning sun. He had to find out whether it was her.

With one smooth motion, the dark-haired man opened his door, slid out of his car, and hurried around the concrete cresent in front of the school. He caught a look at the Mercedes's driver as she turned onto the street; she was a blond all right, but she wasn't Jennifer Bennett. By the time the child who'd emerged from the car reached the school steps, the man was only half a dozen feet behind her.

"Hey! Little girl!" he called to her.

The copper-haired child turned and looked at the man with curiosity.

"Come on over here a minute, honey. I just want to talk to you." He smiled at her eagerly.

The child's expression turned to fear and she began to run up the stairs, heading for the sanctuary of the school.

In the same instant, a woman who'd been standing near the doorway greeting the children as they arrived started down the stairs, taking them two at a time. "Run along to class, Amy," she ordered in a clipped, anxious voice. Her jaw set, the teacher turned toward the dark-haired man and called to him, "Who are you? What are you doing here?"

"I . . . I . . . Nothing." The man spun around and sprinted off the school grounds toward his car.

The teacher watched as he gunned the red Toyota's engine and sped away into heavy morning traffic on San Vicente Boulevard.

13

It was nearly ten-thirty by the time Jennifer picked up Amy at the Averys' house. The pajama-clad child was asleep on the living room sofa.

"Patty and Joey stayed home from school today," Lauren Avery told Jennifer as she opened the door. "But I took Amy in. Probably won't know whether she's going to get their cold for a few more days. So far she looks fine."

Jennifer thanked her friend, woke Amy, and herded her out to the car with her bags, which Lauren had packed and waiting. The poor kid would be a wreck at school tomorrow, Jennifer thought, if she didn't get her home to bed quickly.

Jennifer saw the message light on her phone answering machine blinking as she opened the front door to her apartment. Was Seattle calling with a job offer? Probably not, she realized; nothing would happen this quickly, although she'd left Seattle with a good feeling about the interview. The news director had seemed particularly friendly, and he'd introduced her to all the most important members of his staff.

"Come on, sweetheart, let's get you into bed," Jennifer said to Amy. As she tucked the sleepy little girl in and bent down to kiss her good night, Amy reached up and hugged her mother extra tight.

"I'm real glad you're back, Mommy. It wasn't very fun at Patty's house. She's sick and her momma wouldn't let her play with me."

"I know, sweetie. I'm sorry you didn't have a good time, but we're both back home now and it's very late. Go to sleep real fast so you're not too tired for school tomorrow and we'll do something special together—just you and me—tomorrow afternoon."

Within minutes, Amy had dozed off. Jennifer reached out and gently brushed the child's reddish blond bangs off her smooth porcelain forehead, then tiptoed out of the bedroom and closed the door behind her.

Before tending to her messages and the unpacking, Jennifer poured herself a glass of chardonnay from the refrigerator. The first sip tasted cold and sharp and soothing as she held it briefly on her tongue. Soon the wine began to relax her and she turned to the phone machine. The display told her she had three messages.

The first was from last night—Forrest Hathaway, telling her that he hoped her trip would be successful. Jennifer felt an emotional wrench as she heard his voice. So Forrest hoped her trip would be successful. What exactly did that mean? Perhaps it was nothing more than a polite statement, the kind one makes to a neighbor. If she moved to Seattle, it would probably mean nothing to him. And why should it? She and Forrest barely knew each other. Certainly it was far too early in their relationship for her to be thinking of them as any kind of couple.

The phone machine beeped after Forrest's call and a second male voice boomed out into the room. "Jen-babe, hi, it's me." She recognized Howard Whittaker's baritone. "It's Sunday night, little after nine. Just got in from a four-day turnaround to Tokyo and Hong Kong. Rough schedule, but

I had plenty of time to think over there. I, ah—I miss you, babe. How 'bout we get together tomorrow night and talk things over? Take you to Spago. Call me."

Howard's message came as a bit of a shock to Jennifer. It had been only a couple of weeks since she'd last seen him, but already he seemed like a character from her distant past. She'd even forgotten that she'd given him her phone number here at the Edgewater. So Howard had been thinking, had he? That probably meant he'd dreamed up yet another plan to sweet-talk her into continuing their relationship under his rules of permanent noncommitment. Particularly if his idea of talking things over was to chat over a meal at Spago. Impress the woman with an expensive dinner and she'll agree to anything, right, Howard?

Not long ago, a message like this from Howard Whittaker would have made Jennifer's heart surge with renewed hope. A few weeks ago, she would have convinced herself that Howard was finally coming around after all. Now, she realized, she didn't even care. If she never saw Howard again, it would mean nothing to her. Was that because she'd met Forrest Hathaway? Or maybe because a new job in Seattle had begun to seem a strong possibility for her? Or simply because she realized she didn't love Howard? Whatever the reason, she decided not to return his call. Let him stew for once; she'd done that plenty of times over the past year. Let him find some other gullible woman to take to Spago.

Another beep preceded the third message. "Ms. Bennett," a woman's cool, cultured voice announced. "This is Ms. Samuels, at Brinton Academy. There was a—a rather nasty incident here at school today involving Amy and I'd like to discuss it with you, privately, as soon as possible." As she listened, Jennifer's grip on her wine glass tightened. Ms. Samuels's voice had an officious edge to it, as always. "I would appreciate it if you and I could speak tomorrow, here at the school," the teacher continued. "I don't have door duty Tuesday morning. The principal's office will know where to locate me before classes begin. Seven-thirty would be most convenient."

Had Amy done something wrong? Jennifer sincerely hoped not. There'd been another "nasty incident" when Amy was in kindergarten, less than a year after they'd moved to Los Angeles. Another child's paint box had been found in Amy's backpack and she'd been accused of stealing it. Amy had denied taking the other child's paints, but nobody believed her. Even Jennifer couldn't be sure. It had happened back in the difficult days when Amy was in therapy twice a week, still working through whatever traumas had preceded Jennifer's adopting her. Children sometimes steal when they're emotionally distressed, Jennifer knew. Amy's therapist had confirmed what she already understood—that trantrums, stealing, lying, property destruction, or worse, all could be ways in which children acted out their anger when they couldn't find the words to express what they were feeling.

In Jennifer's mind, whether or not Amy had stolen that paint box was singularly unimportant. The theft was a small transgression at worst, but Brinton Academy's official stand had been considerably tougher minded. If Amy ever stole again, the principal had warned Jennifer, the child would be summarily expelled. Private, unlike public, schools had the power to do that to a child—banish her without so much as a trial. Presumed guilty as accused.

Was her daughter becoming emotionally traumatized again, Jennifer wondered with a pang of guilt. Was Amy distressed enough to steal . . . or to cheat on a test . . . or what? Surely all the recent disruption in the little girl's home life could have put her development back a notch or two, what with moving away from the house she loved, having her mother out of work and constantly worried about money, even spending the past two days with a sick friend while Jennifer was a thousand miles away.

Jennifer shuddered as she recalled the miserable child Amy had been five years ago—a child who wet her bed almost nightly, a child who could hardly utter a complete, understandable sentence, a child who seemed to hate herself and everyone around her. Jennifer didn't want that child back again—for Amy's sake as well as her own.

As she unpacked her garment bag and got ready for bed, Jennifer found that all thoughts of her Seattle trip quickly disappeared from her mind, as did her romantic musings about Forrest and Howard. Only Ms. Samuels's worrisome call and Amy's future seemed important to her now.

Chapter

14

Jennifer perched on an uncomfortable brown metal folding chair in the tiny cubicle adjacent to the Brinton Academy principal's office. Frightened and worried, she had responded to Ms. Samuels's telephone message by showing up at Brinton Academy well before the suggested meeting time.

The teacher sat behind a large yellow metal desk, obviously the power position in this tiny room, not to mention the far more comfortable seat. Jennifer's knees were wedged against the cold front panel of the big desk. Apparently this room was used by teachers holding private conferences with their elementary school students; for adult-sized conferees, it was far too cramped.

"I didn't mean to alarm you unnecessarily," Ms. Samuels said, "but we at Brinton Academy feel we can never be too careful."

"Of course not," Jennifer said, wishing the woman would get to the point. If Amy was being expelled, why tiptoe through all these preliminaries. "Look, has Amy done something wrong?" she asked. "Because, if she has—"

"Oh, no, it's nothing like that. We're quite pleased with Amy here. She's a delightful child, quite imaginative in her own way. It's—well, I wondered whether you might have an ex-husband . . ."

Jennifer's bristled. Whatever she'd been expecting to hear, it wasn't this. "What did you ask me? If I had an ex-husband? No, no I don't." What made Jennifer's marital status any business of Brinton Academy, anyway? "Why do you ask?" Her voice turned cold.

The teacher made eye contact with Jennifer for the first time since their meeting had begun. "I see. Then this might be more serious than I first thought. She drew in a deep breath. "Yesterday morning, I noticed that Mrs. Avery dropped Amy at school."

"That's right. I had an out-of-town meeting, so Amy stayed overnight with the Averys. I asked Lauren to drive her to school."

"Amy was late—only a minute or two, but I was just about to close up the front door for the morning when she arrived." Picking up a pencil in her long, bony fingers, Ms. Samuels began to draw geometric shapes on a piece of lined paper.

"Yes? So why did you call me?" It certainly wasn't because Amy was two minutes late to school. When *would* this irritating woman spit out whatever she had to say?

"As Amy was approaching the front steps, a man came up and began to speak to her. I thought—well, we've had a few situations where there's been a custody dispute and—"

"I already told you there's nothing like that with Amy." Jennifer's mind began to race. "What kind of man? Who was he?"

"I'm trying to tell you, Ms. Bennett, if you'll just listen." Jennifer forced herself to be patient. Ms. Samuels put down her pencil and resumed her tale. "I called out to her. The child was already late for school, as I told you. When she heard me, Amy hurried up the steps toward the front door, and I headed down the steps to have a few words with this man. I mean, I didn't know who he was, you understand?

We can't have strange men coming up to our children right on the school grounds. Not at Brinton Academy."

Jennifer was quickly getting the impression that Ms. Samuels cared far more about Brinton Academy's pristine reputation than she did Amy's safety. "What did this man look like?" she asked. "Did he call Amy by name?" A vision of the rubbery baby doll left in a paper bag on their front steps back at Seaview Ridge flashed into Jennifer's mind.

Ms. Samuels closed her eyes, as though trying to conjure up a vision of the intruder on the circular drive. "It happened so fast. . . . No, I never heard him call her by name. I think he just called her 'little girl,' or maybe 'young lady,' something like that. My impression is that he was a fairly tall man, maybe around six feet, dark hair, average-to-slender build. But I'm not sure I'd be able to identify him. I think he was wearing some kind of jacket, nothing expensive. Maybe a denim windbreaker kind of thing."

Jennifer tried to remember the man in the dark blue or black Ford who'd driven past her house on moving day. He was dark-haired, that much she recalled. But she'd never actually gotten a clear look at his face. Besides, any number of people she knew could fit Ms. Samuels's description—not only the man in the Ford, but Howard Whittaker or Maria Rodriguez's husband Armando or even Forrest Hathaway. "How old a man was he?"

"Hard to say. Could be anywhere from thirty to fifty. I didn't really get a good look at him, Ms. Bennett. As soon as I started down the steps after him, he turned around and left."

Jennifer thought for a minute. She had to know whether this guy had been after Amy specifically, or if any little girl would do. Or maybe he was totally harmless, just somebody asking directions who'd been frightened off by Ms. Samuels' officious manner. "How did he get there?" Jennifer asked, her knuckles turning white as she knotted her fingers together. "I mean, was he on foot, or did he come in a car?"

"Like I told you, he was on foot when he approached Amy. But, when I started down the steps after him, he ran across the driveway and out to the street. He got into a car that was parked just past the circular drive."

"Did you get his license number?"

Ms. Samuels shook her head. "No, it happened much too fast for that, and I—well, I didn't know at the time whether it was really anything we needed to be concerned about. I think his car was red, though." Her teeth bit down on her lower lip. "Yes, now I remember. The car he was driving was definitely red."

Scratch the guy in the dark blue Ford, Jennifer thought. "What makes you think this man was especially interested in Amy, Ms. Samuels? I mean, maybe he only wanted to ask her for directions, or he might have been looking for another child and he meant to ask Amy about her. Or him."

"Anything's possible, Ms. Bennett, I just don't know. He didn't try to grab Amy or anything like that. I didn't think the incident warranted calling the police right away. I wouldn't have been able to give them a clear identification of the man, anyway. But I thought I'd better talk to you, see if you might have any explanation."

"No, I have no idea at all." The last thing Jennifer was inclined to do was tell this uptight teacher that somebody had left toys on her doorstep. Brinton Academy was so straitlaced that they might even kick Amy out if they felt her presence might put the school in any kind of danger. Besides, Jennifer thought, she and Amy had already moved away from Seaview Ridge; if yesterday's incident in any way involved the man who'd left the toys at their old house, he wouldn't know where to find them anymore. She decided her best move was to go on the offensive. "I expect Amy to be kept completely safe here at Brinton, Ms. Samuels—from the minute she arrives in the morning until I pick her up in the afternoon. If somebody's hanging around here, threatening little girls, I strongly suggest you put on some extra security."

The teacher's eyebrows rose. "We have always been very, *very* security conscious here, Ms. Bennett. There has never been any kind of assault on any of our children or, heaven forbid, a kidnapping attempt. I simply wanted to inform you about yesterday, in case you had a family member or . . . Well, you've already told me that's not the case here." She pushed her chair away from the desk and stood up. "We'll keep a careful eye on Amy, as always. If anything like this ever happens again, we'll call the police immediately. You needn't worry about your daughter while she's with us."

Jennifer picked up her purse and rose to go. She would have to talk with Amy tonight. She would have to find a way to warn her daughter, preferably without needlessly terrifying her. Not that Amy didn't already know strangers could be dangerous, of course. Jennifer had been warning her about strangers for years now, and they'd had a long discussion only a short while ago about the kidnapping of that Petaluma girl. The story had been all over the news for weeks and Amy had been worried that a bad man might break into her house and take her away. Jennifer and Amy had taken that self-defense class together, too. Still, all of those warnings were abstract; this time, danger was threatening to become all too personal.

"I appreciate your letting me know about this, Ms. Samuels," Jennifer said, shaking the teacher's hand. "I'll talk to Amy. And, please, please, take good care of her."

"That's our job, Ms. Bennett."

Jennifer stood and watched as Ms. Samuels marched down the marble-lined hallway to her class. She wanted desperately to believe that Brinton Academy could, indeed, protect Amy from any evil that might threaten her. Still, she was stiff with anxiety and worry.

Maybe, Jennifer thought, that was partly because of the work she did. As a journalist, she had seen far too much tragedy to believe anyone could ever be completely safe anywhere.

Chapter

15

Amy climbed to the top of the jungle gym and perched there for a few minutes, being extra careful to keep her skirt pulled tight around her knees so none of the boys could look up and see her underwear. She shaded her eyes with her right hand and squinted at the horizon. There wasn't much smog today, so she could see the mountains real good. But sitting up here all alone wasn't much fun. If you asked her, recess wasn't fun at all without Patty. Usually, during recess, she and Patty climbed on the playground equipment or played tag with some of the boys from the second and third grades.

Sometimes, on a really good day, Patty's brother Joey and his friends got together a kickball game and they let Amy and Patty play with them. Joey said that Amy and Patty were better at kickball than most of the boys, anyway, so he didn't care that they were only girls. He always made them be on his team and they almost always won. Today, though, Joey was home sick, too, and none of the other children had asked Amy to join in their play groups.

Feeling lonely, she climbed down from the jungle gym and walked over to Tiffany and Joanne, two girls from her class who were sitting on the edge of the sandbox. "Wanna play tag?" she asked them.

Tiffany screwed up her face, shoved a lock of her long ebony hair away from her dark brown eyes, and said, "Tag? Yuck! Who wants to play tag! That's boy stuff. We got our Barbies."

"Yeah," added Joanne, Tiffany's best friend. "Our Barbies are going out on a real important date tonight. We gotta fix their hair."

Boring, Amy thought, feeling rejected. Scuffing the toes of her sneakers on the playground's blacktop surface, she headed toward the grassy area where she sometimes played kickball. Today, there was nobody there. She sat down on the ground and began to pull up blades of grass. As soon as she found a particularly wide blade, she wedged it lengthwise between her two thumbs. If she got the piece of grass just right, she knew, she could make a real good whistle with her hands.

As she brought her thumbs up to her lips and began to blow, she thought she heard someone calling her. She lowered her hands and the blade of grass fluttered to the ground. Looking around, she saw a man standing about ten feet behind her, outside the chain link fence that surrounded the school grounds. She wasn't scared, not really; the fence was eight feet high and it had three fat strands of barbed wire on top. The teachers said the fence was to keep vandals from getting into the playground at night. Amy wasn't sure what a vandal was; she thought maybe it was some kind of animal, like a big dog or a raccoon.

"Hey, little girl! Hey, kid, come over here a minute. Got something for you."

Amy stared at the man. He was big, as big as some of the men her mom sometimes went out with, but she couldn't get a good look at his face. He had on a floppy hat, pulled way down over his ears, plus a huge pair of sunglasses hiding his eyes. Did she know this man?

Amy glanced back toward the school building. The big

clock on the outside told her that recess would be over in only seven more minutes. The two teachers on duty, Ms. Johnson, from the third grade, and her own teacher, Ms. Butterfield, stood together by the doorway, watching the children climbing on the playground equipment. Nobody seemed to be looking at Amy.

"I'm not s'posed to talk to strangers," she told the man. "My mom said."

"That's good advice," the man said, "but I'm not a stranger. Just come on over here a minute and I'll show you. I won't hurt you." He held up a small gold object that glinted in the sunlight. "Got something real special here for you."

"What's that?"

"Something real nice, just for you. Look at it. It's got your picture inside."

The man's smile was sort of creepy, Amy thought, and talking to him like this made her stomach feel funny. Still, if he really had a picture of her, maybe he wasn't a stranger after all. And, if he wasn't a stranger, then maybe it was okay for her to talk to him. Still . . . "Recess is almost over," she told him, getting up off the grass. "I gotta go in now."

"Hey, honey, don't go. Not yet."

"I gotta, or I'll get in trouble."

"Hey, look here." The man bent down and pushed the shiny gold object through the wire mesh of the fence. It fell just inside the fence, on the grass. "See, I'll leave it right here for you. Better come and pick it up, quick, or it'll get ruined." He turned and walked away from the fence, then paused on the sidewalk a few feet away, watching to see what the little girl would do.

Amy checked out the teachers once more. Now they were rounding up the other kids and herding them back inside the school. In a split second, she sprinted over to the fence, grabbed the gold object off the grass, slipped it into her skirt pocket, and raced toward the school building to join the other children.

"Amy," Ms. Butterfield said when she had joined the second and third graders lined up to go back inside. "Did I see somebody standing by that fence?"

Amy looked at her feet, suddenly feeling guilty. She didn't want to get into trouble. "It was just a man," she said, "but I told him I wasn't allowed to talk to him."

"I should think not!" Ms. Butterfield's face was stern, and a little shocked. "Is he still over there? If he is, I think we'd better call the police."

"No," Amy told her, fingering the little gold treasure hidden in the pocket of her skirt. "He went away when I said I couldn't talk to him."

"Well, come on inside, then. I'm certainly glad you have enough sense not to talk to strangers."

On the way back to class, Amy stopped in the girls' restroom. After she had locked herself into one of the stalls, she sat down on the toilet and took the gift the man had given her out of her pocket. Turning it over and over in her hands, she examined it carefully. It was a flat, gold, rectangular case with a tiny clasp on one edge. Across one side was written the word, "Kitty." Amy knew that word from her books; it was short for kitten. She liked kittens, almost as much as she liked puppies. Someday, when they got their own house again, she planned to ask Mommy to get her a puppy of her very own. Or maybe a kitten.

Amy's stubby fingers pried at the clasp until the little metal case popped open. Inside was a photograph, all right, but it didn't look like a picture of her; the face inside was a baby's. Could this really be her picture? Amy wondered. Maybe this was what she looked like when she was a baby. Mommy once told her they didn't have any pictures of Amy before they got adopted together, so she didn't really know what she'd looked like when she was a baby.

Amy stared hard at the picture. This baby had reddish blond hair like hers, but there wasn't very much of it. There was a funny-looking mark on this baby's head, too; it showed up right through its thin hair. The mark was brownish red and it was shaped sort of like the map of California Amy had been studying in geography class.

After she flushed the toilet, Amy washed her hands at the sink, the way she'd been taught. She stared at her round, freckled face in the mirror above the sink. Her auburn hair was thick and curly and her scalp didn't show through it at all. She leaned forward, closer to the mirror, and pushed her bangs up and off her forehead. No mark there. She tried parting her thick hair and holding the two sides flat against her head. Was there a mark like California on her scalp? She couldn't really tell.

"Amy," Ms. Butterfield said, standing at the door. "You're the last one again. Come on, now, no more dawdling. You'll make everybody late for class."

Amy stepped away from the mirror and did as she was told. But several times during the remainder of the school day, as she sat in her desk listening to Ms. Butterfield going over the multiplication tables, she put down her pencil and let her fingers creep into her pocket. The little gold case was smooth and cool to her touch. She wished she could take it out again now and look at the picture some more, but she didn't dare let anyone else see it. If anybody found out she had this little gold case, Amy knew she could get into trouble, really bad trouble. Ms. Butterfield might even say she stole it, like that time in kindergarten, with the paint box. She couldn't risk something like that happening again.

Amy decided she would wait until she got home to look at the baby's picture again. When she was all alone in her own bedroom, with the door shut tight, she could look at it all she wanted to.

She even knew where she could keep this little gold case hidden, a special secret place where nobody but her would ever, ever find it. Smiling to herself in anticipation, Amy slipped her hand out of her pocket and picked up her pencil.

"Eight times eight is sixty-four," said Ms. Butterfield as Amy copied the numbers from the blackboard onto her paper.

Chapter 16

"*I tell you, you just can't trust anybody these days,*" Hilda Bennett said. "They all cheat you, they overcharge, every last one of them does shoddy work. Why, just yesterday, that crooked roofer—well, I gave him a piece of my mind!"

"I'm sure you did, Mother," Jennifer said, holding the telephone receiver a full inch away from her ear. Her mother's angry voice coming over the phone line was so loud that she feared it could damage her eardrums.

"Thirty-five dollars he charged me! Just to patch two lousy shakes that blew off. Just wait till *you're* an old woman all by yourself, Jenny. Then you'll find out. These crooks all figure I've got money I don't need, so they try to take advantage. Women with husbands don't have to worry about this kind of thing."

Jennifer sighed, stretching the wall phone's cord taut so she could reach the kitchen stove. She stirred the spaghetti sauce she was heating for supper, adjusted the flame underneath the boiling water, and braced herself for more of her mother's gripes. The woman had been complaining about the roofer and the garbage collector and the woman who came to clean her small house in Idaho and anyone else she could think of for the past fifteen minutes. Jennifer should have been used to it by now—this was a typical phone call from her mother—but her patience was growing short.

"I'm sure you handled the roofer just as well as you always handle these things," she said, choosing her words carefully. The truth was, her mother's vitriolic attacks had probably alienated half the population of Twin Falls— casual employees and friends alike. The other half undoubtedly hadn't yet met Hilda Bennett.

"Don't you use that tone of voice with me, Jennifer. I know what I'm talking about, you'll see."

Jennifer put the cover back on the pot of spaghetti sauce and laid her spoon down on the counter, where it left a puddle of red sauce on the white tile. "I'm not using any particular tone of voice with you, Mother," Jennifer said, her irritation peaking. She tried to keep it out of her voice. "I know you're angry"—Hilda Bennett was always angry about something—"but you have no right to take your anger out on me. I think we'd better change the subject."

"Or maybe I'll just hang up now, if you can't manage to talk civilly to your own mother when she calls."

"You're not going to goad me into fighting with you, Mother, so you might as well give it up right now." Jennifer sensed that her mother had run out of handy targets for her venom again; she did not intend to take on that job, not today. She took a deep breath. "Did you get that package of Amy's school portrait proofs I sent you?"

"You mean all those little pictures? Yes, they came yesterday."

"So, what do you think? Did you pick out the one you want me to have printed up for you?"

There was a long silence on the line, but Jennifer declined to fill it with chatter.

Finally, her mother spoke. "Honest to Pete, Jenny, I don't know why you bother sending me these things. It's not like Amy's . . . Well, you know."

"You're wrong, Mother." Jennifer peered down the hall to see whether Amy could overhear her conversation, but the child's bedroom door was closed. Still, she lowered her voice, just in case. "It's *exactly* like Amy's your grandchild. She's *my* daughter; that makes her *your* grandchild, whether you like it or not."

The silence returned. Once again, Jennifer waited it out.

"Maybe she's your daughter, legally, anyway." Hilda's voice no longer sounded angry; now it had taken on a whiny tone. "But believe me, Jenny, it's not the same to me, not the same at all. If you'd gotten married when you had the chance, I'd have *real* grandchildren now. You'd have a husband to take care of you and—"

"I don't want to hear this, Mother! We've been over this a million times, and I will not listen to your opinions on my life anymore."

"You always *were* like that. Never gave a damn about anybody but yourself!"

Jennifer held the receiver out in front of her, her hand shaking visibly. Talk about projecting your own personality defects onto other people! she thought, now completely outraged at her mother's gall. If she let herself speak now, she knew she would say something that would sever her relationship with her only blood relative forever. So she settled for swearing under her breath and reminding herself that the woman on the other end of the phone line simply wasn't emotionally healthy. Probably, after all these years, Hilda Bennett simply couldn't help being the way she was. "I'm not going to argue with you, Mother," Jennifer said, when she'd managed to get her temper back under control. "I've got to go now, or our supper will burn. Do you want me to send you one of Amy's pictures or not?"

An overly dramatic sighing sound came over the wire. "Oh, go ahead, if you want."

Don't do me any favors, Jennifer thought, but she said, "Pick one, then. Just read me the number off the back."

"I can't pick. They all looked the same to me. You choose."

Jennifer closed her eyes and pictured smoke streaming out of her own ears. The way she felt right now, the gears of her brain certainly must be smoking. This kind of mental imagery sometimes relieved her irritation with her mother enough so that she could continue speaking to her. But more and more often lately, Jennifer wondered why she bothered trying to maintain any kind of relationship at all with this frustrating, acid-tongued woman.

Yet, every time Jennifer was ready to cut her mother off, she was hit with a terrible sense of guilt. The woman was nearly seventy, she would tell herself, and she'd been unhappy all her life. It was true, too, that Hilda had no one in her life, other than her only daughter. Under those circumstances, how could Jennifer refuse to have anything to do with her? Of course, she realized that tolerating this behavior allowed her mother to continue being rude and self-centered without having to suffer the predictable consequences; Jennifer was acting as a classic codependent, but she felt stuck. As a young child, she'd been taught how to coddle her mother's foul temper, her moods, and she'd learned the lesson well. Now there was no changing Hilda Bennett's sour approach to life, not after all these years.

"How about the one where Amy has a blue bow in her hair?" Jennifer suggested, finally. "That's my personal favorite."

"Blue bow? I don't remember a picture with any blue bow."

"I know there's one with a blue bow, Mother. Look again."

"I *am* looking. I dumped all the pictures out on the table here while we were talking and, I tell you, there is no blue bow."

Jennifer began to wonder whether she was losing her mind. Could she have forgotten to put that particular proof in the package with the others? "Hold on a minute, will you, Mother? I've got to check something." She put the phone down on the kitchen counter and hurried over to her desk. She pulled open the top drawer and grabbed the envelope the photographer's proofs had come in. She looked inside; it was completely empty. "Humor me, look through those proofs just once more," she said, when she returned to the phone. She read off the proof number she'd written on the outside of the photographer's envelope.

"Oh, for Pete's sake, Jenny, I may be old, but I'm not blind yet. I tell you, you didn't send me any picture with a blue bow, and none of these proofs has that number on them, either." The old woman sighed dramatically to underline her irritation. "I really don't give a damn which photo you send me," she said. "Just pick one of the five poses and get it over with."

Jennifer could almost hear the words her mother was undoubtedly thinking but somehow had managed to restrain herself from saying, that Amy's photo would only end up in some drawer, anyway. "All right, Mother," she said. "You win."

"I'll call you again next week," Hilda told her. "Will you still be at this number?"

"As far as I know, Mother. I'll let you know if anything changes." She put down the phone and went to tend to the pots on the stove. Did her mother have a reason to lie about the missing photographer's proof? Jennifer wondered. She couldn't think of any. The old woman could be nasty about all six proofs as easily as about only five.

This made no sense. Where could that picture with the blue bow have gone?

Jennifer picked up a handful of dry spaghetti and tossed it into the pot of boiling water. As she stirred the pasta, watching it soften and cook, her confusion grew deeper.

Chapter

17

"No! No! Don't!"

Jennifer awoke to screams. The clock radio glowing in the dark told her it was after two in the morning. Her heart pounding now, she threw off her bedcovers and forced herself to sit up.

"Stop! *Stop* it!"

Amy was screaming, Jennifer realized, her panic quickly mounting. She streaked across the hall to her daughter's room, threw open the door, and flicked on the light switch. As she ran to Amy's bedside, the child's eyelids fluttered and Jennifer saw that her cheeks were wet. A quick look around the room showed her there was no one else there.

"Wake up, sweetheart," she said, sitting down on the edge of Amy's bed. "Wake up, hon. You're just having a bad dream."

It had been at least two years, Jennifer realized, since Amy had had one of these nightmares. In that time, they'd both grown complacent, they'd become used to restful nights. Since Amy was five or maybe a little older, Jennifer's sleep had been interrupted by only her own demons, not by her daughter's.

Jennifer lifted Amy's head off the pillow and cradled it against her breasts. "Wake up, sweetie. Mommy's here now," she cooed. "Everything's all right now."

Amy's blue eyes were unfocused and her sturdy little body was stiff.

Jennifer stroked the little girl's rigid spine gently with two fingers. "What were you dreaming, Amy? Tell Mommy."

"A bad man, a real bad man." The child's voice was flat, lacking its normal intonation.

Damn, Jennifer thought. Just what she'd tried so hard to avoid had happened after all. She'd spoken to Amy after supper and, as gently as she could, warned the little girl once more that she should never to talk to strangers, at school or anywhere else. It seemed obvious that her brief lecture—no matter how carefully she'd tried to word it—had frightened Amy. At the time, Amy had seemed undisturbed; she'd even insisted that she already knew "all that stuff" and that Jennifer didn't need to tell her again. Still, after Ms. Samuels's warning about the man who'd approached Amy at the school entrance on Monday morning, Jennifer felt that the subject simply had to be broached one more time. If she neglected it and something happened to Amy as a result, well . . . she didn't even want to think about that.

"What about the bad man, honey?" Jennifer asked her frightened daughter. "Tell me."

"He—he—" Amy's breath came in short bursts now, as if she'd just run up a long flight of stairs.

"He what? What did the bad man do? Did he hurt you?" Jennifer continued her stroking motions, but Amy showed no signs of relaxing.

"He was hitting Mommy. He was hurting her real bad and she was crying."

Confused by Amy's description, Jennifer realized that

the little girl was staring straight ahead into space, as though she were in some kind of trance, as though she could still see the terrible, frightening scene being played out in front of her eyes. The child began to tremble.

"It was just a dream, honey," Jennifer told her, firmly but gently tilting Amy's face upward until their eyes met. "See? Mommy's right here with you, and nobody's hurting me. I'm perfectly all right."

Recognition slowly came into Amy's eyes and her body began to relax. "I was scared, Mommy," she said, in a tiny voice. "Real, real scared."

"I know you were, sweetie. I heard you yelling, and I came to get you right away. You don't need to worry anymore. Nobody's going to hurt me, and I'm certainly not going to let anybody hurt you. It was only a bad dream. Are you okay now?"

Amy nodded and crawled back under the bedcovers, curling up into a ball. "Will you stay here with me, Mom, till I get back to sleep? If you're here with me, the man won't come back, I know he won't."

"Sure, honey." Jennifer slid into the narrow bed beside her daughter and cuddled her. With Amy beside her, she gently stroked the little girl's sweat-dampened hair and thought about childhood demons. Poor Amy had had so much stress in her life lately, Jennifer thought, it was no wonder her sleep was being interrupted. "Just relax and go back to sleep," she said. "Everything's going to be okay now."

By a little after three, Amy was sleeping soundly and there was no sign that she would have another nightmare. So Jennifer slowly crawled out of the narrow bed and stumbled back into her own bedroom. It took her another hour before she was able to relax enough to get back to sleep herself.

18

Jennifer picked up her mail in the lobby and sorted through it as she rode the elevator back up to the third floor. As she spotted the return address on the second letter in the stack, her heart sank. It was from the Seattle television station where she'd interviewed for the news anchor position the previous Monday. If she were being offered the job, she knew from experience, there would have been a phone call, not just a letter. This had to be a turn-down.

Jennifer let herself into her apartment before opening the envelope. She needed complete privacy to process another rejection. By now, she thought, she should be used to this kind of thing, but every time she lost out on another job, it hurt all over again. It always seemed like more than the loss of a job, somehow. Whenever she was turned down for an on-camera position, it felt as though every aspect of Jennifer Bennett had been rejected. Not just what it took to do her work—a combination of interviewing skills, basic intelligence, news judgment, and writing ability— was nixed. In this business, Jennifer knew, the management was also saying no to her face, her hair, her body, her smile, her personality, her speech pattern, even that elusive but much-sought-after quality known as sex appeal—virtually everything about her. It was very, very hard not to take it personally.

As she unfolded the Seattle station's letter, Jennifer's eye fell on the middle paragraph. ". . . enjoyed meeting with you in our studios on Monday. However, after much discussion, we have decided to fill this position from within our current ranks . . ." She stopped reading. She'd seen and heard all this before, from a dozen other stations. The bottom line was that she was still unemployed. What's more, she felt like a complete fool; she'd been so confident about her interview on Monday that she'd allowed herself to slack off on job hunting since returning from Seattle.

Jennifer decided to let herself mourn for no more than an hour. This afternoon, she would have to move on, put this disappointment behind her, and follow up on some of her other employment contacts.

She poured herself a cup of coffee and sat down at the kitchen table before going through the rest of her mail. There was a cheery note from an old college friend who was expecting her fourth child shortly, a bill from the company storing her furniture, and a letter from the Internal Revenue Service. It was the wrong time of year for the IRS to be sending out tax forms, she thought, as she tore open the envelope. She sipped her coffee slowly as she read the first paragraph of the enclosed letter. The impact of the words typed on the page hit her hard; her hand jerked, splashing hot coffee across her fingers. She set down the cup, her whole body trembling. A tax audit! The IRS was auditing her tax return from two years back.

What next? Jennifer thought, slamming her fist down on the tabletop. The cup jumped in its saucer, slopping more coffee over the rim. What'll it be—a fire, an earthquake, a flood, a plague of locusts? Damn! She was beginning to feel jinxed. At best, she knew, an IRS audit would cost her a thousand dollars of her accountant's time; at worst—was it possible she really owed some back taxes? And, if she did, where on earth would she ever find the money to pay them? A vision of spending the rest of her life in depressing poverty flashed through her mind.

She felt her entire body tense up. No! she told herself. She couldn't let all this get to her. She had to keep her wits about her or she would never dig out of this hole. Her elbows on the kitchen table, she held her head in her hands and massaged her temples. At times like this, Jennifer knew she had to find something physical to do, a way to loosen up and dissipate the muscle tension she was feeling.

It was only one o'clock. She still had a couple of hours before Amy had to be picked up at school. Jennifer went into the bedroom and changed into a bathing suit. She chose the turquoise one with the flattering bustline; in it, she told herself, she still looked pretty good—at least for a thirty-nine-year-old woman. Then she went downstairs and swam fifty vigorous laps in the pool.

As she climbed out of the water, Jennifer was breathing hard. She felt physically exhausted now, but her neck muscles were definitely looser and she felt more in control of her world. All of her problems could be solved by money, she told herself. Yet, far more important than mere money was the fact that she had a daughter she loved more than life itself. They were both healthy, safe, reasonably happy. Those things alone made them far wealthier than many people who had accomplished greater professional and financial success. Together, she knew, she and Amy would make it through this difficult time.

Thrusting her arm into a sleeve of her aqua terry cloth robe, Jennifer's eyes rose to the bank of windows above the pool decking, but she saw nothing there but sameness—tier after tier of identical white-draped rectangles, at least eighteen or twenty apartments on each floor. She wasn't even sure which windows were hers, let alone anyone else's. She'd had a secondary motivation in coming down to the pool this afternoon, one that obviously was going to remain unsatisfied—she'd hoped to run into Forrest Hathaway. From here, she simply couldn't tell whether or not he was home.

Forrest hadn't been at the pool for the past few afternoons when she and Amy had come down to swim, and Jennifer had missed seeing him. Undoubtedly he'd had meetings with his movie's production company, she told herself. There was no reason to think he might have moved out of the Edgewater. Surely he wouldn't do that without telling her.

By the time she got back upstairs to her apartment, Jennifer had decided she was being silly to wait for a casual encounter with Forrest at the pool or in the lobby or the elevator. If she really wanted to see him, she could simply act like an adult and telephone him.

After she had showered and dressed, she did just that. But when she dialed Forrest's apartment, his phone machine answered. Trying not to sound nervous, she left a message inviting him over about six o'clock for "that long-overdue glass of wine I owe you. I've got a special bottle of Pinot Grigio on ice." Just issuing the invitation made her feel better. She was really beginning to like Forrest a lot, so why not admit it? If he came over tonight, she might even tell him about Seattle. She had a feeling he would understand how she felt.

Jennifer spent the rest of the afternoon on the telephone, calling television stations where she'd submitted her audition tapes. Secretaries in San Francisco and San Diego informed her that letters were en route to her—more rejections. One in Denver told her that the boss had been on vacation all week. "Your tape is in his in basket with all the others," she said in a little-girl voice. The woman sounded about twelve years old, not an encouraging sign. "I'm sure he'll get back to you as soon as he's had a chance to look at it, Ms. Bennett," she said before ringing off.

Last, Jennifer called Bob Harris, the news director at KXXT-TV in Santa Barbara and the man in charge of hiring anchorwoman Christie McNally's replacement. KXXT's receptionist took her name and asked what her business with the news director might be.

"I'm following up on a letter and tape I sent him last week," Jennifer explained. She didn't bother adding that she'd already followed up like this a few days ago, but Bob Harris hadn't returned her earlier call. It never paid to come off as belligerent in these situations.

The receptionist put her on hold for a full three minutes. When she came back on the line, she said, "Sorry, Mr. Harris is on another call right now. Let me take your phone number and I'll give him your message." The same story as last time.

Jennifer gave her number, but she hung up feeling certain she was getting a runaround at KXXT. News directors were legitimately busy people, of course, but it also seemed that they were always "on another line" when they didn't want to talk to somebody. This was really rude, she thought; the least Bob Harris could do was send her a no-thanks letter so she didn't have to keep spending her money on long-distance calls he had no intention of either accepting or returning.

But as Jennifer checked her watch and realized it was time for her to pick up Amy, the telephone rang. Maybe she'd misjudged Harris, she thought, grabbing for the receiver. "Jennifer Bennett," she announced, trying to sound more cheerful than she felt.

"Hi, Jennifer." A man's voice resonated over the line. "It's Forrest. Just picked up my messages and yours gets the award for most enticing."

Jennifer grinned. This call lifted her spirits even more than the one she'd anticipated. "That's what I like to hear," she said. "Can you make it tonight?"

"Wouldn't miss it—as long as you can cope with my possibly being a little late. I'm still here in Culver City. This meeting I just escaped from is supposed to be out before five—producer claims he's got another meeting across town at six—but I'm beginning to find out you can't really count on anything in this business."

"Don't worry about being late, Forrest. I'll go ahead and feed Amy if she gets too hungry. Just come as early as you can."

Forrest promised to call again if he was going to be later than six-thirty.

As Jennifer rode the elevator down to the garage, she thought about what she would wear tonight. Her camel slacks and red sweater would be good—choosing cheerful colors should help lighten her mood. Undoubtedly, so would spending an evening with Forrest Hathaway.

The dark-haired man set down his binoculars on the windowsill and let the white drapes fall back into place. From his bedroom window, he'd been watching Jennifer Bennett swim laps in the pool. She wasn't too hard to look at—a few years older than he liked his women, of course, possibly even older than he was. Still, she had a few good years left in her.

Now she had put on her robe and was heading for the elevator. The show was over. He turned away from the window, hoping that Jennifer's early swim didn't mean she wouldn't be taking the kid to the pool later this afternoon. It was the little girl he really wanted to watch, and he no longer dared try to do that at that snooty private school she went to.

For the past two mornings, when he'd driven past Brinton Academy, he'd noticed a uniformed security guard standing by the front entrance—a new addition to the school staff. He'd ditched his little red car days ago, of course. No sense taking a chance that the guard had been told to watch for a dark-haired man in a red car hanging around the school entrance. His latest wheels were rented from National—a blue Pontiac Sunbird.

He'd gone by the school during the morning recess times, too. But now two or three teachers were always standing close to that high chain link fence that rimmed the playground, instead of at their usual post near the school's back door.

No, he simply had to accept that the school was off-limits for him now, at least until things cooled down. He couldn't risk anybody calling the cops about him. With his background, the last thing he wanted to do was explain what he was doing hanging around an elementary school. Particularly this elementary school.

Undoubtedly the hatchet-faced teacher who'd come after him last Monday, when he tried talking to the kid, was responsible for the security upgrade. At least, that's what the dark-haired man preferred to think. He certainly didn't want to believe the little girl herself had told anyone about their encounter at the playground fence, or that she'd shown anybody the gold case and photo he'd given her. He wanted to think of that meeting, and of his small gift to her, as their secrets, as private things only the two of them would ever know about.

It gave him a deep pleasure to think of the little girl he loved opening that picture case, gazing longingly at the photograph inside it, holding it in her small, warm hands. He hoped that, in time, his gift would become a treasure to her, that it would help her understand that she belonged with him, not with that Bennett bitch who was trying to keep them apart.

If it hadn't been for Jennifer Bennett, the child would have more than just the little gold picture case to remember him by. He wanted to give her lots of things; she deserved to have them. Shit! Every time he thought about that doll the Bennett woman had thrown in the trash, his blood pressure rose. She had no right! She'd probably thrown away the first gift he'd left at her house, too.

Obviously, he had to find a way to give his gifts directly to the child, the way he'd done with the engraved gold case. The little cutie obviously wanted the things he had to give her. The way she'd picked up the picture case and tucked it away in her skirt pocket, where it could be their secret, was clear evidence of that. He wanted the pleasure of seeing her enjoy that baby doll he'd chosen for her, too—it's reddish hair had reminded him of her—along with the dozens of other toys and trinkets he could afford to give her. The cost of the gifts was no problem for him, and he was determined not to let Jennifer Bennett rob him of the pleasure of giving.

The dark-haired man's need to be close to the little girl was growing stronger each day, although satisfying it was becoming increasingly difficult and frustrating for him. He knew he had to come up with a better plan. Simply living near the child here at the Edgewater was definitely not enough. He needed more, far more.

Unfortunately, given his current circumstances, he couldn't simply snatch the kid and take off with her, not that he wouldn't like to. Not that he shouldn't have every right to. But, if he tried anything like that, the cops would be all over him in a New York minute. Besides, the way things were now, he wouldn't be able to get close enough to her to grab her and get away, particularly if she didn't go with him willingly. And he had to face the fact that it might take time for her to get used to him, to realize that she loved him.

You'd think the kid was royalty or the president's daughter or something, the way Jennifer Bennett kept her protected. Brinton Academy was like a fortress these days and, even here at the Edgewater, the little girl never seemed to be left alone. If she went to the pool or down to the lobby, Jennifer was always right beside her. She never played by herself or with any other children on the

Edgewater's grounds, either, at least not as far as he'd been able to observe.

No, he would definitely have to come up with a better plan. Something that would lure both Jennifer Bennett and the child far away from Los Angeles. A plan that couldn't be traced back to him. Then he would be free to get rid of the mother at his leisure. And, once she was out of the picture, the child would be completely his. It might take a while, but she would forget Jennifer Bennett someday.

Eventually, she would learn to need and love only him.

Chapter 20

Jennifer unwrapped a wedge of brie and arranged it on a plate with a selection of crackers. She squinted at the result, which was far from an elegant display. If she'd had her own dishes and kitchen equipment here, she would have put the brie on the walnut cheese board she'd bought from Dansk three years ago, the one with the slot in its side to hold a fancy wooden-handled cheese knife. And she would have arranged the crackers artfully in a small brown wicker basket lined with a bright blue linen napkin. But this was the Edgewater, so a white institutional stoneware plate and an old paring knife would have to do.

"Almost finished, hon?" she asked Amy, who was sitting at the kitchen table, finishing her early supper of macaroni and cheese with raw vegetables.

"Almost." She picked up the last spear of asparagus with her fingers and ate it. "Who'd you say's coming over tonight, Mom?"

"Mr. Hathaway, hon. You remember him."

"The man from the pool?"

Jennifer carried the cheese plate over to the coffee table and set it down, along with a stack of paper napkins.

"That's right, sweetie. He's the man who took me out to dinner last Friday night, too. Remember? When Maria came to stay with you."

"Oh, yeah." Amy pushed her plate away. "Can I have some ice cream for dessert? I'm still hungry."

Jennifer checked her watch. It was almost six-thirty and Forrest hadn't called a second time. He'd promised he would if he was going to be later than six-thirty. "The ice cream's all gone, Amy," she said. "You ate the last of it last night, remember? How about an apple instead?"

Amy wrinkled up her face. "I had an apple for a snack this afternoon."

"You're right." Jennifer picked up Amy's empty plate, carried it into the kitchen, and set it in the sink. "I'll see what else I can find." She opened the refrigerator and found nothing that could reasonably pass for dessert, then turned to the freezer compartment. "How about a nice blueberry turnover?" she asked, removing a small square frost-covered package. "You'll have to wait half an hour or so for it to bake, though."

"That's okay. I can watch TV." Amy slid off her chair and headed for the living room television set. She pressed the power button and the music accompanying a commercial burst from the speakers.

"Hold on a minute, sweetie. Watch TV in my room, will you? I'll want to visit with Mr. Hathaway in the living room."

Amy shrugged and turned off the set. Watching TV from her mom's big bed was more fun anyway.

Jennifer opened the package of frozen turnovers and evenly spaced all four of them on a cookie sheet. The leftovers would be nice with lunch tomorrow. She set the oven temperature at four hundred degrees and popped the cookie sheet inside. As she was setting the timer for twenty-five minutes, the doorbell rang. Momentarily nervous, she smoothed her red sweater over her hips and checked her reflected appearance in the chrome on the refrigerator door.

Amy streaked from the bedroom toward the front door, arriving at the same moment as her mother. "Can I open the door, Mom? Can I, huh?"

"Wait till I make sure who it is. Don't forget, we never open the door unless we know who's out there. Right?" Amy nodded solemnly as her mother peered through the peephole. Jennifer unlocked the dead bolt and stepped back. "It's okay, Amy. It's Mr. Hathaway. You can let him in."

The child grasped the doorknob and twisted, then pulled the door open. On the threshold stood Forrest Hathaway, both of his hands full. "Well, my two favorite leading ladies." He made an exaggerated bow from the waist and offered a cellophane-wrapped bouquet of flowers to Jennifer.

Jennifer smiled with delighted surprise. "How nice." She took the flowers. "How'd you know daisies and irises were my favorites, Forrest? Makes me feel like a star."

Amy and Forrest followed Jennifer into the kitchen and watched while she searched through the kitchen cupboards for a vase. She finally settled for a green plastic juice pitcher, filling it with water from the kitchen faucet.

"Damn. I should have bought a vase," Forrest said, looking at the ugly plastic pitcher.

"Oh, I don't know," Jennifer said, as she arranged the stems in the pitcher. "This has a certain unpretentious charm to it."

"Yeah, if you go for interior decoration by Woolworth's."

Amy pushed her nose up against one of the flowers and sniffed. "How come they don't smell, Mom?" she asked.

"This kind is just supposed to look pretty," Forrest told her.

"They're pretty, all right," she said, smiling up at him shyly.

"Well, these leading ladies thank you," Jennifer said with a grin. Her eye fell on the small box that Forrest still held in his left hand. "What's this, more presents?"

He looked down. "Almost forgot. Found this downstairs when I picked up my mail. It's addressed to Amy."

Amy grabbed for it. "For me? Cool!" Eagerly, she ripped open the box. Her right hand dived inside and reemerged quickly, gripping a red-haired baby doll by its rubber arm.

Jennifer looked at the doll and immediately blanched. "Where did you get that?" she shrieked, snatching it out of Amy's hand. The child flinched and took a step backward, cowering beside the kitchen counter, as though she expected to be struck. Jennifer turned her furious gaze on her guest. "Wh—Where did you get that thing?"

Forrest looked at Jennifer as though she'd gone mad. "It . . . Like I told you, it was just sitting there by the mailboxes, down in the lobby." His face registered complete bewilderment. "It's addressed to Amy, so I thought . . . Is something the matter?"

Amy began to whimper. Jennifer turned to her, quickly becoming contrite about her outburst. She tried to reassure the obviously frightened child. "It's okay, Amy. You didn't do anything wrong." Since coming to live with Jennifer, Amy had always reacted badly to displays of anger. They clearly terrified her. The therapist who'd brought the child through those difficult early years as an adoptee had surmised that she'd probably been beaten as a baby and toddler, either by her own parents or in foster care. So Jennifer always had tried her best to make Amy feel safe with her, to erase all the bad memories she'd brought with her. Jennifer had never once slapped her daughter, and she did her very best to avoid raising her voice in anger.

"Where's the doll from, Mom?" Amy asked in a small, timid voice, standing well back from the object that had caused her mother's explosive reaction.

Jennifer inspected the box, but found no return address. It had no stamps or UPS label attached to it, either, indicating that it had been hand delivered. The only markings on the small corrugated carton were Amy's name and address, including her apartment number, printed in black block letters. "I don't know, Amy," Jennifer said, "but . . . All I know is, it's not ours. We don't want it." Her hands visibly trembling, she thrust the doll back into the box and folded the top closed. Doing her best not to alarm Amy any further, she took a deep breath and tried to regain her composure. "Why don't you go into my room now, sweetie, and watch TV, like you planned?" She spoke slowly and deliberately, in carefully measured tones, to camouflage the hysteria she was feeling. "I'll call you as soon as your dessert's ready."

Amy hung back for a moment, unsure whether she wanted to stay near her mother or to leave the room before she displayed any additional temper. Which was the safer course? Eventually, she turned away and headed for the electronic escape provided by the television set.

When Amy had left the room, Forrest asked, "What was *that* all about?"

Jennifer looked at him sheepishly. Her reaction to the doll—it looked exactly like the one she'd thrown away the night before they'd moved away from Seaview Ridge—had been completely impulsive. Now she felt a little foolish for having let Forrest Hathaway witness it. She obviously owed the poor man an explanation. "Let me pour you a glass of wine," she said, tossing the box containing the doll into the kitchen wastebasket and opening the refrigerator. She took out the bottle of Pinot Grigio and placed it on the kitchen table. "Then I'll do my best to explain things."

As they sat in the living room sipping their wine, Jennifer told Forrest about the anonymous, unwanted fan who'd left children's toys on the doorstep of her house in

Pacific Palisades. Now, she explained as an involuntary shiver ran down her spine, it looked like this guy had not only found her again, he'd somehow managed to find out her apartment number here at the Edgewater Apartment Hotel. Fat lot of good the Edgewater's much-touted security system had done! "I tell you, Forrest, this kind of thing scares me half to death," she said, hugging herself. "You never know what these crazy people might do next."

Before Forrest could reply, the kitchen timer rang. Jennifer went to take the blueberry turnovers out of the oven. She put three of the puffy golden brown triangles on a large plate to cool and the fourth on a smaller plate, which she set on the kitchen table. She poured a glass of milk, set it next to the small plate, and went into the bedroom to fetch Amy.

The little girl was lying on the bed and the television set was blaring as Jennifer entered the room; loud music, heavy on percussion, accompanied some kind of noisy police chase. Great stuff for Amy to be watching when she was already upset, Jennifer thought, reaching over and switching off the set.

"Dessert's ready now, honey," she said, turning toward the bed. "Come—"

As her gaze fell upon Amy, she realized the child was sound asleep. She was lying in the middle of the bed, her small body curled up into the fetal position and her thumb firmly anchored between her lips. Her mouth was making rhythmic sucking motions. Amy had slept in this infantile position every night until she was nearly five years old. Jennifer had thought she'd outgrown it long ago.

With a sigh, she covered her sleeping daughter with a blanket and tiptoed out of the room.

⌒⌒⌒

The dark-haired man drove the Pontiac Sunbird north on the San Diego Freeway, then took the connector ramp to the east-bound Ventura Freeway. His hands gripped the steering wheel of the rental car tightly as he squinted into the bright morning sunlight. Just as he was about to accelerate to cruising speed on the Ventura, the driver of a black Jeep Cherokee cut in front of his car, forcing him to hit the brake pedal to avoid a collision. "Fuck you, asshole!" he yelled, raising the longest finger of his right hand into the air in a familiar gesture and accelerating to within inches of the other vehicle's rear bumper. Goddamned yuppies thought they owned the road!

Today, he was being pulled back into his former life, the identity he could officially document, and he wasn't look-ing forward to it. This stupid drill with his parole officer would keep him away from his surveillance and planning for the entire day, and that made him nervous. Who knew what might happen in Santa Monica while he was away?

Besides, what was the point? In another week or two, parolee Clay Fowler would be long gone anyway. Still, he knew that, if he refused to play this silly bureaucratic game, he could end up back in prison before then—that hellhole where he'd never deserved to be in the first place.

Until today, meeting his parole obligations had been easy. He'd simply called his PO once every afternoon, the way he'd been told. And he checked the answering machine in his rented Studio City condominium a couple of times a day, just in case. He simply returned any calls as though he were safe at home, exactly where he was supposed to be.

Once, he'd been required to travel across town to put in an appearance at the parole office, where he'd bullshitted his PO about how he was attending all kinds of acting and directing classes, not to mention busting his butt full-time, trying to get a job in the movie business. He'd even explained away his newly darkened hair by saying he'd dyed it to audition for a role in a TV series. Yes, sir, keeping his nose clean, staying out of trouble, that was Clay Fowler's professed mission in life, now that he was back on the streets.

But today, Clay's PO wanted to check out his parolee's "living arrangements." What in the hell did the asshole expect to find? That Clay was bunking in with a bunch of other ex-cons? Or maybe running a cocaine cartel out of his living room? Today's drill was one hundred percent unadulterated bullshit. Still, he knew he had to play along. Once he'd discovered that Jennifer Bennett was living in Los Angeles, he'd managed to have his parole shifted there from central California. Her name never came into his negotiations, of course. No, Clay's argument was solely that he needed to be in L.A. to find work in his chosen profession. Where else in California could an actor hope to make a living? Now he was being required to demonstrate just how successfully he was adapting to his new life here in Southern California.

It felt odd taking the Laurel Canyon exit off the freeway

and heading south into the foothills of Studio City for the first time in more than two weeks. Since establishing his phony identity and using it to rent the apartment in Santa Monica, Clay had had no reason to return here to his rented condominium—his official home address.

By now, he almost felt as if he *were* that other guy, the one who lived at the Edgewater and drove rental cars and watched Jennifer Bennett's family. But then, he really had been trained as an actor, and he was good at climbing into the skin of a new character, skilled at living his roles.

He parked a block away from his building and walked—no sense letting some nosy neighbor spot him driving a rental car when his own wheels were parked right here in the condo complex's underground garage. That could spark questions, and answering them wasted time. Not that he wouldn't be able to come up with a convincing explanation if he had to. Clay Fowler took a certain pride in his ability to fabricate a believable lie in a split second. He was damned good at thinking on his feet.

Luckily, the lobby was empty when he came through the front door, so nobody saw him pick up his mail. It had piled up during his absence. When he twisted the key in the mailbox labeled *C. Fowler* and pulled open its rectangular metal door, at least a dozen envelopes flew out and fell at his feet. As he bent over to retrieve them, his eye fell on a corrugated box addressed to Clay Fowler. It was too large to fit into his mailbox, so the letter carrier had left it sitting on the tile floor below. He saw that the return address was Jean's. The date on the postmark was unreadable. How long had the damned thing been sitting here, calling his neighbors' attention to his prolonged absence? Screw Jean, anyway. She was always fucking him up somehow, had been ever since they were kids. If that damned woman had only done what he'd told her to in the first place, none of this—

Clay halted his thought process before his blood pressure began to rise again. He knew it wouldn't do him a damned bit of good to dwell on the past now. Getting all worked up about how badly he'd been fucked over in this deal was a waste of energy, and he would need all of his energy and every shred of his intelligence to get back what rightly belonged to him. He couldn't afford to dwell on Jean and how often she'd let him down. He grabbed the package and carried it, along with the rest of his mail, across the common patio area to his condo.

A foul smell assaulted Clay's nostrils as soon as he opened his front door. He tossed his mail on the kitchen table and cranked open a window to let in some of the morning's warm, smoggy air. Shit! He'd forgotten all about the cantaloupe he'd left to ripen on the counter; now it was thoroughly rotten. Its noxious odor overwhelmed the place, stinking it up worse than a dead body. He lifted the melon with his two index fingers, trying not to get the fluid oozing from it on his hands, then dropped it into the sink. It landed with a splat and cracked open, releasing fumes so pungent they took his breath away. He searched quickly in a drawer for something to use to cut it into pieces small enough to force down the garbage disposal.

He grabbed a butcher knife. Gripping its wooden handle, Clay hacked at the melon with the razor-sharp blade. "Take that, fucker!" he mumbled under his breath, as he repeatedly slashed at the rough gray skin. As the melon began to disintegrate under his blows, he saw Jean's self-righteous face hovering beneath his blade. Then her image faded and Melissa's took over. By the time the melon was nothing but a stinking grayish brown pulp, beads of sweat had formed on his forehead and upper lip, and the back of his shirt was damp. He turned on the water, flipped the disposal's switch, and watched as the remains of the cantaloupe disappeared down the drain.

After opening a window at the front of the town house to create a cross draft, he turned the air-conditioning on high. With luck, the place would air out before his PO showed up to check on him. In the meantime, he headed upstairs to take a shower.

By the time Clay had dried himself and dressed in fresh clothes, the smell lingering in the air had dissipated to a bearable level—either that, or by now his sense of smell had gone numb. He blow-dried his hair and gazed at his reflection in the mirror. Chances were that anyone who knew Clay Fowler before he went to prison would never recognize him now. Except maybe Jean. That's what he wanted, of course. There would be time enough later to get reacquainted.

As Clay buttoned his sport shirt, the buzzer sounded downstairs, notifying him that his PO was at the front gate. He smiled at his face in the mirror, then turned and headed downstairs.

It was show time and Clay Fowler had the starring role.

22

Jennifer stripped the sheets off her bed and tossed them into the corner of the bedroom. Normally she wouldn't change the bed linens until tomorrow, when the Edgewater's maids came to do the weekly cleaning, but today she wanted to do some physical labor, something mindless to help herself relax and sort out her thoughts.

This morning, she'd spent almost an hour packaging up some more videotapes and sending them off with letters of application, but she hadn't been able to keep her mind on her project. She was still thoroughly shaken by the events of last night.

After Forrest left, Jennifer had taken the doll out of the trash and examined it more carefully. As far as she'd been able to tell, there was no difference between this doll and the one she'd tossed out weeks ago at the Seaview Ridge house. But whether this was really the same doll was probably irrelevant anyway. One doll or two—the packages clearly had to have come from the same person. That two unrelated people would leave exactly the same gift was far too weird a coincidence to be believed. No, either somebody had gone through her trash at Seaview Ridge and retrieved the doll after she'd discarded it, or that same somebody had bought a second doll just like the first.

In either case, Jennifer was forced to recognize, that person had access to the Edgewater Apartments. She might well have been close enough to touch him in the elevator or at the mailboxes or in the pool area. That was terrible enough to contemplate. What was even worse was the thought of this psycho, this pervert, this whatever kind of sick creature he was, getting close to Amy.

As Jennifer stretched the contour sheet over the queen-sized mattress of her bed and fitted it over the last corner, she considered her options. She could call the police, of course, but that presented her with the same old dilemma. What could the police really do for her? There was no law against a person's leaving gifts for somebody else.

A short time ago, she'd read in the newspaper that the California legislature had passed a new antistalking law, but she'd probably have to be able to tell the cops precisely who was stalking her for the new law to be any help. She simply didn't know who he was. She hadn't received any threats from her strange, would-be benefactor, either. Surely threats would have to be an essential element in an illegal stalking conviction. Otherwise, every man who had a crush on some woman who didn't return his affections could be found guilty of illegal stalking.

The management of the Edgewater might be able to help, Jennifer thought. She could always lodge a complaint with them about the building's security. Yet she wasn't sure exactly what that would accomplish. This place specialized in accomodating transients, although they were relatively affluent transients. She'd known that when she moved in. As a result, the turnover of residents in the apartments here was unusually heavy. People moved in and out all the time.

With a shudder, Jennifer realized that the man who'd left that doll might live here himself by now. He could have followed her here from Seaview Ridge and rented an apartment nearby. What if this deluded man had the same legal right to walk these halls as she and Amy did? Jennifer's stomach lurched and she bit down hard on her lip as she reached for the second bed sheet.

Unfolding the sheet and spreading it over the top of the mattress, she began to feel more and more like a trapped animal. What she really needed to do, she decided, was get both herself and Amy away from this place, probably completely out of Los Angeles, much as she'd hoped they'd somehow be able to stay.

Sally Donovan had called this morning to alert Jennifer to an opening for a producer of a news magazine show that Channel Three was developing. She'd felt a wave of new hope at first, but now she wasn't sure whether she even wanted to apply for the job. If she got it, it would mean staying here in Los Angeles. It would mean taking the risk that, every time she opened her front door or picked up her mail, another toy from this warped stranger might be sitting there, waiting for her. Or for Amy.

Even worse, that the man himself might be there. Not that the gifts themselves were so bad, of course. They weren't pornographic or violent. Still, Jennifer felt freaked out whenever she speculated about the giver's reasons for leaving them.

Her own bed freshly made up, she carried the soiled sheets into the living room and dropped them on the floor by the front door. As soon as she had changed Amy's bed, she would take all of their sheets, along with the rest of their week's laundry, downstairs to the coin-operated laundry room. Doing the laundry was another mindless task that allowed her time to think.

Amy's room was unusually messy today, a result of Jennifer's allowing the child to sleep a little later this morning. The little girl had awakened, screaming, in the middle of the night again, in the throes of another terrifying nightmare. This time, Jennifer felt completely responsible. That flash of raw anger she'd displayed when Amy found the doll in that cardboard box had obviously frightened the child badly. No wonder she'd had another bad dream.

Jennifer took Raggedy Ann from the bed and seated her on the brown upholstered chair in the corner, then collected Amy's yellow bathrobe and checkered pajamas from the floor and hung them on a hook inside the closet door. She arranged the child's shoes in a row at the bottom of the closet and put the books and toys back in place on the shelves of the small white bookcase that stood against one wall.

When she'd finished, Jennifer looked around the room with a sense of satisfaction. After less than five minutes of straightening up the place, she had it looking neat once again. All she had left to do now was change the bed linens.

As she pulled the bottom sheet off Amy's bed, the narrow mattress slid crookedly across the box spring. Jennifer tossed the soiled contour sheet aside and, using her knee, shoved the mattress back into place. As the mattress slipped jerkily back into position, she heard a thumping sound. Had something fallen to the floor? She looked around her feet, but spotted nothing. Was her imagination in such high gear that she'd begun hearing things? Jennifer didn't think she was that far gone, not yet. She knelt down beside the bed and ran her hand over the low beige carpeting, just under edge of the bed ruffle. Her fingers touched something smooth and cold. They quickly closed around it.

As Jennifer pulled the object out from under the bed, a flash of gold caught her eye. She sat down on the brown chair, next to Raggedy Ann, to look at what she'd found. In her hand was a flat, gold rectangle—a small metal case. She flipped it over and saw the word *Kitty* engraved diagonally across its face. Had a previous resident of this apartment hidden this object between the mattress and box spring and forgotten all about it? Curious, Jennifer forced her thumbnail between the two sides of the case and twisted until the clasp released and it snapped opened.

With a single glance at the picture inside, her heartbeat thudded to a halt. Her fingers stiffened reflexively and she dropped the small gold object into her lap as though it had turned burning hot. Her mind raced in a thousand new directions, every one of them promising a frightening finish line.

If the baby whose photograph was inside this little case was named Kitty, Jennifer knew with a quick flash of fear, she had to be Amy's identical twin. Either that, or this was a photo of Amy herself—a picture Jennifer had never seen before.

Her hands trembling now, she picked up the case once more. Bracing herself, she took a longer look at the photo inside. It was Amy, all right, or her exact double; Jennifer recognized the distinctive birthmark visible beneath the child's wispy pale hair. Did identical twins have identical birthmarks? She didn't know.

The child in the photo looked very young, maybe only sixteen or eighteen months old. Amy had been two when Jennifer adopted her. The red-brown birthmark had been visible on her scalp at the time but, within only a few months, the child's hair had grown and thickened enough to camouflage it completely.

This photo had to be either of Amy or of a twin sister Jennifer knew nothing about. Either way, she could find no comforting explanation for its being hidden here, underneath Amy's mattress. Had someone from Amy's distant past been in touch with the little girl? And, if so, who was he? Or she? And why?

Jennifer thought she'd remembered the head of the adoption agency back in Oregon telling her that the child's parents were dead, and that, for unstated reasons, her only blood relatives couldn't adopt her. That's what she'd always believed, anyway. Unless . . . Unless she'd wanted to adopt a child so badly that she simply hadn't heard any potentially troublesome details about Amy's past.

More likely, Jennifer believed, the adoption agency simply hadn't shared any potentially disturbing information with her. Certainly, months after the adoption was final, when she'd requested more details about Amy's past to help the little girl's psychotherapist work with her, the adoption agency had cited its rules of confidentiality and completely refused to cooperate. So both Jennifer and the therapist had continued working with Amy without having any of the crucial facts behind her obviously severe psychological distress.

Now, well after the child's emotional scars seemed to be healed, her unknown past seemed to be closing in on them again. Only someone from Amy's early life would have access to this photo, Jennifer knew. She began to wonder whether Amy's mother really was dead. And what about her father? Where was he? Or those relatives who'd reportedly been unable to adopt her when she was two? Jennifer shivered as an icicle of fear pierced her soul. If someone from Amy's past ever came and took her away, she didn't know how she'd ever be able to survive. Even a custody battle was unthinkable. Not now, when Jennifer had no savings and Amy already was showing signs of becoming emotionally troubled once more.

Jennifer stared at the photo case as though it might suddenly come alive and talk to her, as if it might explain how it had come to be in this room, under Amy's mattress.

The child had to have put it there herself, of course. There was simply no other plausible explanation. Unless whoever left that doll downstairs last night had also gained access to this apartment. Or unless one of the maids had planted the case there during the weekly cleaning—perhaps paid by somebody to do so.

No, Jennifer scolded herself, *you can't afford to indulge in that kind of fantastic thinking.* She could see she was getting too far afield in trying to find an explanation—any explanation—that would let Amy off the hook. She would simply have to face the facts. The most likely scenario was that somebody—whether a man or a woman—had given Amy the gold picture case, and that she had hidden it under her own mattress.

Jennifer fought against a growing feeling of betrayal that jousted with her raw fear. If Amy had indeed hidden this little photo case under her mattress, there was only one plausible reason—she'd done it so her mother wouldn't find it. Yet Jennifer had always considered herself to be extremely close to her only daughter; certainly the two of them were far better friends and companions than she and her own mother had ever been. She'd always told herself that Amy would feel free to share anything with her, anything at all, without fear of being scolded or punished.

Obviously she'd been very, very wrong.

Jennifer kept turning these painful thoughts over and over in her mind, and they tormented her. Who had given Amy the picture case? For what reason? And why did the little girl want to keep secrets from her own mother? Worst of all, Jennifer wondered, how would she be able to protect Amy from what she now feared was a very real, imminent threat?

A tear tumbled down Amy's cheek and plopped onto her dark blue skirt. "I'm sorry, Mom," she said, her small round face collapsing. "Honest." She lowered her head and stared into her lap, refusing to meet her mother's gaze.

The genuine anguish in Amy's face and voice broke Jennifer's heart. Yet she was determined to continue her questioning, for her daughter's sake as much as for her own. She had confronted Amy about the picture case as soon as they got back to the apartment after school. Now they were sitting side by side on the child's freshly made bed. "I know you're sorry, honey," Jennifer said. "I'm not mad at you—just a little disappointed, I guess. And I'm not going to punish you, I promise. All I want is for you to tell me everything you know about the person who gave you this." She held the picture case in front of Amy's tearful eyes.

"He . . . He said he had a present for me. I just . . . ." Amy sniffled and her voiced faded away.

"You just what?"

"I just wanted to look at it." She wiped her eyes with the sleeve of her blouse. "He told me he had a picture of me. I just wanted to see it."

Jennifer handed Amy a tissue and waited while she blew her nose. "When did this happen?"

"I dunno. The other day, I guess. At school."

Jennifer's hands clenched into fists. At school. So whoever this man was—assuming he'd left the doll at the door—he knew where Amy lived. He knew where she went to school, too. And, not only that, he'd actually managed to talk with her and give her this picture while she was at Brinton Academy. Jennifer's fear quickly merged with anger at the officious Ms. Samuels and the rest of the Brinton Academy staff. The exclusive private school obviously wasn't quite the safe fortress they'd claimed it was. "Was this the same man who tried to talk to you in front of school Monday morning? The day Patty's mom drove you?"

"Huh?" Amy picked up Raggedy Ann and hugged the doll to her chest. "I don't . . . I dunno, Mom. I don't think so. This was at recess."

"On the playground? You mean a strange man was right there on the school playground?" As Jennifer saw Amy cringe and pull away from her, she immediately regretted using a shocked, angry tone of voice. Amy always cowered before loud, angry words, much like a puppy whose master had whipped it. "I'm not angry with you, hon," she said, softening her voice. "I'm mad at the school if they let—"

"No, not *on* the playground, Mom. He was next to the playground, on the sidewalk, over by the fence."

Jennifer sighed with frustration. This interrogation was beginning to remind her of the time she'd tried to interview four male gang members on *Only in L.A.* Her topic had been the violent, antifemale lyrics of the gang members' favorite rap songs. The show was meant to promote understanding between two oppressed groups in society. But the net result of Jennifer's interview was to demonstrate that she and the gang members couldn't even speak the same language. It had turned out to be one of the least informative shows she'd ever done, a total embarrassment.

"Amy," Jennifer said, placing her arm around the little girl's shoulders and giving her a slight squeeze. "Just start at the beginning and tell me everything that happened, and I'll try not to interrupt you. Okay?"

The little girl nodded slowly. "Okay, I guess . . ."

Jennifer waited patiently. Finally Amy began to speak in a quiet voice. "I was all by myself, 'cause Patty was home sick that day, and nobody else wanted to play with me." She twisted a piece of Raggedy Ann's orange hair between her fingers. "The—the man was over by the fence and he started talking to me."

"Did he call you by name?" Jennifer asked, her grip on Amy's shoulders tightening a little.

"Mommm, you *said* you wouldn't interrupt."

"Sorry."

"I don't remember exactly what he said. I think he called me 'little girl' or something." Amy wiggled out of her mother's embrace and tossed the doll aside. "I told him I wasn't allowed to talk to strangers."

Jennifer nodded her approval, keeping her lips tightly pressed together to keep from interrupting Amy's tale again.

"He said he had something for me. A—a picture of me. He wanted me to come and get it, but I told him no, I would get in trouble." Amy began to chew on her thumbnail. "I wasn't gonna. . . . But then the man put the thing through the fence and walked away. It was right there on the grass, Mom, and I just wanted to see—" Amy slid off the bed. "That's all, Mom. I just wanted to see if it really had a picture of me inside." She reached for the case and looked at the photo it held. "Is this really me when I was a baby?"

"I think it is, honey."

Amy pressed a finger against the photograph. "What's this funny thing on my head?"

"That's called a birthmark. It's a kind of special design some people have on their skin. Sometimes they have it when they're babies and then it goes away."

"It looks like California."

Jennifer smiled. "You're right, Amy, it is shaped sort of like the California map."

"Is it still there?" The little girl pulled her hair away from her forehead with her free hand and leaned her head toward her mother. "Look and see."

Jennifer touched her daughter's scalp gently, parting the strands of soft, curly hair. "Maybe just a little bit," she said. "You've got so much hair now, I can't really tell anymore."

The child wrinkled her nose. "I'm glad it doesn't show. Kids would make fun of me."

"Then those kids would be really, really stupid." But Jennifer knew that Amy spoke the truth; children quickly mocked what was different, anything they didn't under-stand, and they could be extremely cruel to other children. "This man, Amy. Did you ever see him before that day?"

She shrugged. "I dunno. Maybe."

"Why don't you know? Was there anything about him that looked familiar to you?"

"I dunno. See, he had these big glasses on, and a big hat, so I couldn't see him too good. 'Sides, I didn't want to get too close."

"That was smart, sweetie. Try to picture him again, in your mind. Can you see what color hair he had?"

Amy gave her mother an exasperated look. "Mommm! I *said* he had a hat on. How could I see his hair?"

"Okay. Then try to remember how big he was."

Amy shrugged. "Big, I guess."

All men probably seemed big from Amy's perspective, Jennifer realized. She got up off the bed and stretched to her full height. "Was the man bigger than me?"

Amy nodded.

"Bigger than . . ." Jennifer tried to think what man's height Amy might easily recall. Forrest Hathaway was the only man who'd been at the apartment recently. "Uh, bigger than Mr. Hathaway?"

"Nope."

"Between me and Mr. Hathaway?"

"Nope. 'Bout like Mr. Hathaway, I think."

Jennifer guessed Forrest Hathaway's height to be about six feet, maybe six feet one. "How about Mr. Whittaker?" she asked, seeking additional confirmation. Howard Whittaker was also right around six feet tall, and Amy had known him for more than a year. "How about Howard? Was he bigger than Mr. Whittaker?"

"Mommm." The exasperated look was back on Amy's face. "Mr. Hathaway and Mr. Whittaker are the same."

"I think you're right, hon." She sat back down on the bed, placed her elbows on her knees, and leaned toward Amy, meeting her gaze at eye level. "Anything else you can remember about this man?"

The child shook her head. "Not really. Just . . . I think he had on jeans and a jacket, a big blue jacket."

"That's good, hon, very good. Did . . . Think real hard now. Do you think you might have seen this man anywhere before? I don't mean just at school. Anywhere at all."

"Like I told you, Mom, I dunno. I couldn't see his face so good and I—I was just looking at the present."

Jennifer kept her facial expression neutral, free of disapproval or surprise. She knew that either might put Amy back into her shell and inhibit her from sharing whatever she might be able to remember. She could understand Amy's being tempted by the gold case, particularly when the man told her that her own picture was inside. What child wouldn't be curious? Still, it was terrifying to think what might have happened if that fence hadn't separated him from Amy. "What about the man who tried to talk to you on Monday morning, hon? Do you think the man at the fence could have been the same one?"

Amy looked at her shoes. "I really dunno, Mom, honest. I didn't even look at that man. I was late for school and I was scared my teacher would be mad and I'd get in trouble. All I did is run up the steps, and Ms. Samuels—"

"What did Ms. Samuels do?"

"She came down the steps. She told me to get inside to class, so I did. That's all."

"You did the right thing, sweetie." Jennifer tried to think what else to ask Amy that might help identify the man at the fence. "What about the man's voice, hon. When he talked to you by the school fence, what was his voice like? Did he sound like anybody you know?"

Amy thought for a minute before answering. "He was all kind of whispery," she said after a while. "Like nobody but me was s'posed to hear."

A man in a hat and sunglasses, about six feet tall, whose voice was whispery, probably because either he didn't want to be overheard or because he didn't want Amy to recognize his voice. If this was the same man that Ms. Samuels had frightened away on Monday morning, he also had dark hair and drove some sort of red car. Not much to go on, Jennifer realized. Certainly the police couldn't sweep the streets for tall, dark-haired men who drove red cars and wore hats, sunglasses, and blue jeans. That description would fit half the men in L.A. "If you can remember anything else about him, Amy," she said, "anything at all, I want you to promise you'll tell me right away. Okay?"

"Okay. I'm sorry, Mommy. Honest I am." Amy's lower lip began to quiver again. "I . . . I just didn't want to get in trouble."

"What kind of trouble?"

"I wanted to see the picture. And then I thought I would get yelled at because I talked to the man when I wasn't s'posed to. And . . . And I thought the teachers would think I stole it." Two fat tears rolled off Amy's cheeks and dripped onto her blouse.

Jennifer's heart sank. The poor kid. She obviously was still scarred by that awful time in kindergarten, when she'd been accused of stealing a cheap little paint box. "I would never think you stole that picture case," she said, holding out her arms. Amy slowly moved into her mother's comforting embrace. "I know my girl is no thief."

"I was scared, Mom," Amy confessed. "I hid the picture 'cause I was scared about what you'd say."

Jennifer pulled her daughter onto her lap and stroked her hair gently. "Words can't hurt us, Amy. But sometimes being afraid of them can."

"What do you mean?"

"Well, for instance, you didn't want to tell me about the man at school because you were afraid of what I might say. But if I *hadn't* found out about him . . . Well, what if he tried to take you away from me, sweetie? I couldn't stand for that to happen. So it's really, really important for you to come and tell me right away when something like that happens. Understand? That way, I can protect you and nobody will ever be able to take you away from me."

Amy chewed on her thumbnail. "Okay, Mom, I promise I'll tell you first thing if he comes back again."

Jennifer gave her a quick squeeze. "You remember all the things we talked about doing if anybody ever tried to grab you, don't you, Amy?"

"Yeah."

"What were they?"

"I'm s'posed to yell as loud as I can and kick and hit and try to get away, right?"

"That's right. And what else?"

Amy's face was somber, her forehead deeply furrowed. The tracks of her tears were still wet on her cheeks. "Try to find a policeman right away, or else a telephone and call nine-one-one."

"Very good, hon." Jennifer wished she could really feel the sense of confidence she was trying to convey to Amy. In her heart, she wondered exactly how much good Amy's kicking and screaming would really do if a grown man tried to snatch her off the street. Yet fighting back had to be a lot more effective than passivity. If Amy could create a big enough ruckus, someone might hear her and come to her aid. Better yet, Jennifer vowed, she simply wouldn't let her daughter be alone where something like a kidnapping could be attempted. When she wasn't at school, Jennifer would watch over her every minute.

"I won't ever let anybody take you away from me," Jennifer promised.

Chapter

24

Jennifer carried her brown leather briefcase out of the West Los Angeles storage facility and unlocked the door of her station wagon. She'd been at the massive warehouse ever since delivering Amy to school before eight o'clock this morning, shifting boxes around in the cramped locker that now held the bulk of her worldly possessions. Now it was nearing eleven.

Luckily, the boxes Jennifer wanted were all well labeled, so she hadn't had to open carton after carton to find what she needed. Still, she'd located all three of the containers she was seeking near the bottom of their stacks. She'd had to lift and carry at least two dozen heavy cartons before finally getting access to the right ones. Then, after she had removed the items she needed, she taped the boxes shut again and put them back where the moving men had stored them.

Now Jennifer's back began to ache from her uncustomary physical efforts. But she felt good that she'd actually managed to find everything she'd come here for. In her briefcase now were the income tax records and receipts she needed for the IRS audit, as well as her file containing all of Amy's adoption papers. The third item she'd come to the storage facility to get—that can of mace she'd hidden for years on her bedroom closet shelf at Seaview Ridge—was now in her purse, where she would be able to get her hands on it in a hurry.

It began to rain as Jennifer drove underneath the Santa Monica Freeway and up the Robertson Boulevard on-ramp. She switched on her windshield wipers and watched as they streaked grime across the glass. As she merged the car into traffic, she pulled a lever and windshield washer solution squirted onto the windshield, clearing her view of what was quickly becoming the proverbial Los Angeles parking lot.

At least there would be no outdoor recess at Brinton Academy this morning, she thought. Amy and her friends would be unhappy about being kept indoors and missing their customary active games, but Jennifer couldn't help feeling somewhat relieved. This was one day that no man would be approaching her daughter on the school playground.

Traffic was crawling westward slowly and it took Jennifer almost half an hour to reach her exit at Centinela Avenue. Los Angeles freeways and side streets always turned slick and dangerous in the rain; the coating of dirt and oil that accumulated on them during months of dry weather turned slippery and slimy as soon as a little water was added. As a result, drivers had to be extra cautious whenever it rained, resulting in even slower traffic than usual. But the natural desert of L.A. badly needed the rain and, after a good hard downpour, the air was always refreshingly clear and clean.

After she finally exited the freeway past an art storage warehouse advertising bargain rates, Jennifer turned left on Pico Boulevard and circled around a fender bender. The two drivers involved were discussing the accident, one of them waving his hands angrily, as she slowed almost to a stop and stared at them. The car that had been rear-ended was a red Volkswagen Rabbit. Its driver, the man gesturing with such animation, was tall, dark-haired, around forty. She rolled down her side window. Could he—

The driver of the stretch white limousine behind Jennifer's station wagon tapped his horn twice, startling her out of her reverie, and a siren wailed in the distance. She pressed down on the accelerator and headed toward the Edgewater, feeling momentarily foolish. She could hardly stop and stare at every man who fit the descriptions Amy and Ms. Samuels had given her. For all she knew, the man at the playground fence and the man who'd spoken to Amy near the school entrance weren't even the same guy. Except for his suspiciously quick exit when Ms. Samuels approached him, Jennifer could conclude that the latter man had simply been looking for directions, or maybe he was trying to find some other Brinton Academy student.

As soon as she got back to the apartment, Jennifer made herself a cup of coffee. Her phone answer machine notified her of only one message—from Howard Whittaker an hour ago. He was calling to ask her out tonight. This time, his suggestion included dinner at Santa Monica's Chinois on Main, plus he offered to pay for a babysitter for Amy. "Know things are a little tight in the wallet for you right now, Jen-babe," he said. "So I'd be willing to pop for a sitter. Call me."

Jennifer cringed as she listened to Howard's recorded message. How could she ever have thought she was in love with this man—a man who spoke in insufferably dated clichés and whose inflated ego assumed that she would always be available whenever he called at the last minute? "—tight in the wallet—" "—pop for the sitter—" Indeed! She decided not to return this call, either. As far as she was concerned, Howard Whittaker was now ancient history.

Instead, Jennifer sat down at the kitchen table and looked through the adoption file while she sipped her coffee. The information the file held was sketchy at best. There was a copy of Amy's birth certificate, legally altered to include only Jennifer's name as the infant girl's parent. Amy's biological parents' names, as well as the child's own birth name, had been removed. The file also included a few letters and legal documents, the name, address, and phone number of the Oregon adoption agency that had placed the two-year-old with Jennifer, and a payment receipt from the attorney she'd hired to handle the official paperwork.

With a pang of frustration, Jennifer remembered calling the adoption agency once before, shortly after she'd moved to California. Madeleine Fariday, Amy's psychotherapist, had asked Jennifer to collect any available information about Amy's early life. She'd wanted clues about why the child had lost her ability to speak, and about the source of the little girl's vast reservoir of unexpressed rage. But the head of the adoption agency had been no help whatsoever.

Maybe this time would be different, Jennifer told herself. Adoptions were more open nowadays. In some of them, the birth parents and the adoptive parents actually met each other; occasionally, they even became friends.

She reached for the telephone and dialed the number of the Portland-based agency. "May I speak with the director, please?" she asked after the receptionist had answered.

"Who's calling, please?"

Jennifer explained who she was and what she wanted. She was put on hold to wait for the agency's director, Marian McCrary. She'd hoped that Mrs. McCrary might be retired by now, replaced by someone younger, someone more flexible, someone more modern. She remembered Mrs. McCrary all too well from five years ago—a stocky woman in her late fifties who wore tobacco brown suits that matched her dyed hair and insisted on being called *Mrs.*—never *Ms.*— McCrary.

"This is Marian McCrary," the woman's clipped voice announced after Jennifer had been kept waiting on the line for at least five minutes. "What can I do for you, Ms. Bennett?" There was no warmth in her tone.

Jennifer briefly explained about the man who had been trying to make contact with Amy here in Los Angeles. "He has to be someone from my daughter's past, Mrs. McCrary, because of that photograph he gave her. I don't know who— maybe her natural father, an older brother, an uncle, someone she was in foster care with. But I'm scared to death, and I've got almost no information about Amy's—about her people, or her life before she came to live with me."

Jennifer nervously drew circles on the outside of the manila file folder with a pencil while she spoke. They lengthened into little funnel clouds, miniature black tornadoes. "I was hoping you could help me find out who this man is, Mrs. McCrary, so I can put a stop to what he's been doing. Before—before something terrible happens to my Amy."

A sigh echoed over the phone line. "Your feelings are understandable, Ms. Bennett. This certainly does sound like a trying situation for you. But you have to understand that I'm not at liberty to give out information from the agency's files."

"Surely something like this has to be an exception, Mrs. McCrary. My daughter's being physically threatened, and I—"

"I'm very sorry about that, Ms. Bennett, really I am. But just think for a minute. You really must consider the agency's position in this kind of thing. Anybody could call us up on the phone, just like you're doing right now, tell us their child is in some sort of danger, so they need immediate access to our files. We have no way of knowing whether what they're telling us is true or not. We can't—"

"I'll send you a copy of the photo," Jennifer offered. She could easily picture Marian McCrary right now, sitting at her desk, wearing one of her old brown suits, a smugly officious expression on her pudgy, sagging face. "That should change your mind. In this photograph, you can see for yourself that Amy's way, way younger than she was when I adopted her. There's simply no other way I could have gotten this kind of picture except what I told you."

"I'm not trying to imply that you're lying, Ms. Bennett. It's just that we have *rules*. Look at it this way—how would you feel if Amy's birth mother called me up with some cock-and-bull story about the child's being in danger and I opened up my files and gave her *your* name and address? I'm sure you'd—"

"Amy's *birth* mother? You told me her birth mother was dead!" That had been one of the few pieces of vital information the agency had parted with five years ago.

There was a long pause in the converation, while the sound of papers being shuffled sounded in Jennifer's ear. "I . . . I can see here that you're right, Ms. Bennett." Marian McClary cleared her throat. "I really can't be expected to remember details about all the children we place, right off the top of my head. There've been hundreds of them. But it does say here in the file that the birth mother is dead. The child apparently went to live with relatives briefly, but they felt they couldn't keep her permanently, so they brought her to us. As you know, the child was put into foster care prior to our placing her for adoption with you, but that was only for a month or two."

Jennifer sighed. Marian McCrary was not giving her so much as one new fact. "What about Amy's birth father? Is he still alive? And, if he is, where is he now?"

"I simply can't tell you that, Ms. Bennett. I'm not even sure we have the answer. You know, the way we see it, you should really feel reassured that our agency has such a strict information policy."

"Just how do you figure that?" Jennifer could hear sarcasm and bitterness creeping into her own voice.

"Think about it. If we won't give you information about Amy's original family, you certainly can rest assured we're not going to tell any of them about you. Complete privacy for everyone involved in an adoption—that's our motto. We find that keeping our records totally secret works out best for everybody concerned. That way, nobody has to worry about a child they gave up for adoption years ago someday showing up on their doorstep, upsetting their entire life. We make a pledge to our mothers and our adoptive parents, and we stand by it." Marian McCrary's voice became more and more patronizing as she droned on. "Why, Ms. Bennett, do you realize that we've been state licensed for more than forty years now? And, in all that time, I'm proud to say, we've never had so much as one intrusion into our confidential records."

Bully for you, Jennifer thought, growing angrier by the minute. "How about if I get a court order?" she asked, grasping for something—anything—that might worry the agency director, that might spur her into some kind of action. "If I get a court order, you'll *have* to give me the information I'm asking for."

"It's just not going to happen, Ms. Bennett, so you may as well save your time and money. Don't think you're the first person who's tried this kind of thing with us. You get a court order, we'll fight you all the way to the Supreme Court if we have to. As we both know, that could take years, and the only ones who'll make out in the end are the lawyers."

Jennifer's grip on the telephone receiver loosened and it slipped in her moist palm. She could tell when she'd been matched, when she'd come up against someone at least as stubborn as she was. Unfortunately, this someone had all the power here, and she knew it. "I want to leave you with just one thought, Mrs. McCrary," she said. "Just how are you going to feel if something happens to my Amy, and you could have prevented it?"

"I'm sure you're worrying about nothing, Ms. Bennett. Things will work out and Amy will grow up happy and healthy. You'll see. You've given her a good, stable life now and—well, in my opinion, you're both far better off not knowing too much about where she came from. Often our children's backgrounds are quite, uh . . . unusual, you might say. Sometimes even rather unpleasant."

Obviously. Otherwise these kids wouldn't be up for adoption, Jennifer thought, and asked, "Shouldn't whether we want to know about Amy's background be our choice?"

"We've already been through all that, Ms. Bennett, more than once. Now, you really must excuse me. I'm late for a meeting. Do have a nice day."

Another irritating cliché, Jennifer thought. She seemed to be surrounded by them today. "No doubt my day will be absolutely fantastic," she said angrily, slamming down the receiver. Her petty final action did not make her feel any better.

Chapter

25

Jean Fowler Morton used her left hand to pull a large-size box of Quaker oatmeal off one of the Foodmart's cereal shelves. She dropped it into her shopping cart and reached for a box of the store's own brand of corn flakes. With her right wrist encased in a bulky plaster cast for the past five weeks, grocery shopping had been taking her a lot longer. And, with five growing children to feed, she needed to shop a minimum of twice a week. Today she was trying to hurry the chore along. Salem was threatened by rain again this afternoon, and Jean wanted to get home before the downpour hit. She wheeled her cart around the corner into the paper aisle.

"Wait a minute, I'll get that down for you," Jean's friend and neighbor Connie Wilynski offered. The two women had come to the Foodmart together in Connie's car. Jean's old clunker had a stick shift, and driving it made her injured wrist ache, so she'd gratefully accepted Connie's offer of a ride. Standing on tiptoes, Connie hoisted a twenty-four-roll economy pack of toilet paper off the top shelf and handed it to Jean.

"Thanks." Jean took the toilet paper, bent down, and wedged it into the bottom section of her cart. A short, slightly overweight woman in her middle thirties, she had a pretty face, but she looked at least five years older than she really was, particularly on a day like today, when she wasn't wearing makeup. Her naturally red hair, once her most striking feature, had been messy and unstyled for the past few weeks. With her wrist out of action, she'd been unable to do much more than keep her hair clean.

"That thing comes off next week, right?" Connie pointed at Jean's cast.

Jean grimaced at the grimy white casing that imprisoned her wrist. "Sure hope so. Doctor says he has to X-ray it once more. I tell you, Con, my skin itches so bad underneath this thing sometimes, I can hardly stand it, especially at night." She added two jumbo rolls of paper towels to her load. "If he doesn't cut the damned thing off, I think I will."

"I still think you should have called the police about that bastard, Jean. I can't understand how you could let him get away with hurting you like this." Connie was a tall woman, slimmer than Jean, with a pointed chin and thin lips. She was not naturally as pretty as Jean Morton, but Connie obviously cared about her physical appearance and did her best to make herself look good. As a result, people here in Salem who'd met both women were more likely to describe Connie as attractive than Jean.

"We've been over this a dozen times, Connie," Jean said, unconsciously rubbing her left cheek. The purple bruise that had marked it a short while ago was nearly healed now. "Clay's my only brother. If I'd filed a complaint against him, he probably would've been sent right back to prison. You know that."

"So what's the problem?"

Jean circled her cart around to the refrigerated case and added four half gallons of low-fat milk to her purchases. "Yeah, right. You want to raise my kids? 'Cause, if I turn Clay in to the cops, you can bet your life savings he'll kill me the minute they let him out. Or maybe you won't have to take my kids in—he'll probably kill them, too."

"Look, I know you're scared of your brother. But are you gonna let him beat you up whenever he feels like it?" Connie put a carton of milk into her own cart.

Jean squared her shoulders. "You make it sound like it happens all the time. For God's sake, Connie, before that day, I hadn't even seen my brother in five years."

"Only because he was locked up in California."

"Even before that, he was hardly what you'd call a frequent guest around here. Before all his trouble, he and Melissa came to visit us here just that one time—for two lousy days. Besides, Clay hadn't laid a hand on me since we were kids."

"Hooray for Clay! Mr. Self-Control. Why don't we just nominate him for sainthood while we're at it?"

"You're not being fair, Connie." Jean stopped in her tracks and turned to face her friend. She felt her anger rising fast, and she didn't want to react in her usual way—with tears instead of words. Who was Connie Wilynski to lecture her on what she should do about Clay, anyway? Clay wasn't Connie's brother. Connie'd never had to grow up in a family like the Fowlers', either; she couldn't possibly know what their childhood life had been like. "You're forgetting one thing, Connie," Jean told her, her voice quavering with emotion. "I did a pretty crappy thing to Clay. He had every right to be mad at me."

"So, now it comes out—the real reason." Connie's knuckles were white on her grocery cart's handle. "I wondered how long it would take you to admit it. Little Jeannie Morton feels guilty for not adopting her brother's poor, homeless kid, so now big bad Clay gets to punish little Jeannie for the rest of their natural lives. That how you figure it?"

As she thought about how to answer her friend's question, Jean lifted two cans of green beans off the shelf and added them to her cart. Finally she admitted, "I . . . It's just that I understand how Clay feels, Connie. I mean, he figured on Kitty's being here in Salem with us. He thought she'd be waiting for him to come and get her when he got his parole. I let him down."

Jean truly did feel guilty about Kitty, but she didn't know what she could have done differently. She'd spent night after sleepless night trying to find the answer to that haunting question. Five years ago, she'd been caught squarely between her brother and her husband—and afraid to cross either of them. It was true, too, that Kitty had been a severely disturbed little girl, much more of a handful than the Mortons had been prepared to handle.

Bruce hadn't wanted to take in Jean's niece in the first place. He was adamant that there was no reason they should have to clean up Clay's mess. When she'd first approached her husband about adding Kitty to their family, Bruce had screamed at her, "We've already got five brats of our own, Jeannie. What the hell do we want with another one? Specially a kid like that." Still, he'd finally agreed to give the toddler a chance—Jean had to give him credit for that much.

Bruce had put his foot down firmly, however, when Kitty began acting out. That terrible day Jean and Bruce heard ear-splitting shrieks coming from their baby son's room would be engraved on her mind forever. She and Bruce had shared a terrified look, then raced into the nursery, where they found little Kitty standing next to the wailing infant's bassinet, beating him with a sharp stick she'd found in the yard.

Kitty was only twenty-two months old at the time. The next day, Bruce put the child into foster care and wiped his hands of her forever. Jean had seen her little niece only once after that day—she'd seen her only once in the flesh, anyway.

"Sometimes . . . Sometimes, I think Clay can't really help himself," Jean said. "It's like he has this terrible rage inside him and—"

"So, who doesn't? Honestly, Jean, I love you like a sister." Connie shook her head in exasperation. "But sometimes I just don't know about you and men. First Bruce, now Clay. Maybe you should just paint a target on your forehead, or get yourself a T-shirt that has *victim* written in bright red letters across the front."

Jean swallowed hard, fighting back tears. She couldn't start crying here, in the middle of Foodmart's canned goods aisle. In her heart, she knew that Connie was right; still, she felt attacked by her friend, not helped. She *was* afraid of men, had been ever since she was a small child, that much was true. She'd been in therapy once, for a few months after her divorce, but she'd dropped out when her health insurance stopped paying for it. Still, she'd learned a few things. One of them was that she had an extremely strong fear of men, which the counselor had chalked up to her early relationship with her father. Henry Fowler had generally ignored his only daughter when she was a girl— unless he needed a target for his anger. Jean learned early on that avoiding her father meant avoiding trouble. And, when she couldn't hide from him, she tried her very best to be a good little girl. If she was only good enough, she remembered telling herself, maybe this time Daddy wouldn't attack her—either with his strong, punishing hands or with his sharp, crippling tongue.

Jean knew it probably was about time she learned to stand up to a man, any man. Both her therapist and Connie had told her the same thing. Still, knowing what she should do and doing it were two very different things. "He's my brother, Con," Jean said, feeling every bit as wimpy as she knew she looked. "I just can't."

Connie shrugged and shoved her grocery list into her purse. "It's your funeral. Got everything?" She turned her cart around and aimed it toward the checkout stands.

Jean double-checked her list. "Except bananas. They all

look overripe today, and the kids won't eat them if they're already getting soft. Would you mind stopping by Hardy's on the way home? I can run in real quick." Hardy's Produce was only a mile or two off their route home.

"Just for bananas? You need them that bad?"

Jean avoided making eye contact with her friend. "The kids like them," she explained. "And Stevie won't eat his cereal if I don't put a banana on it."

Connie rolled her eyes skyward. "Sure, why not. Just don't complain to me when Stevie grows up to be just like his father and his uncle."

"I don't know how you can say that, Connie. Poor Stevie doesn't even see his father or his uncle anymore. None of my kids do." Since their divorce two years ago, Bruce Morton had taken up residence in Seattle with his new girlfriend, a buxom twenty-two-year-old blond who taught aerobic dancing for a living. He'd been back to Salem to see his children a grand total of four times.

"I know, Jean. Your kids have a rotten father, and they have a rotten uncle. That stinks, and I feel bad for them. But you can't make up for the failings of a couple of grown men by being a doormat, or by indulging your kids' every whim." Connie pushed her cart into the shortest checkout line and began to unload her groceries from the cart onto the counter. "Well, at least you must feel good about one thing," she offered.

"What's that?"

"Poor little Kitty will never have to live with that piece-of-scum father of hers. Because of what you did, she's got herself a good home with normal parents. And Clay Fowler will never be able to bother her again."

Jean began to search through her purse for her check-book, a ploy to avoid letting her friend see the guilty expression that was quickly creeping into her eyes. She knew Connie would go ballistic if she ever found out everything that had happened on that day five weeks ago, when Clay showed up on her doorstep.

All Jean could hope for now was that Connie's prediction—that Clay would never find his daughter—might still come true, in spite of the help she'd reluctantly given him. Kitty would be far better off in her adoptive home. But Jean wished for something else even more—that her brother would never again show his face here in Salem.

By the time the two women left the Foodmart and began wheeling their carts across the parking lot toward Connie's car, the first drops of rain had begun to fall. Jean frowned and cursed her timing. "Let's go straight home," she said as Connie helped load her grocery bags into the trunk. "I guess Stevie can do without his banana for one day."

Connie glanced at her old friend with approval. "Well, hallelujah," she said, and grinned.

Chapter

26

*Jennifer checked her watch. She'd been waiting at the local police
station to talk to a police officer for more than twenty minutes.* The waiting room was chaotic, with telephones ringing constantly in the background, people shouting for
attention, and both cops and civilians running in and out
of the station's back door, all of them looking seriously
worried about something.

Jennifer got up off her bench and walked over to the
counter. "I'm sorry, but I can't wait much longer," she told
the clerk, a pretty black woman in her early twenties. "I
have to pick up my daughter at school before three." It was
already after two o'clock. Brinton Academy was only three
or four miles from the station but, in the rain, crosstown
traffic would be slower than usual.

"I'll check and see if anybody can see you yet, ma'am."

"Thanks. I'd really appreciate it." Jennifer returned to
her seat.

Five minutes later, a man wearing an ill-fitting gray pinstripe business suit, a white shirt, and navy tie came into the
waiting area, took some papers attached to a clipboard from
the receptionist, surveyed the half dozen people sitting

there, and called out, "Ms. Bennett?" He was in his early to middle forties, about Jennifer's height, and approaching total baldness.

Jennifer stood up. "That's me."

He walked over to her. "Hello, ma'am, I'm Detective Mike Jenrud." He thrust out his hand and Jennifer shook it. His hand was warm, but not damp. "Let's go find someplace more private to talk." He led the way along a narrow institutional green corridor, then opened the door of a glass-fronted cubicle and entered it. The tiny room reminded Jennifer of the one she'd shared with Ms. Samuels at Brinton Academy a few days ago. It was quieter in here than in the waiting room. Here, the telephones' insistent bells were muted by the glass partition.

"Now," Detective Jenrud said, when they were both seated on hard wooden chairs with a table between them, "why don't you start at the beginning and just tell me what's on your mind."

Jennifer told him everything she could remember about the man who'd approached Amy at school, then took the gold photo case from her purse and showed it to the detective. "I figure the man who gave this to my daughter has to be somebody from out of her past," she said, prying open the case. She placed it on the table and turned it around so Jenrud could look at the photo inside. "See, this picture here had to be taken several months, maybe even a year before I adopted Amy. She was two when I got her, and you can see here that she's still a baby." She snapped the case closed again. "And notice this, here on the outside? The name Kitty is engraved across the front."

Jenrud looked at the case where it lay on the table, but didn't pick it up. "Let me see if I've got this right. You say this guy gave this picture to your daughter—Amy, is that her name?" Jennifer nodded. "You say he gave this to Amy while she was playing on the playground at Brinton

Academy?" He leaned back in his chair and chewed on a pencil eraser, as though it were a cigar or a pipestem, while he listened to his visitor's reply.

"That's correct, Detective. Amy told me he pushed it through the chain link fence—you know, the high fence that surrounds the entire school playground. She picked it up off the ground and kept it. Like any kid, she was curious."

"So both you and Amy have handled this case."

Jennifer blanched as she realized the implications of the detective's question. "Yes, I'm afraid we have," she admitted. "Amy carried it around with her for a while, and then she hid it under her mattress. Since I found it there, I've touched it quite a bit myself."

Jenrud's face displayed his frustration at the stupidity he so often found in the civilian population. "Won't be able to lift any of the guy's prints off it, then. What about that doll you say he left at your place?"

Jennifer stared at the table. Someone had inked initials into its surface on her side. Outside the cubicle, she could still hear telephones ringing, muffled voices speaking. "Sorry," she said. "I . . . I didn't want it lying around the apartment where Amy would find it, so I put it down the trash chute at the Edgewater," she confessed. Her impulsive action now made her feel incredibly foolish. "I see now I should have kept it for evidence."

"How long ago did you throw it out?"

"A few days, at least."

"It's in some landfill by now." Jenrud made some notes on the paper fastened to the clipboard, then looked up at Jennifer again. "You know, you look sort of familiar. You an actress or something?"

Jennifer responded with a weak smile, pleased to be recognized by the public once more, however obliquely. That wasn't happening to her all that often anymore. "I used to be host of *Only in L.A.*, on KNLA-TV," she explained.

"Yeah, now I remember you. You did one of those Rodney King interviews, right?"

Jennifer felt Jenrud's manner toward her cooling. She tried to phrase her answer carefully. "I did several interviews on my show, with different people involved in the King beating case." The infamous Rodney King case, in which four white police officers were charged with using excessive force against a black man, following a high-speed chase, had been a political lightning rod in Los Angeles. Jennifer was proud of her role in helping to shed light on the various issues the incident raised within the community. "I tried to present all the different viewpoints on *Only in L.A.*," she told Jenrud, watching his reaction carefully. She knew that many members of the police force had strong feelings about the federal convictions of two of the cops involved in the King beating. Some of them blamed the so-called "liberal media" for inciting public sentiment against the police. At the very least, the case had heightened tensions among the cops, the news media, and the public they were both pledged to serve.

"Show got canceled, huh?" Jenrud asked.

Jennifer detected the hint of a smirk on the cop's lips, and she didn't appreciate it. She began to suspect that Jenrud had just mentally categorized her as one of the enemy. Perhaps, if she still had her show, she thought, he would be forced to show her more respect; then, at least, she would have the implied power of being able to shower him with negative publicity if he didn't treat her right. But now, she not only was one of the enemy, she'd lost all of her weapons. She looked at her watch. "I don't want to be rude, Detective," she said, "but I do have to pick Amy up at school in a few minutes. I'd appreciate it if you would tell me how you plan to catch this guy."

Jenrud's chair snapped into an upright position as he leaned forward abruptly. He made another brief notation on his clipboard and stored the pencil he'd been chewing under the clip. "I'll go talk to a few people over at Brinton Academy, see what they can tell me about all this, either this afternoon or tomorrow morning. See if this guy meets the description of any child molester known to be in the area. Beyond that, Ms. Bennett, there's not a whole lot we can do."

"What? What do you mean, there's not a whole lot you can do? Someone's trying to take my daughter! And I don't think you're going to find him in your child molester files, either. Like I told you, this has to be somebody who knew Amy when she was a baby."

Jenrud held up his right palm. "Let me spell it out for you, ma'am. What we got here simply isn't a crime. At least not so far. We find out this guy's harassing your daughter further, or he tries to snatch her or one of the other kids at Brinton, something like that, then maybe we got enough to go on. Right now, all we got is a guy who maybe said a few words to your daughter. No threat, no physical contact, nothing illegal."

"What about the toys?"

Jenrud shook his head slowly. "No law against giving somebody a gift, ma'am. You're in show business, you ought to be used to that." He said the words "show business" with clear contempt in his voice. "Besides, you can't even be sure the guy who talked to your daughter at school left that doll. Fact is, you don't even know it's a man that left it."

"You think there's two different people bothering us at the same time? That's ridiculous." Jennifer held up the photo case between her index finger and thumb. "And what about this? Isn't this proof that this man plans to . . . I don't know." Her chin started to quiver and she inhaled slowly until she'd regained control. "I'm just terrified that he's going to try to snatch my Amy away from me,

Detective. I mean, why else would he give her this? Why else would he be hanging around this way?"

Jenrud crossed his arms across his chest. His expression was not sympathetic. "Just what would you like us to do, ma'am?"

Her anger and frustration mushrooming, Jennifer's voice became incrementally louder. "What I want is for you to find this man and make him stay away from my daughter. Is that asking so much?" She ran her fingers through her hair absentmindedly. "What is it with you people, anyway? Do I have to wait until he's kidnapped Amy before you even try to do anything about it?"

Mike Jenrud sucked in air loudly, then let it out again. "If you really think this guy's the child's real father or uncle or whatever, Ms. Bennett, I'd suggest you go see your adoption agency, get them to help you find out who this fellow is. If you can prove your theory, get yourself a name, you can probably get a restraining order and—"

"I already *tried* that, Detective. I talked to the adoption agency today, in fact. They told me this was *my* problem. Basically, they won't give me one damn bit of help if it means opening up their precious files." Now Jennifer was so angry that she was having trouble keeping contempt out of her own voice. "Any more suggestions?" she asked.

"Yeah. Keep an eye on your kid, if you're really worried about her."

Jennifer tossed the photo case into her purse. "I don't believe this. *If* I'm worried about her! What do you think I'm doing here?"

Gripping the clipboard at his side, Jenrud rose from his chair. "This kind of thing could be worth some publicity, couldn't it?"

Jennifer's jaw dropped. "Publicity! You have no right! You have no right to say something like that to me."

"Just asking a theoretical question, ma'am," Jenrud said.

"You asked what I can do for you. I'll do whatever I can, but you gotta understand that the police department simply doesn't have the manpower to provide bodyguards for private citizens—celebrities or not. Wouldn't be appropriate, even if we did. I can go talk to the staff at Brinton Academy, however. If anything else happens, don't hesitate to let me know." He reached inside the pocket of his suitcoat and drew out a business card, then handed it to Jennifer.

She swallowed hard and took the card. She knew that displaying the rage she was feeling right now probably wouldn't help her convince Detective Jenrud to pay more attention to her dilemma, but she couldn't stop herself. "I certainly hope that 'if anything else happens' doesn't include my daughter's being kidnapped," she said, slipping the card into her purse, next to the little gold case. "And I will definitely be in touch with you again, Detective. You can count on that."

Jenrud opened the door to the cubicle and stood to the side. "Can you find your way out?" he asked without smiling.

Jennifer straightened her spine. "Absolutely, Detective. As a journalist, I've been trained to pay attention to every little detail. Besides, I wouldn't feel right, wasting your time by asking you to show me the way."

By the time she reached the parking lot, Jennifer's anger was threatening to dissolve into tears of frustration.

"Hurry along now, Amy," Jennifer said, *as she climbed out of* the station wagon in the Edgewater's underground garage. Amy still hadn't unbuckled her seat belt. "You've got homework before bed." The two were returning home after a quick dinner of make-your-own salads and bowls of homemade soup at the Souplantation in West Los Angeles.

As Jennifer was closing her driver's side door, a red BMW streaked down the ramp into the garage and braked to a stop in the aisle right behind her. Noting the car's red color, she froze in place for an instant, sucking in acrid exhaust fumes. Was the dark-haired man at the wheel? She couldn't see; the BMW's roof obscured her view of the driver.

She heard a click as the BMW's door began to open. Sprinting around the front of her station wagon, she thrust herself between the little red car and Amy and opened her purse. She fumbled around inside of her bag, searching for her can of mace until her fingers finally closed around it. Anyone who wanted to snatch her daughter would have to get past her first.

"Jennifer, Amy, hi, there!" A deep male voice Jennifer couldn't quite place echoed across the concrete and steel cavern. A man's dark head began to emerge from the driver's side of the BMW.

Jennifer thrust her arm across Amy's door to prevent it from opening, then just as quickly lowered it when she recognized Forrest Hathaway's grinning face. "Forrest, hello." Embarrassed, she dropped the mace can back into her purse.

"Hey, sorry, didn't mean to scare you." Forrest's handsome face registered what looked like genuine concern.

"No, no, you didn't scare me," Jennifer lied. "Just didn't recognize your car. I thought you had a . . ." She tried to recall the color and make of the car Forrest had used to drive the two of them to dinner at Ocean Avenue Seafood on their only date. "A Buick, wasn't it? A blue one."

"Used to have an American car, all right, but it was a Dodge. You're right about the color, though." Forrest broke into a self-conscious grin. "One of the other writers at the studio took me aside, told me I was driving the wrong wheels for an up-and-coming screenwriter. Clued me in that my Dodge gave me the completely wrong image."

"You're kidding."

Now it was Forrest's turn to look embarrassed. "What can I tell you?" He shrugged his muscular shoulders. "Gotta have the right kind of status symbols or my work just doesn't cut it, I guess."

Jennifer opened Amy's car door and stood aside so that the little girl could get out. She put an arm around her daughter's shoulders and gave her a quick squeeze. "You're in a crazy business, Forrest, in case you hadn't already figured that out," Jennifer said. "So you bought a new car."

"Yeah, a while back. Right after that night you and I went to dinner, in fact. Traded in my old wheels and went totally Hollywood." He rapped his knuckles loudly against the BMW's roof. "It's not new, I'm afraid—in fact, this one's a year older than my Dodge—but there's no way my budget would cover a brand-new car. Apparently this baby's one of the prescribed brands, though. At least the guards at the studio don't smirk anymore when I drive up to the gatehouse."

Jennifer laughed outwardly, but inside she felt a seed of suspicion she'd been ignoring for the past several days beginning to take root. Mistaking Forrest for the man who'd been pursuing her and Amy was now forcing her to recognize that she really knew nothing about this man she felt so attracted to, nothing except what he'd told her. Forrest was, after all, a tall, dark-haired man who lived at the Edgewater, a man who'd gone out of his way to strike up an acquaintance with her and her daughter. He'd brought that discarded doll into her apartment, too. Sure, he claimed he'd found it by the mailboxes, but she had nothing but his word for that. And now he was driving a red car as well. Shuddering, Jennifer recognized that Forrest Hathaway could actually be the mysterious man from Amy's past. She didn't *want* to suspect him, but dared she risk Amy's safety by trusting him too much? Yet she knew the worst thing she could do right now, if Forrest was really the man stalking them, was to let him know she suspected him. "Studio guards, eh? Sounds like the acid test," she said, forcing her smile to broaden and gripping Amy's shoulder a little tighter.

"Apparently." Forrest cocked an eyebrow and leaned across his car's roof. "Say, how about doing it again? Dinner, I mean."

Jennifer felt her face grow warm and her stomach flip-flop. "I . . . I don't know. When?" Stall him, she told herself, stall him until you know for sure.

"Tomorrow night, maybe. Or Saturday, if that's better for you."

"It'll depend on whether I can line up Maria to sit for

Amy, Forrest. Tomorrow's too soon. Why don't I call you after I reach her?"

"I could go to Patty's tomorrow," Amy suggested, looking up at her mother eagerly. "I could go to Patty's after school and maybe stay overnight, play with their puppy."

"No way, kiddo. Besides, it's Patty's turn to stay overnight with you." Jennifer ignored the theatrical frown on her daughter's freckled face. Obviously, Amy had no suspicions about Forrest. Still, the man at the school fence had worn a hat and sunglasses and he'd spoken to Amy in a whisper. Jennifer herself might not have recognized Forrest under those circumstances. How could she expect a seven-year-old to be more perceptive? "I'll let you know, Forrest," she repeated. Forrest grinned, his green eyes twinkling, and Jennifer felt herself waver. He looked so genuine, so sincere, and she was lonely. Still . . .

"Talk to you later, then," he told her. He got back into his car and drove off in search of a vacant parking spot.

When Jennifer reached the elevator, she looked back into the garage to see if Forrest was approaching, feeling a strange mixture of attraction and apprehension. But he was still driving up and down the aisles in his little red car, searching for an empty parking space.

Relieved, she herded Amy into the elevator and pushed the button for the third floor.

Chapter

28

"Sweet dreams, hon," Jennifer said as she kissed Amy's forehead and switched off the overhead light in her bedroom. She had just finished reading her daughter the final chapter of *The Secret Garden.*

"'Night, Mom." Amy was snuggled warmly under her bedcovers, hugging Raggedy Ann close. "Leave my door open a little bit, okay?" The recent recurrence of her nightmares had left the little girl feeling reluctant to be left alone in the dark.

"Just a crack," Jennifer agreed. "I'll hear you and come right away if you call me, sweetie. Don't worry."

She went back into the living room, and spent the next half hour at her desk, packing up more audition tapes and résumés. Increasingly nervous about her lack of employment prospects, Jennifer was now expanding her job search to include television stations in the midwestern states.

When she'd finished her correspondence and stacked her new bunch of padded mailers by the front door, Jennifer tried to read the Anne Tyler novel she'd checked out of the library yesterday, but her thoughts kept wandering off the page. In her mind, she alternated between an examination of her suspicions about Forrest Hathaway, which she prayed would turn out to be unfounded, and a replay of her frustrating encounter at the police station.

Until she knew for certain that he was unconnected to Amy's past, Jennifer reluctantly concluded, she would have to keep her distance from Forrest. She would tell him that Maria was ill and couldn't babysit, postpone his suggested dinner date indefinitely. But was that enough? Maybe, she thought, she should ask the police to check the man out, see if he had some kind of police record. But what if she was wrong and Forrest somehow found out that she'd suspected him? Besides, Jennifer told herself, Detective Jenrud had made it quite clear that the police weren't particularly interested in her problems, at least not before the mysterious dark-haired man—whether he was Forrest Hathaway or not—had harmed, kidnapped, or possibly even killed one of her small family. Feeling helpless and frightened, she realized she was completely on her own.

The printed words on the page began to swim before Jennifer's eyes. She put her book down and went into the kitchen to fix herself a cup of peppermint tea. Maybe it would help her relax and get to sleep, she thought. As the tea steeped and the pungent odor of mint filled the air, Jennifer took the little gold picture case out of her purse and sat down at the kitchen table to look at it one more time. Maybe there was some clue here she'd been overlooking.

The case itself seemed unexceptional. The gold color had rubbed off of one of its corners, revealing a grayish metal underneath. At best, the case was gold-plated, Jennifer realized. Yet it was certainly better than dime-store quality, and someone had gone to the trouble and expense of having it engraved.

"Kitty," Jennifer read aloud. Was Kitty the name Amy's birth mother had given her? Or maybe Kitty was a shortened version of Katherine or Kathleen. She had an eerie feeling in the pit of her stomach as she thought about how shrouded in mystery her daughter's origins were, and would probably always remain. Yet those unknown origins now seemed to present a very real threat to Jennifer's family, a threat against which she felt completely defenseless.

Amy's natural mother was dead, that much she knew. But what about the child's other relatives? Had her natural mother been married? And, whether she had been or not, what had become of Amy's father? Could he possibly be Forrest Hathaway?

Jennifer had read about cases where a natural mother had given up her child for adoption, only to have a man claiming to be the natural father later try to wrench custody away from the adoptive parents. There were laws nowadays requiring that both natural parents sign off before a child was legally adoptable, but sometimes the system didn't work right. Thinking about something like that happening to her gave Jennifer nightmares.

Still, whatever the circumstances surrounding Amy's birth, nobody could hope to lay claim on her after five long years, could they? Besides, Jennifer told herself, if anything like that were happening now, the adoption agency would certainly be the father's first point of contact. And his approach would undoubtedly be through an attorney, not through a schoolyard fence.

Her sinuses soothed by the relaxing fumes of the peppermint tea, Jennifer removed the teabag from her cup and discarded it, then took a long sip of the steaming liquid. Somehow, peppermint tea always smelled better than it tasted, she thought. Still, she needed something to help her relax and collect her thoughts, and the ritual of making tea always seemed to help somehow.

She put down her cup and picked up the gold case again. The baby pictured inside looked more pensive than happy, Jennifer thought. She wondered what this child's life had been like. Had it been a happy life until the mother's early death? And just how had the mother died? Probably, Jennifer thought, in a car accident or from some tragic incurable illness. Certainly she had to have been a young woman still, with many years of a normal lifetime remaining. Whatever the cause of death, this baby had been wrenched from her mother's arms at a terribly young and impressionable age. Sometimes the scars still showed.

As she gazed into the eyes of the baby who had grown into the seven-year-old now sleeping down the hall, Jennifer used her fingernail to pick at the metal rim holding the photograph in place. It was stuck tight, seemingly welded into place, probably by the metal's corrosion over the years. There had to be some way to remove it, though, Jennifer figured; how else could the picture have been inserted into this case in the first place? Her fingernail wasn't strong enough to do the job. When its tip began to splinter and peel, she gave up and went to get a paring knife out of the kitchen drawer.

The tip of the paring knife's blade bent precariously, threatening to break off, when Jennifer wedged it hard into the same corner that had resisted her fingernail's efforts. She withdrew the blade and set to work on another portion of the framing. Finally she was able to slide the point of the knife under one of the top corners. She twisted the blade while, at the same time, prying upward sharply. Suddenly the entire frame broke loose. It flew toward her face, startling her, then arced and nosedived toward the table, where it landed with a sharp ping.

She would never get this case put back together again, Jennifer realized, as she examined the two broken prongs that had held the frame in place. But then, why should she need to? The police had shown no particular interest in it; they could hardly blame her now for destroying evidence.

She slid her damaged fingernail underneath the small

photograph and lifted it gently. The picture curled slightly as Jennifer slowly peeled it out of the case that had held it for years. Her breath caught as she held the small photograph in her hands and turned it over. There it was, just as she'd hardly dared hope—on the back of the photo was the faded blue impression of a rubber stamp. She held it up, closer to the hanging light above the table, and read the words, "Babcock Photography, San Luis Obispo, CA." Underneath the photo studio's name was a long number, "132-847-388."

Finally, Jennifer thought, a clue that might actually help her solve the mystery of Amy's origins. She knew San Luis Obispo was a small city near the central California coast. She'd been there once or twice, driving through on her way between Los Angeles and San Francisco. If Babcock Photography still existed, and if it still kept its old records, she knew she might be able to find out who had brought Amy there to be photographed all those years ago.

Her hands trembling, Jennifer reached for the telephone book. She checked the area code for San Luis Obispo, then dialed the long-distance information operator for that section of the state. In less than a minute, a computerized voice gave her the telephone number she was seeking.

Jennifer punched the numbers into the telephone. After four rings, a recorded message came on. "You have reached the studios of Babcock Photography," a deep male voice told her. "Sorry, we can't take your call right now. Our office hours are nine A.M. to six P.M., Mondays through Saturdays. Evenings by special appointment. We're located on Monterey Street, two blocks south of the Apple Farm Motel and Restaurant. If you wish to leave a message, please wait for the beep and we will return your call as soon as possible. Thank you for calling Babcock Photography."

When the beep sounded, Jennifer hung up. Her message

was far too important to be left on an answering machine. Feeling a sense of hope for the first time in days, she slipped the little photo into her wallet and tossed the disassembled gold metal case into a drawer.

It would take her about three hours to drive to San Luis Obispo from Santa Monica, she knew. She could get there and back in one day easily enough, but she couldn't count on being able to make the round trip during Amy's school hours. Dared she ask Lauren Avery to let Amy come home from school with Patty tomorrow or Friday? Jennifer was hesitant to ask for another favor after having begged Lauren to keep Amy while she went on her job interview trip to Seattle. Besides, with the dark-haired man possibly lurking around the school grounds, Jennifer felt better picking Amy up herself each afternoon.

No, she decided as she poured the remains of her tea down the drain of the kitchen sink, she would wait until Saturday, then take Amy with her to San Luis Obispo. They could make the trip into a fun family outing, maybe stop for a while on the beach on the way back home. If they left Santa Monica early enough, they could be in the university town well before noon.

Chapter

29

"Ouch, that hurt!" six-year-old Ginnie Morton complained, scraping her chair across the floor to avoid her brother's reach. "Mom, Stevie's poking me again."

"Stevie, stop poking your sister. I mean it—right now! You should be ashamed of yourself."

Hearing his mother's sharp words, Stevie Morton pulled back the finger he'd been using on his younger sister's rib cage, then quickly stuck out his tongue.

"Mom, now he's making faces at me," Ginnie whined. "Make him stop."

Jean finished slicing the meat loaf she had prepared for her brood's supper and transferred it from the cutting board to a platter. Her wrist still ached, but the despised cast was gone. She carried the platter over to the big round kitchen table, where all five of her children were seated, engaged in their usual dinnertime ritual of teasing and squabbling. The Morton children had become increasingly unruly since their father had left Salem. Now, as they grew older, Jean could feel the little authority she still maintained over them eroding a little more each day.

"Stop it and eat, all of you," she barked. Only the

youngest two, six-year-old Ginnie and five-year-old Tommy seemed to pay any attention to her. Ginnie grabbed the platter and helped herself to a thin slice of the grayish hamburger concoction.

"Meat loaf *again?*" Seven-year-old Stevie pushed away the platter Ginnie offered him, gripped his throat, and feigned vomiting into his plate. His theatrics were accompanied by loud urping noises.

"Cut it out, Stevie," said the oldest Morton child, nine-year-old Lynn. "You're a disgusting little creep."

"I *hate* meat loaf," Stevie complained.

"Then you just can go hungry," Jean told her middle child, fed up with hearing her children's complaints. She tried hard to stretch her inadequate food budget to feed all five of them healthy meals, but it was impossible to do that and also serve them only the foods they liked. "Honest to God, I'm so sick of hearing you kids griping all the time I could scream." She carried a large bowl of mashed potatoes to the table and set it down in the middle with a loud thump. "Complaints, complaints, complaints. That's all I hear around here."

"*I'm* not complaining," Lynn said, a superior smirk on her face. Naturally a bossy child, the nine-year-old frequently tried to usurp her mother's position as the Morton family's head. She speared a slice of meat loaf with her fork and transferred it to her plate. "I think Stevie should go to his room without supper, see how he likes that. Maybe he'll starve to death—*if* we're lucky."

"Shut up, bitch."

"Steven Morton!" Jean grabbed her son's arm and spun him around in his chair until he sat facing her. "Don't you dare use that kind of language around here! Apologize to your sister, right now."

Stevie yanked his arm out of his mother's grasp, his blue eyes clouding with anger. "No way. Lynn's always bossing me around. Make *her* apologize."

"Mom, these potatoes are cold." Ginny spit a mouthful of her mashed potatoes back onto her plate.

"Stop it, all of you," Jean said, clapping her hands over her ears. She had an overwhelming urge to walk out the front door and keep going. Either that or to climb back into her bed and pull the covers over her head. Anything to shut out this constant cacophony. The telephone rang. "Just shut up and eat!" she yelled over her shoulder as she hurried into the living room to answer it. If she tried to hold a phone conversation on the kitchen extension, she knew she would never be able to hear over the children's noise. Relieved at having an excuse to leave the kitchen, she slammed the door behind her, picked up the receiver, and said, "Hello."

"Don't send me any more of your damn packages, Jean."

Startled, Jean had to think for a moment before she realized that it was her brother on the line. "Clay, what . . . What are you talking about?"

"Just don't send me any more fucking packages, you fool. That goddamned box you mailed me sat in the lobby of my condo for who the hell knows how long. Shit, I can't even get away for a few days without you calling everybody's attention to my being gone."

Jean's grip tightened on the receiver as her mind raced in circles, trying to understand what Clay was talking about. Packages, packages, what the— Finally the memory clicked into one of her overloaded circuits and she recalled boxing up Clay's brown pullover, the one he'd left at her house, and mailing it to the Studio City address he'd given her. But that was two or three weeks ago. "I just thought you'd want your sweater back, Clay." Her voice sounded small and frightened, even to her own ears.

"I don't give a shit about any old sweater," Clay shouted at her. "Damn the sweater. I can buy a dozen new sweaters anytime I want to. Just use your head for once, and quit trying to blow my goddamned cover!"

"Okay, okay, I was only trying to do you a favor. It's your money. I guess you're entitled to waste it any way you want to." And it was his money, Jean thought, bitterly, all of it. Their father had left the bulk of his estate—well into seven figures—to Clay, his only son. The way old Henry Fowler had figured it, his daughter Jean had a husband to provide for her, the way women were supposed to; she didn't need her father's money. A measly ten-thousand-dollar bequest was all he'd left her. It had been spent long ago. Now her husband was living in another state and she was stuck with five kids to raise all by herself.

"I don't want any more of your favors," Clay said.

"Okay, okay, whatever." What was it about her, Jean wondered, that invited this kind of ingratitude, this kind of abuse, from everyone in her family? "What did you do, take a vacation somewhere?" she asked wistfully, wishing she had that luxury. What she wouldn't give for a real vacation—to anywhere, she didn't care where, as long as she could go all by herself, without the kids.

"Vacation!" A sarcastic chuckle came over the phone line. "Shit, woman, I told you I had a job to do and I'm doing it. I'm still working on cleaning up the mess you left on the last fucking favor you did me."

"Clay," Jean said, a queasy feeling forming in the pit of her stomach. "I hope you're not getting yourself in more trouble. You know you—"

"She's my kid, Jean. If you'd kept her like you were s'posed to, I wouldn't have to be here now, trying to figure a way to get her back."

"I told you I'm sorry, Clay. If it wasn't for Bruce . . . Well, I feel really bad about it, you know I do, but there's nothing I can do to fix things now. Besides, you know what that judge told you. Trying to track Kitty down after all this time's only going to get you in more trouble. The child's gone, she's got a good life. You can get used to it, if you just try."

"Used to it! You don't get used to somebody stealing your kid, you stupid idiot. Kitty's *mine*, Jean, and don't you forget it. Nobody—I don't care if he's a fucking judge or fucking Bruce Morton or fucking God himself—is going to keep my kid away from me."

Her brother's venomous outburst reminded Jean of their childhood years on the ranch in California. Clay had always been possessive of his property and he'd always had trouble realizing that people weren't just objects he could own. Even as a boy, Clay had been obsessed with controlling everyone and everything around him, and he never seemed to care what he had to do to accomplish that goal. Even the frequent beatings their father had given him had never deterred Clay. Punishment meant nothing to him; it just made him that much meaner.

Jean had never forgotten the time her brother hanged her cat in the barn, but today she could no longer remember why he'd done such a horrible thing. It didn't have to be anything all that important to set Clay off, to jump start his nasty streak. Jean was ten years old the year her brother had killed her cat; Clay was twelve. She'd been completely terrified of him ever since.

Her brother had always been filled with a terrible kind of rage, Jean realized. He'd never known where to draw the line, when to quit, no matter what the result. He'd crossed well over that line in trying to control Melissa, and look where that had ended. Now he wanted to do the same thing with Kitty. . . . Jean shuddered. "Clay," she begged. "Give up this crazy search, *please*, for Kitty's sake if not for your own. Don't ruin her life like—"

"It's not crazy, don't you dare call me crazy! I'm entitled to have my own kid and I'm going to get her back, whatever it takes, you stupid bitch."

"I don't have to let you call me names, Clay." Jean's chin was beginning to quiver now, and she felt close to tears. "I can just hang up this phone if I want to." But she knew she didn't have enough courage to do that. If she hung up on her brother, there would be consequences, consequences she didn't want to face. Instead she waited with the receiver against her ear, trembling and listening to the crackle of dead air on the phone line. In the background, she could hear the muffled arguments of her own children, filtered through the closed kitchen door.

Finally Clay broke the impasse. "I already found her," he said, sounding now like a small boy who'd put something over on his teacher. "I found my Kitty."

Jean wasn't sure whether to believe him or not. Clay was a very accomplished liar. She remained silent.

"What's the matter?" Clay asked, taunting her. "Don't believe me?"

"It's just—"

"You're the one handed me the lead, sis. Only smart thing you did in this whole fucking mess."

"What—" But Jean could guess. "The clipping," she said.

"Hell, yes, the clipping."

Jean felt a pang of guilt as she remembered Clay's finding the story she'd cut out of the *Oregonian* about five years ago—a feature about single professional women who'd adopted children. There was Kitty's photo, in full color; the little girl was sitting on then-Portland TV anchorwoman Jennifer Bennett's lap, wearing her familiar troubled expression. Of course, the toddler's name was no longer Kitty Fowler; the photo caption identified her as Amy Bennett. But Jean had recognized her instantly. She'd torn the story from the newspaper and hidden it away with the few things Kitty had left behind here in Salem. In the months afterward, she'd made a habit of tuning in to Jennifer Bennett's newscasts. Every night, as she watched the television set, she tried to reassure herself that this woman was a good mother for the child she'd been forced to give away. In time, her guilt began to fade . . . until Clay was released from prison and he soon afterward showed up at her house, expecting to claim his daughter.

"I shouldn't have kept it," Jean said, mainly to herself. Yet she knew she might well be alive today only because she *had* saved that clipping. Clay's finding that box of Kitty's things—including the yellowed piece of newspaper—had halted his angry rampage on that terrifying day when he broke her wrist. His rage over not finding Kitty here in Salem suddenly dissipated, he took the box Jean had stored in her garage, and raced out of her house. When she was sure her brother was gone for good, she called a taxi-cab and went to her doctor's office, where she made up a story about falling down the stairs to explain her injuries.

In the weeks since then, she'd prayed that Clay wouldn't be able to find either Jennifer Bennett or her adopted daughter. After all, the woman had left her job with the Portland television station years ago. She had to be miles and miles away from here by now.

"Kitty's gotten real tall."

Jean could hear the note of pride in her brother's voice, as though he were personally responsible for his daughter's physical growth. "She'd be older now, over seven," she said.

"She's a strong, healthy kid. Swims like a real tadpole, too."

Jean stiffened. Either Clay was embellishing his lie to torment her, or he really *had* found Kitty. She couldn't stop herself from becoming a participant in his little game. "Swim? How do you know Kitty can swim?"

"I'm watching her right now, that's how. There she goes again, a nice, clean swan dive off the side of the pool. A real little expert; she's my kid, all right. Gets halfway across the pool before she even has to surface. Just like me at that age. Remember that old pond we used to swim in back on the ranch, Jeannie?"

"Yeah, I remember." Jean felt completely exhausted. She was relieved that her brother's anger seemed to be gone now, but worried that he might be telling the truth about Kitty. If he really was watching the child while he talked on the phone, he was much too close to the little girl. Jean didn't want to think about what he might do next. Poor Kitty didn't deserve a father like Clay Fowler. "I gotta go," she said. "It's dinnertime. I gotta feed my kids."

"Yeah, okay, whatever. Just remember what I told you—no more packages. I'm probably gonna have to disappear for a while, so don't try calling me, either."

Apprehension crawling down her spine, Jean murmured a good-bye and hung up the phone. She stood in place for a long moment before taking a deep breath, squaring her shoulders, and heading back into the war zone that was her own kitchen.

Chapter

30

Jennifer loaded her briefcase and an old beach blanket into the back of the station wagon, then climbed into the driver's seat. It was a little before nine o'clock on Saturday morning. "All buckled up, Amy?"

"Uh-huh. How far to where we're going, Mom?"

"About two hundred miles. Take us three hours or so, like I told you," Jennifer said. "It'll be nice, just you and me together all day." She started the car and backed out of her parking space in the Edgewater's garage. "We can sing songs and see who can count the most cars."

Amy wrinkled up her face, not yet completely convinced that this morning's outing was going to be as much fun as her mother was predicting. "But how come we have to go to this 'Bispo place, anyway?"

"It's San Luis *Obispo.*"

"San Luis *Obispo.* How come?"

"Because I've got some business to do there, hon. It probably won't take us too long, but it's really, really important. You can help me a lot by being an extra good girl today."

"Is it about a job, Mom? Is somebody in San Luis

Obispo gonna give you a new job?" Amy's forehead was
furrowed with what looked like worry.

Sighing, Jennifer drove out of the garage past Forrest
Hathaway's red BMW, which was parked near the doorway, then merged slowly with the light traffic heading
northbound on Centinela Avenue. She wished she could
tell Amy that this trip was about a job. With a sharp pang
of guilt, she realized anew that her daughter was becoming
far too aware of their increasing money troubles. Just yesterday, she'd found the child eavesdropping on a phone
conversation she'd been having with her accountant. Then
she'd spent the next half hour reassuring Amy that she
hadn't really meant it when she'd told the accountant they
would "end up in the poorhouse" if they bombed out on
the upcoming income tax audit. Now it looked as if
Jennifer hadn't done such a great job of reassuring her
worrywart daughter after all. "This isn't about a job,
Amy," she told her. "It's about this mystery I'm trying to
solve. And it's kind of about you, too."

"Me?" Amy's blue eyes opened wider and her fingers
began to play with the loose end of her seat belt.

Jennifer drove up the ramp and onto the Santa Monica
Freeway westbound. "It's about that picture in the little
gold case the man gave you, anyway. The photographer
who took that picture has a studio up in San Luis Obispo. I
want him to look at the picture again."

"How come?" Amy's jerked her legs out straight, so her
sneakered feet rubbed against the underside of the dashboard.

Jennifer wondered if she was making a mistake in giving Amy this much detail. She didn't want to upset the
child any more than she already was, yet Amy was far
from stupid. She would surely figure out what was going
on as soon as Jennifer took the photo from her wallet and
showed it to the photographer. "I want to see if he can tell

me who Kitty is," she explained. "If I can find that out, maybe I can figure out who that man who gave you the picture really is, too."

Amy leaned back in her seat and bent her knees again. She wedged her toes against the front of the glove compartment. "I don't like that guy," she said, frowning.

"Me, either."

"We're not gonna have to try and find him, are we?"

"No, hon. But if I can figure out who he is, then I think I can make him stay away from us." Jennifer prayed she was right.

The car's interior quickly darkened as they entered the tunnel at the end of the Santa Monica Freeway, then brightened again as they emerged on northbound Highway 1, skirting Santa Monica Beach. "Can we go to the beach after we're done with the picture stuff?" Amy asked, leaning forward against her shoulder harness and peering longingly out the car window at the nearly deserted stretch of pale sand to the west.

"If we have time and it's not too cold, maybe we'll go to a brand-new beach," Jennifer promised, relieved that Amy's agile mind had wandered onto a new topic. "Want to count cars? First one to a hundred wins."

"Okay." Amy grinned, her usual competitive self.

"What color do you want?"

"Red," she said, decisively. "You can have green."

"Okay," Jennifer agreed, guessing that red cars were far more common in Southern California than green ones. But winning the game was not her goal; what she wanted was simply to keep Amy happy and occupied during their ride north. "There's a green car already," she said, pointing out a dark green Saab in oncoming traffic.

"I already got two," Amy shouted triumphantly. "And there's three." She jabbed her finger excitedly in the direction of a Jaguar that was turning onto the highway from the Jonathan Club's beachside parking lot. "Four, and here comes five . . ."

Amy won the game easily, counting one hundred red cars before they'd passed all the way through the northern limits of the city of Ventura, about sixty miles north of Santa Monica. Jennifer had counted only fifty-three green ones, but she'd missed more than a few, her mind frequently wandering away from their little contest.

"What do I win, what do I win?" Amy asked, when she'd reached one hundred. She bounced in her seat, caught up in the heady excitement of victory.

Jennifer thought for a minute as she gazed out over the ocean, with its smattering of working oil wells to mar the otherwise breathtakingly beautiful scenery. "Tell you what, sweetie. I'll take you out to lunch at the Apple Farm when we get to San Luis Obispo, and you can have a real special apple dessert. How's that?"

"You mean like pie or something?"

"Yes. Or maybe an apple dumpling."

"What's an apple dumpling?"

"It's a whole peeled apple with the core taken out of it. Then it's wrapped up in a big piece of pie crust with sugar and cinnamon inside and baked. Tastes a lot like apple pie, but it's round like a ball and you can put cream on top of it if you like. Trust me, you'll love it."

"Okay," Amy agreed. "How about we sing now?"

"Sure."

"You can pick the first song."

"Okay. I pick . . . 'Once in Love with Amy.'" Jennifer knew her daughter had loved the ancient Ray Bolger theme song ever since she'd taught it to her a few years ago. It made Amy feel special to know there was a song about a girl who had the same name she did.

"Hey, great, Mom." Amy beamed with pleasure.

As they drove north, they sang three choruses of

"Amy," followed by half a dozen songs Amy had learned in school. By the time they'd finished a seemingly endless duet of "Ninety-nine Bottles of Coke on the Wall," they were well past Buellton, with its gaudy billboards advertising Pea Soup Andersen's tourist-oriented restaurant.

As she drove and sang along, Jennifer mused about how silly the two of them would look right now to any stranger watching them . . . and about how much she would miss this kind of corny togetherness with her daughter if she ever lost it. Her eyes suddenly began to tear up and she had to clear her throat before she could continue singing.

But Amy never noticed.

Chapter

31

The Babcock Photography studio was located on the bottom floor of a narrow white frame building on an old San Luis Obispo street just east of Highway 101. Its paint was peeling and its general look was one of aged shabbiness. Jennifer pushed open the front door and entered the small pine-floored reception room, with Amy following close behind her. As the door swung shut behind them, a buzzer sounded somewhere in the back of the dusty little shop, far beyond the curtained doorway that stood behind a long, vacant counter with a cash register at one end.

A short, burly man in his late forties emerged through the bright blue curtain. He wore a white dress shirt with the sleeves rolled up to his elbows and a pair of faded jeans. "Morning," he said, nodding briefly in the direction of his visitors. He smelled faintly of a combination of photo-developing chemicals and cheap aftershave lotion.

"Good morning," Jennifer replied. "Are you Mr. Babcock?"

"I'm Owen Babcock, Junior. They call me Obie. You looking for my dad?"

"I—I'm not sure." Jennifer approached the worn wooden

counter. Out of the corner of her eye, she watched as Amy wandered off and began to tour the reception room, checking out the many framed photo portraits of both individuals and groups that were mounted on the walls.

"Fact is, my dad passed on, end of last summer." The man pulled on one of his long, brown sideburns; his greasy hairstyle was early Elvis Presley. "Me and my brother took over for him," he said, with no enthusiasm. Babcock seemed to be one of those men for whom life had peaked in the late 1950s and had been downhill ever since. The same appeared to be true of his family's photo studio.

"Sorry to hear about your father," she told him. "Guess that means I'm looking for you." Feeling a little nervous now that she'd reached her destination, she smiled at Obie Babcock and set her camel leather handbag down on the counter. "I'm hoping you can give me some information about a photo that was taken here in your studio a few years ago, Mr. Babcock." She opened her purse.

"See what I can do." Babcock hooked his thumbs into the pockets of his jeans and waited while his visitor pulled out a wallet and removed a small photograph from one of its compartments. His ample belly strained against the buttons of the white shirt.

"This is it," Jennifer said, laying the photo flat on the counter. She flipped it over, face down. "See here? It's got your studio's name and a number stamped on the back."

Babcock removed his right hand from his pocket and ran his index finger lightly over the stamped name and number on the back of the photograph, as if to check its authenticity by touch. "Sure does."

"I'm hoping you can look in your records and tell me who ordered this. Maybe dig up an address for him as well."

"Wait a minute, lady. You tellin' me you don't know who this kid here is?" Babcock flipped the photo over again and stared at the baby's sober face.

Jennifer sneaked a glance at Amy. She seemed to be fascinated by a series of mounted photos of children with their pets. They ranged from the predictable kittens and sweet-faced puppies to a pair of baby red foxes posed with three adolescent sisters and a colorful parrot perched on a young boy's shoulder. Jennifer wondered briefly whether these photos were the work of the late Mr. Babcock or one of his sons. "I'm quite sure I know who this is," she told the photographer. "But I need to know who ordered the photo, who paid for it. Please, it's really very important."

Babcock shook his head. "I dunno, lady. First of all, this here's from before we computerized our records. I'd have to go through my dad's old files—we got boxes and boxes of 'em out in the back room. Second, if you ain't the one ordered this, how's it any of your business who did?"

Jennifer felt her shoulders and neck muscles turning to marble as she began to realize how reluctant Babcock was to help her. "Someone's been stalking my daughter," she began in a quiet voice, hoping that Amy wasn't paying attention. "He gave her this picture. So if I can just find out where the picture came from in the first place, I might be able to—" Babcock's face was completely deadpan, a study in boredom. Either he didn't believe what she was telling him, Jennifer realized, or he just plain didn't give a damn. She decided to try another tactic. Opening her wallet, she added, "I'm willing to pay for your time, of course."

Finally, a spark of interest flared in Babcock's dark eyes. "Ain't got too much of that. Not today, anyhow." He cocked his head toward the large wall clock mounted above the blue curtain. It was a few minutes before noon. "We got a wedding to shoot tonight. Got to be over at the church by two, two-thirty at the latest, give me time to get all the equipment set up. My brother Hermie—he's the artsy one in the family, takes after our dad—Hermie throws a fit if his cameras and lights ain't set up on time."

"Please, Mr. Babcock. I've come all the way up here from Los Angeles, and this is really, really important to me. It honestly could be a matter of life and death." Jennifer felt a little melodramatic, but she was willing to use whatever it took to get Babcock to help her. She turned and saw Amy approaching the counter, either bored by now with the framed photographs or attracted by her mother's increasingly frantic tone of voice and body language. Jennifer withdrew a twenty dollar bill from her wallet and laid it down on the counter, next to the baby photo. Babcock didn't reach for it. She withdrew a second twenty and laid it on top of the first. Now the photographer began to look a little more interested, but he still didn't pick up the money.

"Any idea when this thing was shot?" he asked, his thumbs hooked back into his jeans pockets.

"Had to be at least five and a half years ago, maybe as much as six. But no longer than six years."

"Looks like my dad's work, all right," he said. "Recognize that background effect he used to use. Looks kinda like a foggy day at the beach with the sun just startin' to break through around the edges." Babcock picked up the two twenties. His eyes darted briefly toward the cash register at the far end of the counter, then back to the money. He folded the two bills in half, then in quarters, and slipped them into his shirt pocket. "This buys you one hour of my time, lady, not a minute more."

"Tell you what," Jennifer said, quickly checking on her remaining cash supply. "I'm going to take my daughter up the street to Apple Farm. We'll have some lunch and check back with you afterward. If you've got the information I need ready by then, I'll pay you another forty bucks. Deal?" Perhaps, she hoped, the promise of an additional payment would prompt Babcock to actually go into the shop's back room and check those file boxes. As things stood now, she didn't trust this strange man to do anything at all for her, once he was out of her sight.

"Gotta be cash," Babcock told her, "and no receipts."

Jennifer nodded her agreement. "I need a name and an address," she said. Paying Obie Babcock cash would mean she'd have to put the lunch and gas for the station wagon on her credit cards; she had only a few dollars more than forty left in her wallet. "Be back in an hour or so." She took Amy's elbow and piloted her out the door. As they were leaving, she saw Babcock pick up the photo and disappear with it behind the bright blue curtain.

"Mom, how come you gave that man all that money?" Amy asked when they'd reached the street. Her blue eyes were wide.

"Sometimes things cost more than you expect," Jennifer said vaguely, hoping her costly investment would pay off. "Come on, sweetheart, let's go find you that apple dumpling. We can leave the car here and walk." The Apple Farm was only a few hundred feet up the street. "Race you."

Amy turned and streaked down the sidewalk, her short legs pumping hard and her auburn curls bouncing as she ran. Jennifer had all she could do to keep up with her.

"*May I have your key, please?*" the bank's assistant vice president asked Clay Fowler, holding out her open hand. Her fingernails, curling upward, were long and tapered and painted with a pearlized shade of fuchsia polish. Into her waiting palm Clay dropped a small silver key attached to a red plastic disk with his safety deposit box number imprinted on it.

The young woman inserted the bank's master key into one slot and Clay's into a second, then turned both of them simultaneously clockwise. There was a sharp click and the little door in the wall sprang open on its hinges, revealing a long gray metal box inside. While Clay watched and waited, the bank officer slid the box out of the wall cavity and carried it over to the table.

"Just press that buzzer on the wall over there when you're finished in here, Mr. Fowler," she told him, flashing her plastic, bank-officer smile. "I'll be right outside the door."

Clay nodded and waited for the bank employee to leave him alone in the privacy cubicle. She had a nice, trim little ass, he thought, as he watched her bounce toward the door. Nice pair of tits, too, although she was definitely shorter than he liked his women. Those three-inch heels she was wearing didn't fool anybody. This broad was no taller than five feet one, five two, tops. He preferred the ones with long legs, always had; it was the tall, slender fashion-model type for Clay Fowler.

As he heard the cubicle's door snap shut, locking him in, Clay felt instantly claustrophobic, the predictable result of nearly six years spent behind bars. He stood perfectly still, his grip on his black leather briefcase growing damp. He took a few deep breaths and willed his pulse rate to slow down. In less than two minutes, his panic had dissipated and his feeling of control slowly began to return.

Clay laid his briefcase flat on the table next to the safety deposit box, unlocked it, and lifted the cover open. Inside was this morning's withdrawal from his account at Farmers State Bank—a stack of ninety hundred-dollar bills, totaling a neat nine thousand bucks. Adding it to the stash already inside the metal box, he would have a total of fifty-five thousand dollars in ready cash. Plenty to cover his immediate needs, he decided.

Now Clay had only one more bank account left to liquidate, the one he'd opened last month at First California Savings. That one contained almost seven thousand dollars. He planned to close it out this afternoon.

There were other things in Clay's safety deposit box as well, things that were far more valuable than the cash. With his late father's entire fortune now in his own name, fifty-five grand was pocket change to Clay.

He pushed the stack of bills to the left side of the metal box and took another look at his other treasures, just to reassure himself that they were still there, that they remained safe where he'd left them only days ago.

There were half a dozen bearer bonds here, each one of them exchangeable for more than half a million dollars anywhere in the world, as well as the two United States passports he'd bought on the black market earlier this week. The best thing about the passports was that they were the genuine article, not those cheap forgeries the Customs people were always on the lookout for. Clay's contact had assured him that these passports had been stolen a mere three weeks ago from the home of a Chicago stockbroker who had a daughter right around Kitty's age. They'd cost him a cool fifteen hundred bucks apiece, but they were absolutely perfect.

Clay picked up his own official blue folder and held it in his hands. Right now, it was more valuable than diamonds to him. He opened the cover and saw his own face staring back at him, complete with the official U.S. seal across his forehead. His photo had been switched for the stockbroker's, but that was the only altered portion of the passport, and it had been done seamlessly. Everything else in the document matched the official information in the government's files.

When he boarded that plane bound for South America, Clay Fowler would become Preston Charles Ames III. He smiled to himself; God, but he loved the pretentiousness of that moniker! Who would ever suspect a guy with Roman numerals following his name of being an ex-con fleeing his parole? Especially when he had a little kid in tow.

The second passport now had his daughter's picture in it—a copy of that photographic proof Clay had stolen from Jennifer Bennett's outgoing mail at the Edgewater. Of course, the child would also be using a false name to get out of the country; until the two of them cleared foreign customs, she would be Claudia Huffington Ames, age eight.

Clay was more than satisfied with the intricate preparations he'd been making, and with himself. At least half of his pleasure in this quest to get his daughter back lay in knowing he was going to outsmart everybody who'd ever tried to screw him during the past few years. It was in showing those bastards who'd stolen six of the best years of his life who was boss now. This kind of thing took brains. And it took more than good planning—it took an abundance of sheer balls. Most men could never pull off a deal like this, but Clay Fowler was confident he was going to succeed. Nobody was going to stop him now.

He closed the passport covers and put the two official documents back into the safety deposit box. By this afternoon, he would have the last of his cash in place as well. And on Monday morning, he would sign the lease and pick up the keys for that office building he'd found in Santa Barbara—using yet another false name, of course. Clay was certain that the building's owner wouldn't question his paying the deposit and first month's rent in cash. How often did a landlord have a chance to lease an entire building these days, especially after years of recession in the Southern California commercial rental market? Most building owners hereabouts were more than ready to grab the money and run.

Clay had the phone line for his new business enterprise all lined up, too. The phone company had agreed to switch it on no later than Monday noon. Not that the phone line was likely to be needed, he thought. Still, he never liked to leave any loose ends flapping in the breeze, not when there was any chance whatsoever that he could trip over them. There was far too much at stake here to be sloppy.

Clay transferred the nine thousand in cash from the briefcase to the metal box, stacking it on top of the passports and bearer bonds. He snapped his briefcase shut and shifted it into a standing position, then closed the cover of the safety deposit box, pushing down hard to make sure it was securely fastened. He felt reluctant, as always, to leave this much of his wealth—his entire future—behind here, entrusting all of this to a mere bank. Yet he dared not carry it around with him, and he certainly couldn't leave anything so valuable lying around his apartment at the Edgewater or in his Studio City condo.

No, this way was best. He would come back here again for the last time early next week, once everything was completely set up, both here and in Santa Barbara. He would buy his plane tickets and clean out this box at the very last possible minute. That would minimize the risk of anything happening to his treasure chest before he and Kitty could board that airplane leaving San Francisco.

Clay rested his hands on the top of the safety deposit box for a moment, enjoying the sense of security and, most of all, the feeling of raw power that it gave him. Then he stood up and pressed the buzzer on the wall that would gain his release from this tiny, locked room.

When the door had opened and the bank officer was standing aside to let him out, Clay felt his usual rush of sheer relief. Once again, he was free. He strode out of the bank at a slightly quicker pace than usual.

Chapter

33

It was after one o'clock by the time Jennifer and Amy had fin-ished their lunches at Apple Farm. The popular place was crowded, mainly with tourists attracted by the many bill-boards along Highway 101 that advertised the Apple Farm Motel and Restaurant. Amy had eaten most of her gigantic hamburger and french fries, leaving almost no room in her small stomach for the special dessert she'd won by count-ing a hundred red cars on the highway.

"Don't try to eat any more now, sweetheart," Jennifer urged, fearing that Amy would have an upset stomach during the car trip back to Santa Monica if she tried to cram any more food into herself. "I'll buy you your apple dumpling to take home."

Amy rubbed her tummy with her open palm. "Okay, Mom, guess I'm pretty stuffed. But we better get two dumplings—one for me and one for you."

"You got a deal." Jennifer asked the waitress to bring them two apple dumplings "to go" and add them to her lunch check. When the dumplings arrived in a crisp white bakery bag, she handed the waitress her credit card to pay for them and their lunches. Opening the bag, she peeked inside. The tantilizingly sweet odors of apple and cinnamon drifted upward. "These sure do look great, don't they Amy?" Jennifer held out the open bag so that Amy could look inside.

"Real, real yummy," the child agreed, sniffing the bag's contents and running her tongue across her lips. "I wish I could just eat 'em all up right now."

"They'll taste even better later, when you're hungry again. Wait and see."

Amy reached for the bag. "I wanna carry 'em, Mom." Jennifer handed it to her, glad to be rid of something else that had to be carried.

On the way out of the white frame building, they passed through the Apple Farm's old-fashioned gift shop and stopped briefly to survey the goods on sale there. They included a variety of apple-inspired products—wooden apples for the teacher, brass bells shaped like apples, apple-shaped candles, bright red aprons decorated with pictures of apples, apple cookbooks, small jars of golden apple jelly—as well as more typical gift shop merchandise. "Come on, now, Amy," Jennifer said, glancing at her watch. "We better get back to the photo studio and see if Mr. Babcock has found that information I need."

"Hey, Mom, can I have one of those T-shirts?" Amy pointed upward at an adult-sized garment suspended from the ceiling. It was decorated with a mammoth red apple that had a jagged bite taken out of it.

"I can't afford anything else today, hon. Besides, that shirt'd be way too big for you."

Amy shrugged her small shoulders and didn't argue with her mother. She was willing to settle for the special lunch and her bakery treat. Gripping her white bag tightly in her hand, she followed Jennifer to the front door and out through the crowded parking lot to the street.

The two walked along the sidewalk to the photo shop at

a noticeably slower pace than they had before they'd eaten lunch. Both felt a little sluggish now, after their unusually large midday meals. As Jennifer pushed open the front door of the Babcock Photography studio, the bell chimed in the back.

This time Obie Babcock emerged from behind the blue curtain far more quickly than he had that morning. There was a grin on his face as he waved a large white envelope in the air. "Found 'er," he announced with a note of pride in his voice.

Jennifer's pulse quickened and she flashed him a relieved smile. "Let's see," she said.

"Got that extra forty?"

"Uh, sure, okay." Jennifer delved into her purse and brought out her final two twenty-dollar bills. A quick accounting told her that she had only four ones and some change left. It would have to be enough to get them back home. She laid the larger bills on the counter. "Let's see what you've got there."

Babcock opened the flap and turned the envelope upside down. Four photographic proofs slid out, landing on the counter. The top one was the same pose that the man at school had given to Amy; the others were clearly its mates, taken on the same day. They showed baby Amy looking even less happy than she did in the photo from the gold case. In one, the toddler's big blue eyes were wet with tears and the corners of her mouth were turned decidedly downward. It was obvious that the tiny girl had not enjoyed having her picture taken, for whatever reason.

"These photos look like the right ones, all right, but who ordered them?" Jennifer asked, feeling a surge of impatience now that she was so close to having the information she'd come all this way to find.

"Keep your shirt on, lady," Babcock said. He reached inside the envelope and yanked on a flimsy yellow receipt that was stuck inside. It had blue carbon-paper writing on it. "It's a woman ordered these shots, not a man," he said. "Name of Melissa Fowler." He read an address on Mountain Avenue in San Luis Obispo off the receipt. "Something seems familiar about that name, but I just can't seem to place 'er."

Melissa Fowler, Jennifer thought. Who was she? Probably Amy's birth mother, or possibly her grandmother. Melissa Fowler. Melissa was a pretty name, one of Jennifer's all-time favorites. And Amy's birth name had been what? Not Amy Fowler—Jennifer was the one who had named her Amy. She'd probably been known as Kitty Fowler when that photo was taken, if the engraving on the little gold picture case meant anything. Or maybe Katherine Fowler, if Kitty was the Fowler family's nickname for Katherine. Hearing the name and address of the woman who'd ordered these pictures of her daughter so long ago gave Jennifer an eerie feeling in the pit of her stomach—part excitement and part raw fear, overlaid with her naturally intense sense of curiosity.

She stole a glance at Amy to see if the child was displaying any recognition of the Fowler name, but she was standing near the door, busily examining what was inside the white bakery bag. Her hand darted inside and emerged holding a wedge of golden pie crust. She quickly shoved the sugary treat into her mouth, licked her fingertips clean, and slid her hand back inside the bag. Normally, Jennifer would have admonished her daughter to stop picking at the dumplings, but now she felt relieved that Amy was occupied with something other than eavesdropping on the adults' conversation. "May I take these things with me?" she asked Babcock, laying her hand lightly across the receipt and the proofs.

Pulling on one of his sideburns, Babcock considered the request for a moment, then shrugged. "Can't see what harm it'd do now, after all these years." He picked up Jennifer's forty dollars and put it into the same pocket where he'd stashed the cash she'd paid him earlier.

"You have a phone book I can use?" she asked.

"Huh? Yeah, sure, I guess so." Babcock pulled a telephone directory from a shelf underneath the counter and dropped it with a thud in front of Jennifer. Dust mites flew upward and floated in the air above the counter. "Help yourself."

Jennifer quickly thumbed through the white pages in the front of the book. When she reached the *F*s, she efficiently ran her finger down the listings, but found nothing between the local Foursquare Church and Fox, Alan M. There were no Fowlers. That Melissa Fowler wasn't listed came as no surprise to Jennifer, really. If she was Amy's birth mother, she'd supposedly been dead for at least five years, so she would hardly be listed in the current telephone directory. Unless Melissa was the grandmother, or she was the mother but wasn't really dead and she had an unlisted phone number. And what about Melissa's husband, if she'd had one? Was he still in town, or was he now in Santa Monica, watching Amy's home and school?

An old black dial telephone next to the cash register caught Jennifer's eye. "May I use your phone for just a second?" she asked. Babcock was waiting impatiently behind the counter now, his arms folded on top of his ample belly. "It's only a local call," Jennifer added with a tentative smile.

The paunchy little man sighed, uncrossed his arms, and reluctantly slid the instrument along the counter toward Jennifer. "Don't take too long now, y'hear. I gotta close up this place and get my gear over to that wedding, or Hermie'll blow a gasket."

Jennifer nodded, then dialed the phone number written on the old yellow receipt. It rang four times before an answering machine picked up. "Hello," a chirpy woman's voice said. "You have reached the Andersons' residence. George and Trixie can't come to the phone right now, but we sure don't want to miss your call. Wait for the be—"

Jennifer hung up, abruptly cutting off the saccharine voice in midchirp. She wasn't sure whether she felt more relieved that a still-alive Melissa Fowler hadn't answered the phone, or confused about what to do next. "Thanks," she said, pushing the old black telephone back toward Babcock. Her mind spinning, Jennifer picked up the white envelope and slid the proofs and receipt back inside it.

She had to find out whether Melissa Fowler was really Amy's birth mother, she realized, and, if she was, how the woman had died. Perhaps if she had that information, it would lead her to the name of the man who'd been following her and Amy. "Where would I find the nearest public library?" she asked.

Jennifer listened carefully as Babcock gave her detailed directions. She thanked him and herded Amy out the door ahead of her.

As they reached the sidewalk, Jennifer heard the door being locked behind them. She spun around on her heel and peered through the shop window just in time to see the odd little man retreating through the blue curtain into the rear of the old studio.

Chapter

34

"Are we still gonna get to go to the beach? Huh, Mom, are we?"
Amy was bored. For the past hour, she'd been sitting at a
table in the library, leafing through the stack of books her
mother had found for her in the children's section. Now
she ventured over to where Jennifer sat hunched over in
front of the microfilm reader.

"What, hon?" Jennifer's vision was growing blurry from
trying to scan the microfilmed pages of the local newspaper's back issues. She plunked one of her last few quarters into the slot and waited for the whirring sound the
machine made as it copied the microfilmed newspaper
page she'd designated. "Oh, right, the beach." She looked
up at the big clock on the library wall. It was almost four
o'clock. "Gee, I don't think we're going to make it today,
honey. I said we'd go to the beach if we had time, remember? It's getting awfully late now."

"But I'm tired of this place, Mom. It's boring." Amy
twisted the toe of her right sneaker against the beige carpeting. A clump of hair fell across her eye.

"I know, sweetie, but I've still got a little bit more work
to do here. Please be a big girl for me. Just be patient a little

while longer, and then we'll go home. I'll take you to the beach in Santa Monica tomorrow if it's a nice day. This time I promise."

Amy started to pout, sticking out her lower lip, then thought better of it and settled for a loud, dramatic sigh. She reached for the pile of copied pages sitting next to the machine her mother was using. "What is all this stuff, anyway?"

Jennifer stiffened and took the pages out of Amy's hands. "It's just my work," she said vaguely. "Tell you what. You keep your eye on the clock up there. When it says four-thirty, I promise we'll go, whether I'm ready or not, okay?"

Amy's eyes rose to the clock. "That's when the big hand gets down to the bottom, right?" Her generation had been weaned on digital clocks. The library clock was a traditional style and she felt far less confident that she could read it correctly.

"Right. You can read your books that much longer, can't you?"

"Yeah, I guess so. But I have to go to the bathroom."

Jennifer looked around the room. There were only a few other people in the library now and she didn't want to leave her microfilm in the machine while she accompanied Amy to the restroom. "You remember where the women's room is, right, where we went before?" Amy nodded. "Okay, then you can go there by yourself, but come right back here when you're through."

"Okay." Amy skipped off in the direction of the restroom.

Jennifer returned to a task that she was finding to be increasingly depressing. In her hurry to collect all the articles about Melissa Fowler and her family in as little time as possible, she was simply copying each one, not taking the time to read it thoroughly. Jennifer would have time to read the old newspaper entries at home tonight, after Amy was asleep. Still, the headlines alone hinted at a terrible, sordid story. The articles Jennifer had copied ranged from a 1985 announcement of the wedding of Melissa O'Mara and Clayton Fowler to a series of far less happy stories: "Local Woman Victim of Domestic Violence," "Fowler Heir Held for Brutal Murder," "C. Fowler Pleads Guilty to Reduced Charges," "Fowler Sentenced in Wife's Killing," and the like.

So, Jennifer thought grimly as she plunked her last coin into the copier, little Amy's father had killed her mother. That much was clear from the bits and snatches she'd read off the microfilm reader. No wonder the poor child had been so disturbed when she was adopted, growing up in a violent home like that one, with her own mother murdered. Jennifer folded up the copies and slid them into a side pocket of her purse. She didn't want Amy to see them. The little girl was reading only at a second-grade level, but she might recognize some of the words printed here. And one of the articles included blurry photographs of Melissa and Clayton Fowler, along with their baby daughter—the same child pictured in the proofs Obie Babcock had turned over a few hours ago, the same child that Jennifer had named Amy. If Amy saw these newspaper pictures, would she remember her birth parents? Jennifer wondered. She didn't know, but she didn't care to find out this way, either. Poor little Amy had endured enough trauma in her life.

It was twenty after four when Jennifer finally rewound the last roll of microfilm and put it back into its storage box. She looked over her shoulder and jerked to attention. Amy was not at her table. How long had it been since she'd left for the restroom? Fear suddenly rising in her, Jennifer scraped her chair backward and stood up. Her eyes searched the room, but she didn't see Amy anywhere. She grabbed her purse and rushed toward the women's room.

Jennifer threw open the restroom door and called out her daughter's name, but she could see the place was empty. Feeling increasingly panicky now, she headed back toward the main portion of the library. Where could Amy be? Jennifer could see only four other people sitting at the tables, all of them alone, plus one standing at the counter, checking out a book. None of them was Amy.

Just as she was considering calling the police, Jennifer heard a familiar giggle. Her adrenaline flowing freely, she rushed toward its source and found Amy walking between the book stacks with a brown-skinned boy about her own age. The two youngsters' arms were piled high with children's books.

"Amy!" Jennifer yelled.

Startled, Amy turned and the top book on her pile slid to the floor. "Oh, hi, Mom. Me and Jason are helping out."

"You're *what?*" Jennifer's heart rate began to slow down a little.

"We're helping the library lady, Mom. She's real nice." Amy grinned at her mother, obviously proud of herself. "She's Jason's mom."

Jennifer closed her eyes for a long moment and took in a slow, deep breath as she tried to control her temper. There had been no reason to panic, she lectured herself, no reason at all. Amy had simply found a way to keep herself occupied here in the library, precisely what Jennifer had suggested she do only a couple of hours ago. "Hello, Jason," she said calmly, when she'd opened her eyes again. "I'm Amy's mother."

"Hi," the boy said shyly, looking at the floor. "I gotta go give these books to my mom. She works in the children's room. Comin', Amy?"

"She'll be along in just a minute," Jennifer told him. The boy scurried through the stacks and out of sight.

"I couldn't find you, Amy." Jennifer could hear the edge

of anger still lingering in her own voice. "You didn't come back like I told you to and I was really worried."

"Sorry, Mom." Amy's grin disappeared. "Do we have to go now?"

Jennifer nodded. "Here, I'll help you carry these back to the librarian." She knelt down and retrieved the book that had fallen to the floor, then took three slim volumes off the pile in Amy's arms. "Then we'll be on our way." Amy's frecked face registered disappointment. "What's the matter, kiddo?" Jennifer asked her. "I thought you were in a big hurry to get out of here."

"Yeah, I guess, but that's when I wasn't having fun. Now I am, Mom. Me and Jason're playing librarian."

Now that her fright had dissipated, Jennifer couldn't help but smile at her daughter. Once again, Amy had demonstrated her incredible adaptability. If the child had learned nothing else in her erratic, difficult young life— and Jennifer was only today beginning to find out just how tragically that life had started out—she'd learned to adapt to her circumstances, however they might change. Amy had taught herself how to find a morsel of happiness— some small thing to help herself survive—anywhere.

"Okay, sweetheart," Jennifer said, ruffling the little girl's auburn hair with relief and affection. "You can spend ten more minutes with your new friend. Then we're heading back home."

"Yippee! Thanks, Mom, I love you." Amy streaked toward the children's section of the library, the books she still carried precariously shifting in her arms as she ran.

Chapter

35

"*Be sure to brush your teeth and wash your face before you climb into bed,*" Jennifer told Amy when they got back to their Santa Monica apartment. "You can have your bath in the morning." It was well after nine o'clock and they both were exhausted after their long day.

Amy rubbed her eyes and yawned. Her cheek was smeared with grease from the fried chicken supper they'd eaten at a Santa Barbara drive-in restaurant and there was a fleck of pie crust stuck to her chin. She'd finished the last of her apple turnover in the car as they drove home along the Malibu coast. Thinking about what a poor diet she'd fed her daughter today, Jennifer felt a sharp twinge of guilt. She would have to go heavy on the fruits and vegetables for the next few days to balance things out.

"Will you tuck me in?" Amy asked. She was slumped against the wall, half asleep.

"Of course I will, sweetie. I always tuck you in, don't I? Just call me when you're ready."

Amy nodded sleepily and dragged herself off in the direction of the bathroom.

Jennifer hung up their windbreakers in the coat closet and

walked over to the answering machine. The light was blinking and the digital readout told her she had received one phone call. She held her hand poised above the machine's playback button for a long moment, half hoping, half fearing that this call was from her neighbor, Forrest Hathaway. This was the Saturday night he'd asked her out for dinner but, worried about whether this handsome man down the hall was really who and what he claimed to be, she'd put him off, citing her lack of a baby-sitter. Still, a big part of Jennifer wanted Forrest to continue his romantic pursuit. She knew she would feel a definite loss if he turned out to be genuine and her suspicion resulted in his getting away forever.

Screwing up her courage, Jennifer pressed the button. "Jen," a woman's gravelly recorded voice said, "it's Sal." Sally Donovan, her friend from KNLA. "Sorry I missed you. Listen, don't call me back tonight. Got a hot date with a first AD from Fox—a little dinner, a little dancing, a little who knows what might follow. Lord knows, I could use some 'follow-up' these days. Hell, there's still plenty of life left in this old girl. Just gotta ignore the sags and wrinkles and go for it, eh?"

Jennifer listened as the recorded Sal laughed at her own feeble attempt at self-deprecating humor, then took a long drag on her cigarette and loudly exhaled into the telephone receiver. "Got a juicy piece of gossip," she continued. "Thought you'd want to hear it.

"Word is you made the cut for that producer's job at Three I put you onto a while back," Sally said. "Brandenberg—he's that new executive producer from New York, remember? Anyway, Brandenberg plans to start interviewing 'round the end of next week. Downside is that the GM, major-league asshole that he is, you might know him—Roger Lincoln, that prick with the coke habit, used to be sales VP at Channel Twelve? Anyway, son of a bitch's got a twenty-four-year-old he's been putting it to behind his wife's back. Wants to put her in this job—the bimbo, that is, not the wife.

"Brandenberg says he's gonna fight him, though, so you still got a chance, maybe a pretty good one if Lincoln's wife finds out about his extracurricular activity. Rumor is, that might be arranged by a few disgruntled folks in the news department if Lincoln doesn't cool his management style. Anyway, just wanted you to know. Keep in touch." Sally made a loud smacking noise that sounded like a kiss, then hung up.

Jennifer rewound the tape, hoping that Amy had not been listening to Sal's colorful language. She didn't know whether to feel encouraged that she apparently was a finalist for a producer's job at a Los Angeles TV station, or discouraged that the usual industry power games were being played to fill that job. Once again, Jennifer felt she had little control over her own professional and economic future. Yet, the truth was, right now she was far more interested in reading those newspaper stories she'd photocopied at the San Luis Obispo library than in speculating about whether she would be offered a producing job at Channel Three.

"I'm all ready, Mom." Amy stood in the hall, wearing her yellow nightgown and holding her Raggedy Ann doll by one arm. Her face was clean now, but her reddish hair was stringy and falling over one eye. It badly needed washing, Jennifer decided, but tomorrow would be soon enough to tend to it.

"Okay, go climb into bed and I'll be right in," Jennifer said.

After she had tucked the little girl into bed and kissed her good night, Jennifer poured herself a glass of wine and sat down at the kitchen table to look through the newspaper clippings. She forced herself to read them in chronological order, although she was sorely tempted to start with the much more sensational later ones. She knew it would be best to learn about Amy's birth parents' story from its beginning; that might well help her understand why it had apparently ended so tragically.

Jennifer spread the first of the stories, a wedding announcement, out on the table and read it. In 1985, when she married Clayton Fowler, Melissa O'Mara had been a graduate of Cal Poly, as the California State University campus in San Luis Obispo was known. Melissa had majored in secondary education at the university, but the announcement mentioned nothing about her being employed as a teacher . . . or as anything else. Clayton Fowler was identified here as the owner-manager and leading actor of a local dinner theater. Obviously seen as more important by the local newspaper was the fact that Clayton was the son of Henry Fowler, a central California real estate developer and international investor. Apparently the elder Fowler was one of the most influential businessmen in the central part of the state.

A clipping dated less than a year later told Jennifer that Henry Fowler had died of an apparent heart attack. Sixty-eight years old at the time of his death, he was survived by his two children, Clayton and a daughter, Jean Fowler Morton of Salem, Oregon, and one grandchild. Jennifer figured that Clayton Fowler and his sister must have inherited a great deal of money when their father died.

There was no news of the Fowlers in the newspapers for more than a year following Henry's death. Then came a paragraph-long story in the social column, announcing the birth of Clayton and Melissa Fowler's first child. Their baby daughter weighed seven pounds eight ounces and had been named Kitty Melissa.

A few favorable reviews of plays at Clay Fowlers' dinner theater followed, but the bulk of the remaining newspaper stories were much more sensational. They were dated toward the end of the 1980s, and Jennifer read them with an increasing sense of dread. The first of these told of the death of Melissa O'Mara Fowler as the result of head wounds. She'd been severely beaten, according to a police spokesman. "Mrs. Fowler suffered multiple blows to the head," Jennifer read. "Officers on the scene said that the young mother's face was so battered and bloody that it was nearly unrecognizable when they found her."

The next day's newspaper reported the arrest of Clayton Fowler. He was charged with first degree murder in the death of his wife and denied bail. What about the Fowlers' baby? Jennifer wondered. What had happened to poor little Kitty during all this? But the arrest story didn't mention her at all.

Jennifer read a later story about Clay Fowler's arraignment and an interview with his attorney, who was identified as one of the most prominent and expensive criminal defense attorneys in California. She recognized the man's name; he'd defended a number of celebrity clients as well as some notorious criminals. But there was nothing in the paper about Kitty Fowler until just before her father's designated trial date.

In the end, there was to be no murder trial for Clay Fowler. His famous attorney arranged a plea bargain for him, although, thanks to the judge, it turned out to be a particularly unusual one. Clay agreed to plead guilty to the lesser charge of manslaughter, but the judge imposed a strict condition before he would accept the deal that Fowler's attorney and the district attorney had negotiated.

"Judge Addison Kemp insisted that Fowler sign away all parental rights to his twenty-month-old daughter before he would accept his guilty plea to a lesser charge," Jennifer read in the newspaper. "The judge, who has been well known locally for his creative sentencing, insisted on this condition for what he termed 'the future protection of the minor child.'

"Judge Kemp agreed that young Kitty Fowler could be adopted by relatives in another state, as long as her father retained no legal access to her. Those relatives were later identified as Mr. and Mrs. Bruce Morton of Salem, Oregon, who have five children of their own. Mrs. Morton is the former Jean Fowler, Clayton Fowler's sister.

"'Seldom have I seen a case where a father has shown less care and concern for his own family,' Judge Kemp lectured Fowler. 'Young man, the best possible situation for your young daughter would be that she never sees you again.'"

Jennifer's stomach lurched as she read the rest of the article. The judge's conclusion, after examining all the evidence and speaking directly with the arresting officers, was that Kitty, who'd been less than a year and a half old at the time, had witnessed her mother's brutal murder. Police called to the crime scene had found her mute and cowering in a bedroom closet, her face and clothes spattered with her mother's blood. As a result of the trauma Kitty had experienced on that night, the judge said, she had regressed both mentally and emotionally to the point where she now required professional help.

The judge also told the press about earlier events in the Fowlers' lives. Neighbors had summoned the police to the Fowler home several times during the years of the marriage, he said. Police logs stated that Melissa Fowler had shown evidence of cuts and bruises on each of these occasions, but she had refused to press charges against her husband, claiming that she had fallen and injured herself. No charges were ever filed.

The judge further stated that baby Kitty herself had shown evidence of physical trauma when she'd been given a medical exam in foster care. Feeling nauseated as she read the terrible story, Jennifer swallowed hard and continued reading. Hairline fractures of both of the child's arms had healed, she learned, but Kitty Fowler still had a large bruise on her head and her left shoulder was stiff, as if someone had severely wrenched it.

Jennifer's eyes filled and she had to stop reading for a few minutes. What kind of monster could hurt a baby that way? That this baby was to become her own daughter made it that much harder for her to imagine. Yet she knew the answer to her own question—the same kind of monster who could beat his own wife so severely that her face became unrecognizable, the same kind of monster who could murder that woman in full view of their young daughter, then leave the child cowering and terrified in a closet.

Clayton Fowler—heir to a fortune, wife and child batterer, and, in the end, murderer. Was he the man at Amy's school, the man who'd left the doll? Jennifer shivered as a chill ran down her spine. The newspaper said that the wife murderer had agreed to the judge's terms—what choice had he really had?—and was sentenced to twelve to fifteen years in a state penitentiary. With time off for good behavior, Jennifer knew, this violent husband and father could easily be back on the streets by now. He could be right here in Santa Monica. He could be living at the Edgewater, just a few apartments away from her own.

Could Forrest Hathaway and Clay Fowler be the same man? Jennifer spread out the copy of the story that included the Fowlers' photographs on the table, then bent over until her face hovered only about six inches above the printed page. But the photos remained blurry, no matter how closely she examined them. Many of the words in her microfilm copies were barely decipherable, causing her to squint to make them out; it came as no surprise that the photographs were far from clear. About all she really could tell about Clayton Fowler from this copy of a newspaper photo was that, some six years earlier, he'd had longish light-colored hair and worn a full beard. What his face looked like underneath all that hair was anybody's guess.

Still, seeing Fowler's pale hair gave Jennifer a brief spurt of hope. The man at Brinton Academy had had dark hair and so did Forrest Hathaway. Yet, she reminded herself, Clay Fowler had once been a professional actor. Changing his hair—either on his face or on top of his head—was a ridiculously simple alteration of appearance for any actor. If Fowler had not wanted to be recognized—and with the judge ordering him to stay away from his daughter forever, he certainly wouldn't want to be spotted hanging around her school—he would undoubtedly try to modify his appearance in every way he reasonably could.

What about Amy? Jennifer wondered whether the child would still recognize her father after all these years. She might go either way. Jennifer had heard about kids who were taken away from their parents in babyhood and who later retained absolutely no memory of them. That wasn't surprising; even adults who'd had normal, happy childhoods often had no memories of their lives before they reached the age of two or three.

Amy's having seen her father murder her mother might have burned the horrific event into her memory forever, or it might have been so painful that, years ago, she'd buried it somewhere in her subconscious mind, never to be retrieved. Jennifer was inclined to think the latter was far more likely, especially considering the years Amy had spent in psychotherapy. Despite all that probing of her young mind and memories, Amy had never spoken about her early childhood trauma.

Jennifer ran her finger over the fuzzy photograph of Clayton Fowler. If she darkened this man's hair, removed his beard, and added a few years to his age, would he be Forrest Hathaway? Or maybe someone else she'd seen here in the building? She simply could not tell. She needed a better photo of Clay Fowler. And she needed to find out whether he was still imprisoned somewhere in the state, or if he'd already been paroled.

Jennifer reached for the telephone. She had a news

reporter friend at KNLA-TV, Lucas Paulsen, whose job was to cover the state's criminal justice system; undoubtedly he could help her get the details she needed. But after she'd dialed the first two digits of Lucas's home telephone number, she realized that it was already after midnight, far too late to call him tonight. She hung up the phone.

For now, all Jennifer could do was go to bed and try to get some rest. It was nearly two by the time she fell into a troubled, restless sleep, dreaming about a young mother brutally beaten to death and her blood-spattered baby.

Chapter

36

Sunday was a difficult day for Jennifer. She was haunted by the shock waves from what she'd learned the night before and she couldn't help looking at her daughter with new eyes. Finding out about Amy's early life answered so many questions: the reason why Amy for so long demonstrated a strong, almost pathological fear of men; why she had always cringed and cowered when anyone, particularly a man, raised his voice in her presence; why, when Jennifer first adopted her, Amy had displayed distinct tendencies toward destructive and violent behavior, particularly whenever she felt cornered; even why the little girl had been an angry mute at age two.

Perhaps, Jennifer thought, lacking the language skills to describe the horrible events she'd witnessed, the child had temporarily lost her ability to talk about anything at all. Now she felt certain Amy no longer had any conscious memory of that fatal night in San Luis Obispo; yet its fallout still affected her daily life in numerous ways. It probably always would.

Jennifer took Amy to the beach in the late morning, as she'd promised she would. The day was far too cool for swimming in the sea, but they picnicked on the sand, played catch with Amy's Frisbee, and built sand castles alongside Santa Monica Pier.

Jennifer frequently felt close to tears as she looked at Amy and thought about her tragic origins. She couldn't stop her mind from filling up with terrifying pictures. It was as though she were being forced to watch a horror movie that played over and over again, each time becoming more gruesome than before.

When a drip of grape jelly from Amy's sandwich landed on her chin as she was eating her picnic lunch, Jennifer reached over to wipe it off and suddenly saw a much younger Amy, her face spattered not with grape jelly, but with her mother's blood. Later, when Amy clasped her hands across her face to protect herself from a Frisbee that sailed too close, Jennifer pictured her daughter reacting in the same way to a huge man's threatening fist. And Amy's skinning her elbow as she dove into the sand to catch the Frisbee sparked Jennifer's vision of her as a baby lying in her crib, with hairline fractures in both of her tiny flailing arms.

All day Jennifer tried her best to act normal and happy about spending a day at the beach with Amy. But her mind was so troubled that, at times, she could hardly manage to breathe normally.

"Hey, Mom, look at me!" Amy called as she turned cartwheels on the packed, wet sand along the water's edge. She landed squarely on her bare feet and looked to her mother for approval.

"Great, Amy!" Jennifer said, clapping her hands loudly. She tried to convince herself that Amy was completely healed now. This strong young girl, who could flip head over heels half a dozen times in a row without even breathing hard, was no longer the vulnerable, damaged toddler who'd hidden in a closet to escape from her murderous father. Still, Jennifer's mind insisted upon conjuring up the most hideously violent pictures; every one of them saw Amy in grave danger and crying for Jennifer to save her.

By three o'clock, Jennifer was exhausted, both physically and emotionally. It was time to go home. "Come on, sweetheart, help me pack up all this stuff," she said. "It's time we headed out of here."

For once, Amy didn't argue, as though she sensed her mother's distressed mood and didn't want to add to it. She obediently folded up her beach towel and stuffed it into the beach bag, then carried the remains of their picnic lunch to the nearest trash can.

"My feet are all sandy, Mom," she complained when everything they'd brought to the beach had been collected. "I can't get my sneakers back on. This icky old sand hurts my feet too much."

"Just carry your sneakers until we get over to the concrete," Jennifer told her. "You can brush the sand off your feet with the towel and put your shoes on over there."

Holding her red sneakers in her hand, Amy sprinted across the wide expanse of golden sand toward the bike path and the parking lot beyond. Jennifer, burdened by the beach toys, the carrying bag, and her own heavy thoughts, followed at a considerably slower pace.

As she unlocked the door to their apartment twenty minutes later, Jennifer heard the telephone ringing. She dropped the sand toys and soiled beach towels she was carrying onto the floor and grabbed the receiver just as the answering machine clicked on to pick up the call.

"Hi, Jennifer, glad I caught you." It was Lucas Paulsen, her friend from NLA's news department, whom she'd contacted for help that morning. Luke's voice, as always, was full of energy and enthusiasm. He was young, still in his late twenties and, unlike so many of his co-workers, he hadn't yet been burned out by the intensity and competition of television news.

"Luke, hi. Say, that was fast. Were you able to get anything for me on that—" A quick look told Jennifer that that Amy was still within earshot, so she chose her words carefully. "About that, uh, person we were discussing?"

"Yeah, got lucky. Didn't think I could do it on a Sunday, but one of my contacts with the cops did me a favor, went over and checked the central computer for me." Luke was obviously proud of his accomplishment.

Jennifer immediately tensed up. She desperately needed to know what Luke had learned about Clayton Fowler, yet she was equally afraid to hear what he might tell her. "Don't keep me hanging, Luke," she said finally. "Is he out?" She held her breath as she waited for the answer.

"'Fraid so. Your man was paroled a couple of months ago."

Another piece of the puzzle fell into place. "Do you know where they sent him?"

"Nope, but the typical routine is that these guys're paroled to the jurisdiction where they committed their crime. Unless they've got some reason to be sent somewhere else, that is. Either way, Fowler could be your guy— San Luis Obispo County's only a few hours away from L.A. Nothing to stop him from getting in his car and driving down here."

"I know. I drove that same trip yesterday. Only takes about three hours each way."

"You need an address for this guy, Jen?" Lucas sounded noticeably less enthusiastic now. "I don't really know how many markers I want to pull in on this thing, so if you can do without it . . ."

"I could use an address, sure," Jennifer told him. "A good, up-to-date photo of him, too. But let me try another route before you call your cop friend back." She figured Detective Mike Jenrud, the surly cop who'd taken her report at the local police station the other day, ought to be able to do at least this much for her. She'd already managed most of what she thought should rightly be his job. "If I bomb out," she told her friend, "I may have to call on you again, but—well, I'll try my best not to. Listen, Luke, thanks, thanks a lot. I really owe you one."

"Hey, no problem. Sorry I wasn't able to tell you the bastard's still locked up in Soledad and you've got nothing to worry about. Say, how's the job search going?"

Jennifer tried to sound upbeat as she told Lucas Paulsen she was pursuing several hot leads at the moment. She did all right, she thought; her lies sounded fairly convincing, even to her own ears. Still, she felt a strong sense of relief when the phone call ended.

Sending tired, sand-speckled Amy off to take her second bath of the day, Jennifer waited until the little girl was out of earshot, then dialed the local police station. She asked to speak to Detective Mike Jenrud, but the officer on duty told her he had weekends off. Predictable, she thought, targeting her building frustration against the cop who'd treated her and her problems so rudely the other day. She was forced to settle for leaving a message for him to call her back.

If she hadn't heard from Jenrud by tomorrow at noon, Jennifer vowed, she would simply call back and insist upon speaking to him, or maybe she would go back down to the station and wait to see him. If Clayton Fowler was here in Los Angeles County, stalking her and her daughter, surely the very least the police ought to be able to do was arrest the man on some kind of parole violation.

And, if the police wouldn't help her, Jennifer vowed, she would deal with Clayton Fowler herself . . . somehow. No way was she ever going to let that man near Amy again . . . no matter what she had to do to prevent it.

37

Clay Fowler had planned a busy Monday. He left the Edgewater early to drive up to Santa Barbara and, by ten-thirty, he was at his new office building, signing a phony signature on the lease papers. The building's owner never even flinched when Clay handed over two months' rent and the damage deposit, all in fifties and hundreds. The man simply pocketed the cash and, with a relieved look on his face, handed Clay keys to the building itself and to each of its ten offices.

As soon as the owner left the building, Clay checked the telephone line he'd ordered and found it working, just as the phone company had promised. It was a good omen, he thought. He hitched up the answering machine he'd bought at Circuit City yesterday and recorded a message for his brand-new "business." He'd always been good with details like that.

Now it was just after one o'clock and Clay was at the third of the service stations he'd mapped out here in Santa Barbara, filling one of the two-gallon gas cans he'd stock-piled over the past week.

"That'll be two sixty-five," the attendant, an acne-faced youth in grease-caked coveralls, told him, holding out his hand. The attendant smelled of a rank mixture of gasoline and body odor.

Clay handed him a fifty.

The youth frowned at it. "Ain't you got nothin' smaller?"

Shit, Clay thought, realizing that he should have changed that bill somewhere else. The last thing he wanted was to attract attention now, while he was filling up these gas cans. Not after he'd been so cautious, bringing no more than one can into each gas station he visited. In brushfire-prone Southern California, Clay knew, anybody trying to buy too much gasoline in cans was immediately suspect, looked upon as a potential arsonist. He'd known a couple of those sorry arsonist bastards in prison, real nut cases.

"Sorry," Clay said, shrugging his shoulders and doing his best to feign contrition. He didn't feel contrite right now, though; what he felt was a wave of bitter resentment toward this miserable little cockroach who had the power to point out his ineptitude, this asshole who had the power to remember Clay and describe him to the cops later on. He would have loved to punch that sneering look right off this filthy kid's face, but he knew he couldn't afford that luxury, not now. "The fifty's the smallest I've got," he said, defensively.

Grumbling under his breath, the attendant shuffled off into the interior of the gas station, taking his time before returning with Clay's change. He handed over the short stack of greasy bills all at once, not bothering to count them out, then dumped a quarter and a dime on top of them. The dime tumbled off the bills and out of Clay's grasp, bouncing with a series of pings across the pavement. Neither of the men stooped to pick it up.

Swearing to himself, Clay stuffed the bills and the quarter into his pocket and climbed back into his current car—another rental, this time a brand-new gold Grand Am from National. It took every bit of his self-control not to burn rubber as he left that gas station and headed down the street toward the next one on his list.

Chapter

38

"*I think this is the guy who's been bothering my daughter,*" Jennifer told Detective Jenrud. She was back in the institutional green cubicle at the police station, her microfilm copies of the San Luis Obispo newspaper spread out on the table in front of her.

"Looks like this Fowler fellow is one of the bad guys, all right." Jenrud seemed less hostile to Jennifer this time, although he was still far from what she considered sympathetic. "But how do you know for sure Fowler's your kid's natural father?" he asked.

Jennifer leaned toward the balding cop; in her hand was the photo she'd taken from the gold case. The suit Jenrud was wearing today was chocolate brown, but it didn't fit him any better than the one she'd seen him wear before. Both outfits looked like something he'd picked up at a Salvation Army resale store. She flipped the photograph over and showed the detective the photographer's stamp on its backside, then described her trip to the Babcock Photography studio. "Babcock told me that someone named Melissa Fowler had ordered those photographs of Amy," she said, "so I went to the library and found all this in the newspaper's back issues." She gestured at the copies spread across the table.

"Not a bad little piece of detective work," Jenrud reluctantly admitted. He scraped his chair backward. It made a screeching sound as its legs rubbed across the worn wooden floor.

"That's not all," Jennifer told him. "I found out Clayton Fowler's been paroled. He's got to be the guy who's been bothering Amy, Detective, he's just got to."

Mike Jenrud picked up another of the newspaper stories Jennifer had brought and tipped his chair backward, balancing it precariously on its rear legs, while he skimmed the copy for information. When he'd finished reading, he lowered the chair and made eye contact with Jennifer. "What exactly do you expect me to do about this?" he asked.

"Arrest Fowler, of course." What had to be done seemed patently obvious to Jennifer. "His bothering Amy has to be some kind of parole violation, right? I mean, according to this, the judge ordered him not to have anything to do with her, ever again. And . . . And I'm really frightened for my child, Detective. Who knows what a crazy man like this might do?"

"The judge does seem to have severed Fowler's parental rights . . . assuming you can believe these newspaper reports, that is." Jenrud sounded doubtful, as though he'd had plenty of personal experience with faulty press reports. "Even so, there's still a big question in my mind about whether the man's simply saying a few words to his kid constitutes a true parole violation."

Jennifer felt her chest tightening, as though a wide belt were fastened across her breasts. Earlier, she'd felt so certain that the police would take over for her from now on, that they would arrest Fowler and her troubles would be over, particularly after she'd managed to tell them precisely who the dark-haired man was. Yet this meeting was beginning to feel like another brush-off, another waste of time and energy. "What about where this creep is supposed to be spending his time?" she asked, indignant. "By rights, he should have been paroled back to San Luis Obispo, right? So what's he doing down here?"

Jenrud took his pencil off his clipboard and chewed it for a moment before answering. "I can check that out, Ms. Bennett. Find out who Fowler's parole officer is, see if he suspects anything funny's been going on. But there's one thing I think I should warn you about."

"What's that?"

"If you're wrong, if the guy who gave this picture to your daughter is *not* Clayton Fowler, then my making these inquiries could hand him a clue to where he can find his daughter."

The belt tightened around Jennifer's chest again and her head began to ache. "I don't get it. Who else could this guy possibly be?"

Jenrud shrugged. "An uncle, a neighbor, some nut who followed the case back in San Luis, somebody connected to that photo studio, maybe some minor-league extortionist who figures on picking up a little cash from you . . . I can think of a dozen people other than Fowler that this could be."

"That's ridiculous." Jennifer's lips were pressed into a straight, stubborn line as she fought against panic.

"Maybe, maybe not, Ms. Bennett," the detective told her. "What about these people who were supposed to adopt the little girl, Fowler's sister and her husband? What happened to them?"

"I have no idea. Something obviously went gone wrong with that, but I don't know the details. The adoption agency told me something about Amy's relatives having kids of their own and not being able to handle another one, so I assume it was their decision not to adopt Amy." That small bit of information was just about all Jennifer had learned from the adoption agency, that and the fact that the little girl's natural mother was dead. She was furious now that she hadn't been told about the unusual and tragic circumstances surrounding the baby she was adopting. That information never would have stopped Jennifer from taking Amy, but it certainly would have been an invaluable aid in finding the right kind of psychological help for the child.

"Maybe these people just crapped out, like you say. But consider this—what if the kid was taken away from them for some reason? They could still be angry about it, even after all these years. Suppose this guy you're worried about is this—" Mike Jenrud's eyes skimmed one of the newspaper articles quickly, searching for a name. "This Bruce Morton fellow. Or maybe somebody else from this Morton family, and not Fowler himself."

Jennifer felt confusion beginning to taint her previous sense of certainty. "Can't you inquire about Clayton Fowler without his finding out you're doing it?" She didn't understand what the big problem was about that, unless Detective Mike Jenrud was basically lazy.

"I can ask Fowler's PO to keep my inquiry confidential, sure. I'm just letting you know that sometimes things leak out, Ms. Bennett, that's all. Plus, let's say it turns out Fowler *is* in this area. Might be the best we'll be able to do for you is try to warn him off." He paused for effect. "Soon as we do that, you better hope he's the one's been bothering you." The detective put down his pencil and leaned across the table. His tone was becoming increasingly irritated and patronizing. "'Cause if he's not, lady, we just told him where to look for his kid."

"I'd like you at least to make the inquiry with the parole officer," Jennifer said firmly. She was willing to take that much risk. "Once we find out where Fowler is supposed to be, then maybe you and I can talk again about whether you should contact him. All right?"

"Sure thing. Give me a couple of days, I'll see what I can find out."

Jennifer gathered up her photocopies and the baby picture of Amy and put them back into her briefcase. "Think you could get me a copy of Fowler's mug shot, too, Detective? I'd really like to show it to that teacher who saw the man at Brinton Academy." She didn't add that she also wanted to see whether the photograph resembled anybody she'd seen around the Edgewater Apartment Hotel. She briefly considered asking Jenrud whether Clay Fowler had ever used the name Forrest Hathaway, but quickly nixed the idea. Fowler would certainly be smart enough to come up with a brand-new alias, and asking the police to investigate Forrest could backfire on her in half a dozen different ways. Jennifer held her tongue.

"See what I can do." Jenrud stood up just as Jennifer did, continuing his pattern of superficial courtesy. "As I recall," he said coolly, "you can find your own way out."

"You recall correctly, Detective. I appreciate your help." Jennifer picked up her briefcase and headed back to her car.

Detective Mike Jenrud's face wore a quizzical expression as he watched his visitor disappear down the hall.

Chapter

39

On Tuesday morning, Jennifer had a brief meeting in Century City with her accountant to hand over her financial records for the year the IRS was auditing. "Listen, Ms. Bennett," the accountant told her as she gave him a fat manila envelope filled with her receipts, "don't worry about this. This kind of audit is really no big deal." He smiled in an obvious effort to be reassuring. "Even if the IRS rules against your deductions—and I'm definitely not predicting they will—this thing can't cost you more than another two or three thousand dollars, four thousand tops, after penalties and interest."

"Four thousand dollars!" Jennifer felt her knees go weak; her sense of desperation mushroomed. "Maybe paying an extra four thousand dollars is no big deal to you, but right now I don't even have a job," she reminded him. "Where in the world am I going to get four thousand dollars?"

The expression that quickly formed on her accountant's face—a potent combination of pity and distaste—only added to Jennifer's humiliation. *You'd think I'd just vomited on his Brooks Brothers suit,* she thought. She should have known better than to refer to her financial fears in this shrine to wealth and power.

As she left the smaller interior office of the accounting firm and headed out, Jennifer looked at the poshly decorated reception room with fresh eyes. The imported leather furniture, the massive inlaid teak desk, the copies of *Architectural Digest* and *Town and Country* set out for clients to read while they waited to see their financial advisors, the panoramic view of Los Angeles's west side from the twentieth floor, the fashion-model-type receptionist—all this had seemed appropriate when she was drawing a big salary as a TV celebrity. Her station manager had originally recommended this firm to her, and she'd been grateful for the advice. But now it seemed like nothing more than a monument to greed and conspicuous consumption, a business dedicated to helping millionaires keep their wealth hidden from the grasping hands of the government, a firm without compassion for all the little people who paid their taxes faithfully. If Jennifer Bennett had ever belonged here, she knew she no longer did.

After she rode the elevator down into the high-rise's massive subterranean parking garage, it took Jennifer nearly ten minutes to locate her car. The garage, with its many levels and numerous branches off each one, was confusing, but she seldom forgot where she'd parked. As she walked up and down the aisles, past showy Jaguars, Mercedes Benzes, BMWs, and occasional Rolls Royces, she felt more and more rattled and out of place. Maybe she was going completely crazy.

Finally she located her station wagon, wedged between some yuppie's Jeep and a large white van with an office supplies vendor's name stenciled on its side. Relieved, Jennifer slid behind the steering wheel and sat for a moment with her eyes closed, struggling to regain her composure. She simply couldn't let herself fall apart now. Amy needed her. With the vicious Clayton Fowler back in the picture, her little girl probably needed her more now than ever before.

When her pulse had returned to normal and she felt a little calmer, Jennifer started her engine and drove up the ramp toward Constellation Boulevard. It wasn't until she reached the toll kiosk and was wedged into a line of cars waiting to escape that she realized she'd forgotten to have her accounting firm's receptionist validate her parking ticket. As she forked over a full five dollars for a mere forty minutes of parking time, she felt her humiliation was now complete.

An hour later, sitting at her kitchen table eating a tuna salad sandwich, Jennifer glanced through her check register. She figured she had enough money left for another month's rent at the Edgewater, maybe two if she scrimped on everything else and made the minimum monthly payment on her credit cards. But if she had to write a check for four thousand dollars in back taxes, she would be dead broke in less than a month. Surely the IRS must have time payment plans available.

If only she had an actual interview appointment for that producer's job at Channel Three, she would feel better. Jennifer wondered if Sally Donovan's tip about interviews taking place at the end of this week was really correct. Here it was, already well past noon on Tuesday, and no one had called her to schedule an appointment. In her current mood, Jennifer was inclined to think the station manager's young girlfriend probably had already been given the job. She made a mental note to call Channel Three this afternoon to follow up on her application. Even if the girlfriend had been hired, Jennifer preferred to know where she stood.

As though in response to her thoughts, the telephone rang, startling Jennifer out of her blue funk. She washed down a bite of tuna sandwich with a gulp of iced tea and answered on the third ring.

"Jennifer Bennett, please," said a male voice Jennifer didn't recognize.

Probably a salesman, she thought glumly. "This is Ms. Bennett."

"Ms. Bennett, I'm so glad I caught you home. My name is Terry Snyder and I'm in charge of a new cable news channel that's starting up in Santa Barbara. I'd like to talk to you about coming to work for us."

Jennifer's grip tightened on the receiver. Santa Barbara? "How . . . How did you find out about me?" she asked.

The caller laughed. "Oh, sorry, guess I'm getting a little ahead of myself. Bob Harris over at KXXT-TV told me about you. Said you applied for a job he had open over there. He's already filled his spot, but he was impressed with your audition tape. Bob's a good guy and . . . well, hope you don't mind his passing your résumé and tape on to me."

"No, no, I appreciate it." Bob Harris, Jennifer thought, that rude news director who wouldn't even return her phone calls. Yet now he'd recommended her to somebody else who was hiring. This certainly *was* a strange business. "Why don't you tell me a little bit about your operation," she suggested.

"We're calling it Family Cable News," Terry Snyder told her, "and as you can figure out from our name, we'll specialize in news that's of particular importance to families all over the country. Not just the predictable stuff like child-rearing information, but economic news, crime news, international, all the regular things. The difference between us and, say, CNN, is that we plan to angle our reports with analysis about what a particular story means to the typical American family.

"Give you an example," he continued. "Let's say there's a new gun-control bill before Congress. What we'll report is what the implications of the bill are for the American family if it passes. Will the proposed law help reduce violence among teenagers in the ghettos? Will it make schools safer? Will it protect all those kids who find loaded guns in their homes and kill or injure themselves or somebody else with them? That sort of thing."

"Sounds interesting," Jennifer said, feeling herself gradually being sucked in by Snyder's obvious enthusiasm. "But where would I fit into this, Mr. Snyder?"

"We're just now beginning to hire staff reporters, Ms. Bennett, as well as hosts for two or three discussion hours." He went on to describe four specific shows he had planned, adding, "I saw the kind of thing you did on *Only in L.A.*, and . . . I can't tell you how impressed I am. I think you and I can do business."

A warm glow began to spread through Jennifer and her gloomy mood began to lift. "Thank you," she said. "I'm flattered."

"I'm not trying to flatter you. I mean it. What we're looking for is someone with maturity, stage presence, good news judgment, and an appealing interview manner. I particularly liked one interview on your audition tape, the piece you did with those two teachers from that junior high school in Watts. Outstanding segment."

"Thanks. I thought that was one of my better interviews, too."

"You see, that's the kind of quality we're looking for."

Jennifer's mind raced forward. "I'm glad you liked it. Tell me a little more about your setup, will you?"

Terry Snyder spat out a mind-boggling amount of detail. Family Cable News was scheduled for an early spring start-up, but he wanted to assemble his staff within the next couple of weeks. His financing was coming from a group of East Coast businessmen who'd offered him carte blanche in hiring. "I chose Santa Barbara for the home base, quite frankly, because that's where I enjoy living," he told her. "The anchoring job I have in mind for you would be based here, too, but we'll also have reporters stationed around the country. Hope you don't have any objection to living in Santa Barbara?"

"Uh, no, I've always liked the city," Jennifer told him. "My daughter and I passed through there just over the weekend; we stopped and had dinner." She did not add that they'd eaten in the car, parked outside a drive-in chicken restaurant.

"We'll have the funds to pay highly competitive salaries," Snyder continued. "I think I can improve upon the money you were making at KNLA, at least a little bit . . . maybe ten percent, assuming that ball park's acceptable to you."

Acceptable? Jennifer thought. That high a salary would be a real godsend, particularly right now. Weeks ago, she'd resigned herself to the fact that she'd have to settle for a substantial cut in pay when she finally got a job. "I expect it would be acceptable," she said, "although I'd have to think it over . . . in the context of what the job would require, that is. And, of course, I have some other irons in the fire right now." What unadulterated crap, she thought as she heard herself playing the expected industry chess game.

"Of course. I understand, Ms. Bennett. You'll want to see exactly what I have in mind for you before you're ready to make a decision. I . . . I don't want to rush you, but I'm on a pretty tight schedule here. I was hoping you and your family might be able to come up to Santa Barbara tomorrow for an interview, Thursday at the latest."

"My family?"

"Right. Didn't I mention that? Sorry. I've talked to so many potential employees over the past few weeks that I sometimes get a little ahead of myself." Snyder paused a moment and Jennifer heard the loud engine of a small airplane overhead as it prepared to land at nearby Santa Monica Airport. "I'm trying to hire only people at Family Cable News who actually have families of their own," he told her. "You know, so our newscasters are honestly in tune with our audience. So, sometime during our first week on the air, I plan to have all our employees introduce their own families to our viewers. The family members won't really have to *do* anything—just say hello and be part of the background on this introductory show. I hope your husband and children won't mind—"

Jennifer felt her heart plummet; this promising job seemed to be slipping out of her grasp. "I'm not married, Mr. Snyder," she said.

"But—I thought you said you and your family had dinner here in Santa Barbara just the other—"

"I said my *daughter* and I did. My family consists of my daughter Amy—she's seven—and me."

Snyder laughed out loud. "In my book, that's a family, Ms. Bennett. I expect a good part of our audience is going to be single moms raising their kids alone. They'll be able to connect with you—count on that. Now, how about it? I'd like you to have you and your daughter fly up here tomorrow morning—flight only takes half an hour. We'll have some time to chat, you can look over my plans for the network, see our facilities. We'll make a reservation for the two of you to spend the night at the Biltmore. Then the following morning, my secretary will put together some maps of the area. She'll mark our nicer neighborhoods— you know, places where you might want to rent or buy a house. Santa Barbara's a small town, really. You should have plenty of time to take a look at the top schools for your daughter, too, before you head back to L.A."

Jennifer felt her head begin to spin with all these details. "Tomorrow? That's awfully short notice, Mr. Snyder and I . . . Well, I'll have to let Amy's school know if I'm going to take her with me. Does she really have to come along?"

"I hope it won't be a problem, Ms. Bennett, but I do feel quite strongly about that. We want your little Amy to be part of this from the very start. This is a *family* operation."

"I understand," Jennifer said, but she wasn't sure she

did. Bringing Amy along on the interview seemed a rather strange requirement, especially in the nineties. It sounded like something from back in the fifties, when men had to bring their wives along whenever they interviewed for a junior executive job. If the wife didn't pass muster as a potential executive's mate, the poor guy didn't get the job. Still, Terry Snyder's requirement sounded harmless enough, and Jennifer badly needed a job. She was in no position to protest too loudly.

"Don't worry," Snyder said. "My secretary will keep Amy occupied and happy while you and I chat about your future here at Family Cable News. Then you and your daughter can go together to find yourselves a place to live. Providing that you accept the job I expect to offer you, of course.

"I don't mind telling you," he continued, "that I have a really good feeling about this." Snyder's speech speeded up, taking on an almost manic quality. "Sometimes I think I'm a little psychic, the way I can tell in advance that I'm going to hit it off with certain people. Your tape tells me you're going to be a real asset to Family Cable News. You have a certain quality about you—a sense that you're really interested in your subject, that you care about people and the things that affect their lives—that sort of thing comes through loud and clear in your interviews. FCN needs people like you, Ms. Bennett."

"Well, thank you, Mr. Snyder, that's awfully kind of you. Tomorrow, you said. Tell you what—let me check a few things on my schedule and get back to you."

Snyder rattled off a phone number in Santa Barbara's 805 area code. "Call and leave a message on my voice mail if my secretary doesn't answer. You know how it is—she's spending most of her time calling out on the other lines these days. Gets a bit chaotic around here. I'll get back to you to confirm everything just as soon as I can." Snyder paused and took a breath. "Only thing is, we'll need a little time to make your airline reservations."

"Oh, don't worry about that, Mr. Snyder, I'd really prefer to drive. It doesn't make much sense to fly such a short distance, and I'd like to have my car with me."

"Then I'll be looking forward to seeing you tomorrow, Thursday at the latest. Shall we say eleven o'clock?"

"I'll let you know," Jennifer said, feeling a little stunned. "I'm looking forward to meeting you, too." When she'd hung up the phone, she stood for a moment with her back pressed against the cool white surface of the refrigerator. Was this for real? Not twenty minutes ago, she'd been lamenting her dismal financial future. Now she'd all but been offered a job with a brand-new cable network. And, best of all, it would pay her at least ten percent more than she'd earned at KNLA.

Jennifer sat down at the table and looked at what was left of her tuna sandwich. But now she felt far too excited to eat it. She picked up the phone and called Sally Donovan to tell her about the phone call from Terry Snyder.

"Never heard of anything named Family Cable News, Jen," Sally told her, "but that doesn't mean much. Cable's coming up with something new every day. Just make sure this outfit is solvent before you sign on—paycheck that bounces isn't much good. Tell you what—I'll check around a little and get back to you."

"Thanks, Sal," Jennifer said, ringing off. She put the rest of her sandwich down the garbage disposal and began to do some mental arithmetic to estimate how long she would have to work for Family Cable News before she could pay off all her bills and be in the black again financially.

Chapter

40

Detective Mike Jenrud picked up the fax that had just come in from the parole board and read it as he walked back to his desk. So Clayton Fowler was now living in Studio City; except during rush hour, it took only thirty or forty minutes to drive from Studio City to Santa Monica. The Bennett woman could be right, he realized reluctantly. If Fowler really was her kid's natural father, he might indeed be the guy who'd been stalking her.

Yet, from what Jennifer Bennett had told him, Mike still wasn't fully convinced that *anybody* was stalking the little girl. The evidence Jennifer had presented him with was slight at best. She claimed somebody had left a doll on her doorstep. Maybe somebody had, but that was no big deal in Mike's book.

Then there was the strange man who'd been sighted lurking outside Brinton Academy. Mike had checked that one out personally and, indeed, one of the teachers—what was her name? He sat down at his desk and reread his notes on the case. Susan Samuels, that was the woman's name. This Susan Samuels had run the man off the school grounds. Still, there was no evidence that Amy Bennett had been this guy's specific target. Maybe he was just the type that liked little girls and Amy was the first one he saw that day.

Jennifer Bennett's most crucial complaint was about the guy who'd allegedly given her daughter that photograph. Yet the Brinton Academy folks insisted they knew nothing about anybody hanging around the fence at the back of the school playground, handing things through the fence to Amy Bennett. If they'd seen anything like that, especially after the earlier incident, Susan Samuels had indignantly told Mike, they'd have called the police immediately.

So, the question in Mike's mind now was, could Jennifer Bennett be trusted to tell the truth, or had she fabricated her story about the photo? Who was to say she hadn't had that photograph for years? Mike figured the adoption agency could have given it to her when she adopted the child, maybe not realizing there was a photographer's stamp on the back of it, and certainly never imagining that the Bennett woman would use that information to track down her child's natural parents.

Certainly, Mike thought, a story about her kid's being stalked by a strange man would be worth a paragraph or two about Jennifer Bennett in the newspapers, maybe even a brief item on *Entertainment Tonight*. That could give her national exposure and, now that she was job hunting, that could be invaluable to her. He wouldn't put this kind of publicity stunt past a woman in her questionable business. After years on the job in Los Angeles County, the detective had developed an inherent distrust of Hollywood types that was almost as strong as his personal dislike of news reporters. He was inclined not to believe Jennifer's story precisely because the woman belonged to both of the subgroups of humanity he most despised.

Still, Detective Jenrud liked to think of himself as a fair man. He'd promised Jennifer Bennett he would check out this Fowler guy, and he planned to keep his word. It would be another day or so before Clayton Fowler's mug shot and rap sheet arrived from up north but, for now, Mike could check with the parole officer assigned to the ex-con and see what he had to say.

It was midafternoon before Parole Officer Sonny Zumbrowski returned Mike's call. Sonny seemed an odd nickname for a man who sounded as though he were a good sixty, sixty-five years old, Mike thought, as he listened to Zumbrowski's weak, scratchy tones coming across the telephone line. Or maybe the poor guy was just a burned-out forty-year-old. POs had a helluva hard job these days, with an impossibly large caseload; they tended to burn out early.

"Did a home visit with Fowler at his digs in Studio City just last week," Zumbrowski reported in response to Mike's questions. "Got himself a nice little condo over there—wouldn't mind havin' one like it myself, if I could stretch a PO's pay that far. Clay Fowler's got family money—ain't *that* sweet? Still busts his ass tryin' to get acting work in the movies, though, and he checks in with me every afternoon, just like clockwork."

"You got Fowler's phone number handy?" Mike asked him.

"Sure. You plannin' on contactin' him?"

"Maybe. Might as well shake his cage a little, see if anything interesting falls out."

"Yeah, well, all my parolees oughta give me as little trouble as Clay Fowler—I wouldn't have this ulcer. You ask me, this one ain't no threat anymore—ain't your typical criminal type. This's just a guy who lost it one night with his wife, let his temper get the better of him and he killed her. Don't get me wrong—I ain't excusin' what he done, but your crime-of-passion murderers usually don't turn out to be your multiple offenders."

Mike wrote down Clayton Fowler's Studio City telephone number as Sonny Zumbrowski dictated it to him. "Thanks for the information," he told the PO. "Let you know if I find out anything you might want to know."

Mike dialed Fowler's phone number next. A machine answered. He left no message. Two hours later, the machine picked up again. So the guy was out for the day, Mike told himself. That didn't necessarily mean anything was wrong. He was probably on one of those auditions Sonny Zumbrowski'd told him about, or maybe he was doing his weekly grocery shopping. There was no valid reason for the uneasy feeling that was beginning to grow in the pit of Mike's stomach.

By the end of the work day, Mike still hadn't reached Clayton Fowler by telephone. What the hell, he thought, as slipped his arms into the sleeves of his suit jacket. Today's was a conservative navy blue striped job that didn't quite button around the detective's thick waistline, so he wore it hanging open. What the hell, he thought, do the job right. He had nothing better to do tonight, anyway; he could drive over to Studio City and check out Fowler's condo. Once he'd done that, he could put his mind at ease, forget about the Bennett woman and her stupid publicity stunt.

In rush hour traffic, it took Detective Mike Jenrud an hour and a half to reach the Laurel Canyon exit off the Ventura Freeway. By the time he rang Clayton Fowler's doorbell, he was beginning to feel sorry he'd ever heard of either the parolee or Jennifer Bennett.

"I'm sorry, Ms. Bennett, but Mr. Harris's meeting is likely to last all afternoon. He'll have to call you back."

The voice answering KXXT-TV news department's telephone was the same youthful, feminine one Jennifer had heard half a dozen times before. "Yes, please ask him to do that," she said with a sigh. "Tell him I just want to thank him for all his help." She started to leave her phone number one more time.

"That's not necessary, Ms. Bennett," the receptionist told her. "Mr. Harris already has your number."

It was the same old story, a confused Jennifer realized as she hung up the receiver. As soon as she'd given the receptionist her name, she'd been told that Bob Harris was "in a meeting" and couldn't talk to her. If this was like all the other times she'd called him, he would never return her call. Yet the man had gone out of his way to help her get a job somewhere else.

Harris probably just didn't communicate with this receptionist, Jennifer figured. The young woman who answered the newsroom's telephone probably had no idea that Bob Harris had sent Jennifer Bennett's résumé and audition tape to a colleague who apparently wanted to hire her.

Still, protective receptionist or not, Jennifer really did want to thank Harris for his help. Even if the anchor job at KXXT had already been filled, who knew what might happen in the future? The FCN position might not pan out for her, and the anchorwoman Harris had hired might bomb out as well. That sort of thing happened all the time in TV news. If he'd really been that impressed with Jennifer's audition tape, Harris might remember her and hire her at KXXT sometime in the future. But he certainly wouldn't remember her very favorably if she didn't bother thanking him now.

She could write to Harris, Jennifer thought, but she couldn't help picturing her letter being opened by some officious secretary—maybe even that receptionist who answered the phone—and routed straight into the circular file.

A bouquet of flowers, or maybe a pretty flowering plant with a note of thanks attached—that would get Harris's attention, Jennifer thought. She grabbed the phone again and punched in the numbers for Florists Transworld Delivery. She ordered a small arrangement of spring flowers in a basket—in deference to her nearly maxed-out credit card, she made a relatively inexpensive selection—and asked that it be sent to Bob Harris at KXXT-TV as soon as possible. Her sending Bob Harris flowers certainly should attract his attention.

"I want this message on the card," Jennifer dictated into the phone. "'Thanks for recommending me to Family Cable News. If I get the job, I'll buy you dinner.' Sign it, 'Jennifer Bennett.'"

"Your flowers will be delivered before noon tomorrow, Ms. Bennett," the clerk informed her.

Perfect, Jennifer thought, feeling proud of her own resourcefulness. She'd bet Bob Harris didn't receive flowers from his other job applicants. He should remember Jennifer Bennett's name for a long, long time.

Jennifer's next call was to the Santa Barbara number of Family Cable News. She decided she might as well go for her interview tomorrow morning. She was anxious to determine whether FCN and Terry Snyder were for real, and tomorrow's weather report looked favorable for a drive up the coast. Snyder obviously wanted to see her as soon as possible and, besides, why should she keep herself in suspense for another day?

A machine answered her call—undoubtedly what Snyder had meant by his voice mail, Jennifer thought. She left a concise message, stating only that she planned to be at FCN's offices at eleven o'clock the next morning.

Within less than an hour, Snyder called her back. "Just confirming our appointment tomorrow at eleven," he told her, repeating the address that he'd given her earlier for FCN's offices and giving her directions from Highway 101. "Your daughter's coming, too, right?" he asked.

"Yes, Amy'll be with me."

"Fine, I'll alert my secretary."

When Jennifer got off the phone, she headed straight for her bedroom closet, where she began to sort through the collection of clothes she'd worn on-camera for *Only in L.A.* She pulled two nearly identical suits off the rack, trying to decide whether she should wear the red or the beige for her interview tomorrow. The beige was more businesslike, but the red was more striking. Which would make a better impression at Family Cable News?

In the end, Jennifer put both the red and beige suits back into the closet and selected a pale aqua-and-peach tweed number with a peach-colored silk blouse, on the theory that this outfit would make her look more feminine, more approachable, than either of the others.

These soft colors were right for a modern young mother's wardrobe, Jennifer decided. This outfit should give her the kind of look that Terry Snyder, with his insistence on a strong family image for his news operation, would undoubtedly prefer.

Chapter

42

Mike Jenrud managed to get past the security gate at Clay Fowler's condo without ringing the man's unit directly. No sense alerting him that the cops were on their way. Now he'd been standing outside the town house's door, ringing the bell, for the past five minutes. Nobody was answering it.

"Hey, lay off the bell, willya, fella? The guy's not home, okay?"

Mike turned to see a thin young man lounging in the open doorway of the unit next door. Naked from the waist up, the youth was deeply tanned and his silky shoulder-length black hair shone in his porch light. Unconsciously, Mike ran his hand across his own bald dome as he approached Fowler's next-door neighbor. He took his police shield from his pocket and showed it. "Know where I might find Clay Fowler?"

The young man's eyes clouded over instantly at the sight of the police ID and he straightened up. "Nope," he replied. "Think he's outta town." Strains of an aria from *La Boheme* echoed from the rear of his condominium.

"What makes you say that?" Mike asked.

"Hey, this guy wanted for some kinda crime or some-thin'?"

"Not necessarily. We just need to locate him, ask him a few questions."

A male voice came from inside the youth's place, "Hey, Arnie, hurry it up, willya? I haven't got all night, you know!"

The youth looked uncomfortable. "Hey, wait here a minute," he said. "Be right back." He disappeared into the interior of his town house for a minute, then returned wearing an unbuttoned short-sleeved plaid shirt. He pulled the door partly shut behind him. "Sorry about that. I got company."

"About Mr. Fowler," Mike prompted. "You said you think he's out of town. Why's that?"

The young man reached around the doorjamb and rapped his knuckles against the wooden siding on the exterior of his townhouse. "These walls are like paper. You hear everything. That's why your laying on that bell was drivin' me—well, I could hear it like you were ringing my bell. Look, I haven't heard a sound from next door for days, maybe even weeks."

The uneasy feeling in the pit of Mike's stomach grew. "Got any idea where Fowler might've gone?"

"Sorry." The shiny black hair shook, shimmering in the artificial light. "Don't really know the guy. His car's still downstairs in his parking space, though, so maybe he took a plane somewhere."

Mike handed the youth his card. "You hear him come back, I'd appreciate a call, okay?"

The young man nodded reluctantly, then disappeared back inside. Mike heard a sharp click as the dead bolt was thrown.

By a little after eight o'clock, Mike had finished the microwaved manicotti dinner he'd bought out of the freezer case at Trader Joe's discount gourmet food store, and he was loading his dishes into his dishwasher. His rent-controlled Santa Monica apartment was slowly becoming a slum, as his landlord refused to replace worn-out furnishings or pay for even minor repairs, but the rent was dirt cheap. Mike had no plans to move out anytime soon. He jiggled the dishwasher's dial until the machine clicked in and he heard a rush of water entering its interior.

Mike's trip to Studio City had been upsetting, and he kept playing it over and over in his mind. If the bare-chested youth next door to Clay Fowler was right, the ex-con hadn't been living in his town house there, despite whatever Sonny Zumbrowski believed. And, if Fowler wasn't living there, where was he living? He had to find out.

Mike traversed the worn-out brown hallway carpeting into his second bedroom, which he used as a combination den and home office, picked up the phone, and called the information operator for Salem, Oregon.

A tired-sounding woman answered the number the operator gave him. "Mrs. Morton?" Mike asked. He could hear a commotion in the background, children's voices arguing loudly.

"Yes."

Mike identified himself. "I'm trying to locate your brother, Clayton Fowler, Mrs. Morton, and—"

"He's living down your way," she replied, a little too quickly. "Got himself a place in Studio City."

"That's why I'm calling you, ma'am. Seems your brother's not actually living at the Studio City address these days. I thought you might know where he is."

"Cut that out this minute, Stevie! You're going to hurt her." Jean Morton's voice sounded muffled now, as though she'd placed her hand across the mouthpiece. "Sorry," she said, suddenly clearer. "Look, Detective, I don't have much of anything to do with my brother these days. The man's nothing but trouble, far as I'm concerned, and I've already got more of that than I can handle right here."

"Have you heard from your brother at all lately, ma'am?"

"Not for sev—look, mister, I really don't need this. To be honest with you, even if I knew where Clay was— which I don't—I'd be way too scared to tell the cops."

"Maybe your husband—"

"Yeah, right, Bruce!" Jean Morton forced a mirthless laugh. "My *ex*-husband, you mean. Sure, call Bruce, ask him. Lives in Seattle these days, with a cute little aerobics instructor he picked up at his health club, you know the type. By all means, be my guest, harass good old Bruce for a while."

Mike could hear the obvious bitterness in Jean Morton's voice as she spat out her ex-husband's telephone number. He wrote it down, but didn't really see any point in trying it. Clay Fowler's former brother-in-law hardly sounded like someone the ex-con would confide in if he were trying to snatch his daughter back. "You indicated that your brother called you recently, Mrs. Morton."

"He didn't tell me where he was, all right? All Clay did was chew me out because I had the bad sense to send him a package." Her hand went back over the receiver and her voice was slightly muffled once more. "Stevie, I said stop it *now!* That's it, young man! Straight to your room."

"Hey, Ma, lighten up," a young boy replied.

"Sorry," Jean said into the telephone. "Look, I gotta go, Detective. I got chaos around here . . . as usual."

"Listen, Mrs. Morton," Mike said. "I sympathize, but it's very, very important that we locate your brother quickly. We have some information that he's about to commit another crime, and you might—"

"Is this about Kit—? No, on second thought, I don't want to know, I really don't. Sorry, I honestly can't help you."

Mike's adrenaline began to flow. "You're right, ma'am,

this *is* about Kitty. I think your niece could be in danger if we can't—"

"No! I don't want to hear about it, mister. I got my own problems. Please don't call me again."

Before he could put any more pressure on her, Jean Morton hung up the telephone. Mike sat in his desk chair, staring at the receiver he still held in his hand, until the dial tone switched to the staccato beeping that warned it was off the hook. He put it back in its cradle.

Mike had an instinctive feeling that Jean Morton knew far more than she was willing to tell about Clay Fowler, but he knew it would take work to get it out of her. Perhaps he should call back, explain that her niece's well-being, maybe even the little girl's life, could depend upon her cooperating with the police. If she was any kind of decent person, Jean Morton might have some sympathy left for the little girl her brother had once been accused of battering. But Mike could see that now was obviously not the time to soften her up. He would have to wait until the woman wasn't being distracted by her noisy brood of children.

In the meantime, Mike knew he should alert Jennifer Bennett that her fears about Clayton Fowler might well be correct, warn her that both she and Brinton Academy should take extra care to protect Amy until Fowler could be located.

Mike Jenrud hated admitting he was wrong, particularly to a Hollywood type who was also a television reporter. It really scorched him to have to call the Bennett woman. But he'd always been a straight shooter. He swallowed hard and dialed her phone number.

Chapter

43

It was late as Jennifer stepped out of the Edgewater's elevator at the third floor, her day's mail clutched in her hand. She saw Forrest Hathaway walking down the hall from his apartment toward her. "Hi," she said quietly, giving him a brief wave and an uncertain smile.

As she watched his long-legged gait closing the space between them, she felt a rush of sexual heat course through her body, but it was quickly replaced by her instinctive sense of self-preservation. Despite her physical attraction to this man, she knew he might be extremely dangerous. She studied Forrest's handsome facial features as he moved closer, trying to match them against the blurred ones she'd memorized from bearded Clayton Fowler's old newspaper photo. She found some similarities, but she couldn't be certain. As she stood there immobilized, the elevator door closed behind her with a soft whine and a thud.

"Hi, there," Forrest said, obviously pleased to run into her. "Tell me Maria's feeling better."

"Uh . . . probably. Don't really know." Jennifer felt embarrassed as she remembered the sick-baby-sitter excuse she'd used to put Forrest off the other night; she'd never been a particularly good liar. "How's your movie?" she asked, anxious to change the subject before a blush could underline her deception.

Forrest shrugged dramatically. "The good news is I have plenty of time on my hands. The bad news is the studio hired some hack to rewrite my script."

"Those bastards." Jennifer held her stack of mail stiffly against her chest, like a shield. She hoped that Forrest couldn't tell how nervous she was.

"Well, it ruined my whole day," he said, grinning broadly, "until one of the other writers took me aside and explained that this is just par for the course in Hollywood." He pulled on his clean-shaven chin. "Hey, the bucks were okay and I'm getting a shared writing credit out of it. So, back on the horse, write another screenplay."

"Makes sense." Jennifer wondered whether the writer who'd clued Forrest in was the same one who'd urged him to trade his American car for that red BMW. Assuming there really was another writer at all.

"And you? Any job leads?"

"Yeah, kinda. I'm interviewing for an anchor spot with a new cable network tomorrow morning."

"Here?" Forrest's eyebrows rose and his voice took on a hopeful tone.

"Nope, Santa Barbara. That's about a hundred mi—"

"I've been there," he said, his eyebrows returning to their normal position. "Nice enough, but a little quiet for my taste." His earlier enthusiasm was quickly waning.

"Yeah, well, uh, Amy's alone." Jennifer was feeling guilty about being out of the apartment longer than she'd planned. "I just sneaked out for a minute to get my mail," she said, as much to justify her brief absence to herself as to illuminate Forrest Hathaway. "Don't want her waking up and finding me gone, so . . . Good luck on that new screenplay." She turned awkwardly and hurried down the hall toward her apartment door.

"Good luck to you, for tomorrow," Forrest said to her back, now sounding less than completely sincere.

As Jennifer turned the key in her lock, she glanced back toward the elevator and caught Forrest Hathaway still watching her, a quizzical expression on his face. He quickly averted his gaze and punched the button that summoned the elevator.

When Jennifer peeked into Amy's bedroom, she was greatly relieved to see the child still sleeping soundly. Something, perhaps the chance meeting with her handsome neighbor, had left her feeling more concerned than ever about Amy's safety during the short time she was away.

At her desk, Jennifer rifled through the mail she'd carried up from the lobby—three bills, a postcard from Brinton Academy announcing that the students' school photos would be distributed to them on Friday, a Land's End catalogue, and a letter addressed to Jennifer in her mother's small, precise handwriting. She tossed the entire pile onto the desktop. There was nothing here she felt in the mood to read right now. She wasn't sure which prospect was worse—finding out exactly how much more money she now owed to her various creditors, or reading another bitter list of complaints from her mother. She decided to open all of the envelopes after she returned from Santa Barbara. Surely, if she had a job offer in hand by then, her mood would be considerably lighter.

The telephone rang. Jennifer jumped to answer it quickly, before the bell could wake Amy. She was surprised to hear Detective Mike Jenrud on the line.

"I wanted to warn you about something, Ms. Bennett," the cop told her, skipping the polite preliminaries and coming right to the point. His voice sounded strained, uncomfortable.

"About what?"

"You could be right about that parolee, Clay Fowler," Mike Jenrud said. "I've been doing some checking up on him. He's supposed to be living in Studio City, but—"

"Studio City! That's practically next door." Jennifer bit down hard on her lower lip and focused her eyes on the stack of unopened mail.

"I know, but the fact is, he hasn't been seen around his place there in a while. Could be a lot closer to you than Studio City . . . unless, of course, he's just got himself a new girlfriend he's moved in with, or something."

Jennifer felt her entire body begin to tremble. Until now, she'd sometimes been able to half convince herself that she was being overly paranoid about Clayton Fowler, that her imagination had somehow been running away with her. Now Detective Jenrud's call seemed to confirm her worst fears. "Why don't you know where he is?" she asked, sounding a little breathless. "Can't you just find him and send him back to prison? I mean, if he's on parole and he's not living where he's supposed to be, you—"

"We *are* looking for him," Mike explained. "I'll talk to his parole officer first thing tomorrow morning but, in the meantime, I wanted to warn you to be particularly careful about your daughter's safety. Try not to let her out of your sight, except when she's at school. Tomorrow morning, when you leave her off at Brinton, be sure to tell the teachers what's been going on. Will you do that?"

"I—of course, I'll watch Amy, I always do. But she's not going to school tomorrow anyway, Detective. I plan to take her to Santa Barbara with me. I've got a job interview up there."

"Good move, Ms. Bennett. Just make sure nobody's following you. Understand?"

Jennifer's breath was coming in short spurts now as her fear increased. "Couldn't you send an officer to be with us for the next couple of days, just to make sure Fowler doesn't break in here or something?" she pleaded.

Mike Jenrud sighed audibly. "I wish I could, Ms. Bennett, but we just haven't got the manpower for that kind of thing. Like I explained to you before, the police department doesn't provide bodyguards for private citizens."

Her request had been worth a try, Jennifer figured, but she'd been expecting the turndown; Jenrud's words came as no great surprise. She wondered whether she should tell the cop about her suspicion that Forrest Hathaway might be Clayton Fowler. The words were on the tip of her tongue, but she bit them off. What if she was wrong? She devoutly hoped she was wrong. No, she decided, she would keep Amy well away from Forrest until the police found Fowler. If Forrest turned out to be the man they were seeking, Amy would still be safe from him. And, if Forrest wasn't Fowler, Jennifer wouldn't have ruined a good man's reputation. Perhaps, after the real Clayton Fowler was found and locked away again, she could still explore a future that included Forrest Hathaway.

"This job in Santa Barbara looks pretty promising," Jennifer told Jenrud, wistfully. "Maybe, if Amy and I move out of town, Fowler will lose track of us." Unless Forrest Hathaway was Fowler, of course. Jennifer mentally scolded herself for telling Forrest she was considering a job in Santa Barbara. She had no good excuse for letting herself run off at the mouth that way; she'd simply given in to her strong attraction to the man. How could she have been so stupid?

The detective paused for a long moment, and Jennifer listened to the silence that took over the line. "I'm afraid you can't count on that, Ms. Bennett," he said finally, sounding a bit more compassionate now. "You simply can't afford to get complacent about this potential danger, at least not until we find this SOB. A woman like you, somebody who's lived all her life in public . . . Well, you're not gonna be hard to find, ma'am, no matter where you might move to."

Much as she didn't want to believe Mike Jenrud's gloomy prediction, Jennifer knew in her heart that the cop was right. Supposedly, the adoption agency had never let Clayton Fowler know who adopted his daughter five years ago. Yet the ex-con had managed to locate the child again, even at this temporary apartment complex. Fowler was definitely not an opponent Jennifer could take lightly.

"I appreciate your keeping me posted on what's happening, Detective Jenrud," she said in a small, frightened voice. "I promise we'll be extra careful."

After she hung up the telephone, Jennifer checked once more that the front door of her apartment was double locked. For extra security, she wedged one of the straight-backed kitchen chairs under the doorknob.

Then she went back to Amy's bedroom and stood in the open doorway for a long, long time, watching over her daughter as she slept.

⌢

Clay Fowler drove out of Santa Monica before dawn, his rented car packed with the few things he didn't want to leave behind at the Edgewater. He'd driven back to the apartment hotel from Santa Barbara last night, slept a few hours, and packed up the car. After today, he had no intention of ever returning there again.

His early start was necessary; there were tasks he still needed to perform to prepare the Santa Barbara office building before Jennifer Bennett and his daughter arrived there. He couldn't afford to be less than one hundred percent ready for them.

Now, shortly after sunrise, he was at the building he'd leased—the headquarters of the fictional Family Cable News—dressed in jeans and an old sweatshirt. The charcoal suit and white dress shirt he would wear later, in his guise as FCN chief Terry Snyder, hung in one of the building's second-floor offices. Some of the chores he had ahead of him this morning were dirty ones, and he didn't want to chance soiling his business clothes.

From the trunk of his car, Clay took his most important possession—the small leather suitcase that contained the valuables he'd taken from his safe deposit box. He carried it upstairs to the office cubicle where he'd stashed his clothes and hid it under the desk. He would return this suitcase to his car's trunk later, maybe half an hour before the Bennett woman was due to arrive. That way, collecting it on his way out wouldn't slow him down. For now, however, Clay was too nervous about the possibility of the bag's being stolen to leave it stashed in the trunk any longer than absolutely necessary.

If some petty thief stole his suitcase, Clay knew his plan would be dead. It contained the thousands of dollars in cash he'd taken from his bank accounts, his valuable bearer bonds, two airline tickets from San Francisco to Brazil—purchased in the names of Preston Charles Ames III and his young daughter, Claudia Huffington Ames—and the Ames family's passports. Everything Clay would need to spirit his little Kitty out of the country in a hurry.

Collecting the money and documents had been the clean part, the more enjoyable part, of Clay's scheme. Now it was time to perform the dirty work. He arranged the pair of three-foot-high decorative glazed pottery urns he'd bought at a garden supplies store so that they flanked the building's entryway. Closing the front door against the possiblility of prying eyes while he worked, he filled each urn with about a gallon of the gasoline he'd painstakingly collected in cans from gas stations all over Santa Barbara. The raw stench of petroleum permeated the air as Clay filled the two receptacles. Wrinkling his nose in distaste at the strong odor, he averted his head and tried not to breathe the fumes while he completed his noxious task.

When the two urns were nearly filled to capacity with the liquid fuel, he replaced their matching pottery covers and propped open the front and back doors of the building to air the place out.

Clay still had another seven nearly full cans of gasoline remaining. These, he decided, wouldn't need to be emptied into substitute containers. He planned to keep them hidden away from Jennifer Bennett's view.

Carrying the bright red cans two at a time, Clay placed one just inside the hallway door of each of the downstairs offices. As he did so, he removed the safety cap from each can, then closed each office's door without locking it. By a little after eight o'clock, this crucial part of Clay's plan had been completed.

Clay expected to be on his way out of this place with his daughter before noon. Jennifer Bennett, of course, would never leave.

Clay didn't expect to have any trouble convincing Kitty to come with him. Once the child recognized him as her father—he'd removed the dark dye from his hair, so he now looked more like the man she must remember—she obviously would want to be with him. Still, if she needed a little convincing at first, he was prepared for that, too. He wouldn't hold any temporary reluctance against his daughter in the long run. After all, she was still a kid.

He had everything planned out, coordinated precisely. If the day went as Clay'd figured, on his way out of the building with Kitty, he would quickly knock over each of the seven open gas containers, releasing their contents so that gasoline would spread quickly across the first floor of the building. Then, as father and daughter left through the front door, he would overturn the two gasoline-filled urns that flanked the entryway.

After Kitty was safely buckled inside his car and he had the engine running to ensure a speedy getaway, all Clay had to do was return to the building's entrance and toss a lighted roll of newspaper through the front door. Within seconds—a few short minutes at the most—the entire two-story building would be engulfed in flames, efficiently cremating Jennifer Bennett while Clay and his Kitty drove north to freedom.

What Clay particularly liked about the scheme he'd

masterminded was that it would undoubtedly take the police a good long time before they could trace anything here in Santa Barbara to Clayton Fowler, ex-con and, up until now, model parolee. Chances were, they'd never make that connection. After all, what was there to link him with Jennifer Bennett, a washed-up television personality? By the time the cops connected all the dots—if they ever did— Clay and Kitty would be safely living in South America.

Originally, Clay had tried to come up with a foolproof way to hide the Bennett woman's identity from the cops. Sure, they might eventually find a few charred bone fragments if they sifted through the ashes of the office building, but they would be hard-pressed to identify those fragments as any particular person's without some additional clues left behind here.

Originally, Clay had hoped the authorities would categorize the office building fire as an arson-for-insurance crime, undoubtedly commissioned by the structure's nearly bankrupt owner. If someone died during the fire, the cops would probably figure it was one of Santa Barbara's many homeless, someone who'd been sleeping inside the empty building without permission, a totally expendable type of human being. Chances were they wouldn't work too hard to identify somebody like that.

But there was a hitch in that plan that Clay hadn't been able to work out. Jennifer Bennett had wanted to drive her car up here to Santa Barbara for her expected job interview, and Clay hadn't wanted to risk alerting her to potential danger by arguing the point.

He would have preferred, of course, that she fly up here. He would meet her and Kitty at the airport himself and drive them back here to this building. That way, there would be no car traceable to the Bennett woman parked outside in the small parking lot. But she'd rejected that idea.

Clay had no accomplice in today's adventure, so there

was no one to help him get rid of Jennifer's car, nobody to drive it to some remote spot and ditch it. It would simply have to stay here in the parking lot. That would mean the cops would soon look for the vehicle's owner inside the burning building, increasing the probability that Jennifer Bennett's remains would eventually be found. Clay decided he could live with that risk; he really had no choice.

As soon as the cops knew Jennifer Bennett was dead, of course, Clay figured they would start searching for her daughter, Amy. But their first guess would probably be that little Amy Bennett had perished in the fire along with her mother. If the fire he set was hot enough, it could be a helluva long time before anybody could prove that Amy Bennett's remains were not in the burned-out building.

Clay Fowler had decided he would have to take a few risks to make his plan work, but then he'd always taken risks. Until that black night six years ago in San Luis Obispo, when his bitch of a wife had provoked him just a little bit too much, when Melissa's refusal to obey him had resulted in his losing six good years of his life, he'd always gotten away with his gambles. If it hadn't been for that whore he'd married—

Clay stopped himself in midthought. He would have to keep his temper under control today if he was going to lure Jennifer Bennett upstairs, if he was going to gain her confidence, catch her off guard, and choke her to death quickly, before she knew what hit her. So far, he was proud of his performance. Hadn't he managed to convince her that he was a television executive, that he had a good job just waiting for her, that she should come to Santa Barbara to interview and bring the little girl with her?

If Jennifer Bennett gave him any trouble once she got here, Clay had a couple of alternative plans for her death. One was simply to execute her with the black-market .38 revolver he'd stashed in the drawer of the desk upstairs. But he didn't much care for that plan; the gun might come in handy later, if something went wrong, but firing it around all this gasoline could endanger his own life and that of his daughter. Besides, the sound of a gunshot could draw unwanted attention, and it might frighten his Kitty as well.

The other alternative would make the woman's death take a little longer and submit her to a great deal more pain. Clay had no doubt that he could overpower Jennifer Bennett if he tried—from his apartment window, he'd seen the woman wearing nothing more than a bathing suit, and she was definitely no body builder. If anything, Clay thought, her muscles were probably quickly turning to middle-aged fat. With at most a minimal effort, he was certain he could stun the Bennett woman long enough to lock her inside one of the upstairs offices. Then he simply would let her burn to death in the quickly ensuing fire.

Clay rationalized that whether Jennifer Bennett's death was quick and easy or slow and painful depended entirely upon how much trouble she tried to give him. It really was her decision. It wouldn't bother him a bit to think about her flesh slowly roasting, then charring in the gasoline-fired flames. Whether she was dead or alive when that happened made no difference to him.

After all, Jennifer Bennett was guilty of what, in Clay Fowler's mind, was an unpardonable crime—she had stolen his property, his only child, and tried to claim it as her own. She had taken his Kitty away from him and kept her hidden. Now he wanted to have what was rightfully his back again. Jennifer Bennett would have to pay for her crime.

When he had put the last of the gasoline cans into position, Clay Fowler mounted the stairs to the second floor, where he would clean up and change his clothes. He had less than two hours left to prepare for the most important acting role he would ever have. The touch of stage fright he was feeling right now would only make his senses that much sharper, more alert, when he finally took to the stage.

Chapter

45

Her makeup carefully applied, Jennifer removed the last of her electric rollers from her hair and picked up her hairbrush. Swiftly she ran the brush through her hair with a practiced hand, then flicked her bangs into place with a rattail comb. When she was satisfied with the results, she closed her eyes and held her breath while she pumped a fine mist of hair spray into the air surrounding her head.

There, she thought, checking her reflection in the mirror once more. She should be able to pass for thirty-five, maybe even a year or two younger than that. Not bad, for a woman nearing her fortieth birthday.

She had been doing her own makeup for the TV cameras for the past several years and, since she'd lost the KNLA job, Jennifer had learned to color and style her own hair as well. That effort saved her a minimum of seventy-five dollars each month. She'd even managed to trim her own bangs evenly. The only thing she hadn't been able to master was cutting the sides and back of her own hair. Her one failed attempt had ended in an emergency trip to the hairdresser for repairs.

In another week or two, Jennifer realized as she

inspected her hair in the mirror, she would have to make an appointment at the beauty shop for a haircut; she was getting a little shaggy around the edges. But by then she hoped she would have a new job and a fat paycheck on the horizon.

Her makeup applied and her hair fixed, Jennifer stepped into the A-line skirt of her aqua-and-peach tweed suit, then tucked her peach silk blouse into the waistband and zipped it up. It was barely eight o'clock in the morning, but she was already completely packed for an overnight stay in Santa Barbara, dressed in her business attire, and ready to leave for her job interview. Whether this anchor spot at Family Cable News turned out to be right for her or not, Jennifer didn't want to queer things by showing up late for the interview. Tardiness was completely unprofessional, an unforgivable habit for a journalist.

"Ready to go, Amy?" she called down the hallway of the apartment.

Since finishing her breakfast of raspberry granola with sliced bananas and orange juice half an hour earlier, Amy had been getting dressed and packing her own overnight bag. Her suitcase for the trip was actually the same blue canvas backpack she used for school each day. She was wearing her "good" clothes, an outfit she never wore to school, except on special days. It was a full rust-colored fine-wale corduroy skirt that almost matched the color of her hair, with a soft yellow turtleneck sweater, brown knee-highs, and her best brown leather shoes. So far, her backpack contained only her yellow nightgown, a pair of tan jeans, her sneakers, and her Raggedy Ann doll. "Almost done, Mom," she yelled.

"Don't forget to take your homework, hon," Jennifer called. "Remember, we promised Ms. Butterfield that you'd finish your lessons in arithmetic and reading before you go back to school."

"I won't forget." Amy tossed two slender textbooks and a workbook into the backpack.

Jennifer came into the child's bedroom. "You look real nice, sweetie," she said.

Spinning around to give her mother a better look at her, Amy beamed. She ran her fingers across the velvety texture of her skirt, loving its soft feel. It was like stroking a kitten.

Jennifer bent over the backpack. "Let's see what you've got in here," she said, quickly checking its contents. "You'll need fresh underwear for tomorrow, and a clean T-shirt, too. I'll put your toothbrush and comb in my cosmetic case with my stuff."

"Okay, Mom." Amy was excited about making this unexpected trip with her mother. It wasn't that she didn't want to go to school, but being kept out for two whole days to go on a business trip with her mother made her feel very, very special. None of her classmates had ever gotten to do anything like this, except maybe the time Yvette got to visit her father in Spain for a week. Yvette's dad was a movie director, which Amy thought was almost as glamorous a job as the one her own mom had on TV.

Amy ran over to her dresser and grabbed the missing clothing out of the top two drawers, then stuffed it into the backpack on top of her jeans. "Should I bring my bathing suit, too?" she asked eagerly.

"I don't think we'll have time to go swimming in Santa Barbara," Jennifer said. "If we get back early enough tomorrow, though, we can swim here, okay?"

"Okay." Amy was in no mood to argue today, not when she was being taken along on this special trip. If her mom got this new job, she'd been told, she might even get to go on TV herself . . . real soon. She zipped her backpack shut and hoisted one of its straps over her shoulder. "I'm all ready to go, Mom."

Jennifer checked her watch. It was eight-fifteen. If they left right now, they should make it to Santa Barbara before ten o'clock. That would give them an hour's margin before their scheduled appointment, in case they hit heavy traffic along the way.

She carried her overnight bag to the front door, set it down on the floor, then hung the garment bag with the outfit she'd selected for tomorrow on the doorknob. Jennifer believed in being prepared—if she had to meet with Terry Snyder again tomorrow, or if, heaven forbid, she spilled coffee all over the suit she was wearing, she would have another outfit to change into.

Amy sprinted across the living room carpet and dropped her backpack next to her mother's bag.

"Use the bathroom just one last time, sweetie," Jennifer told the visibly excited little girl, "and then we're on our way."

Chapter

46

Jean Fowler Morton ushered the last of her five children out the door to school, then collapsed into her chair at the head of the kitchen table. She stared down at the black coffee in the ceramic mug with "Number 1 Mom" written on its side— last year's Christmas gift from Ginnie—and imagined herself being sucked into its dark depths. If she drowned in a bottomless black pool, at least she would finally have some peace, she thought, at least she would stop being tormented by all this guilt.

Jean was tired this morning. No, exhausted was more like it. She'd slept very little last night. First, the kids had refused to go to bed until after they'd watched all three episodes of *The Simpsons* that Lynn had videotaped. They'd seen them all before, but that hadn't mattered—the point was probably to get good old Mom to let them all stay up late, to drive me crazy, Jean thought. *Crazier.*

Then, when she finally did crawl between the bed-covers, Jean hadn't been able to stop thinking about Kitty. If only she'd stood up to Bruce all those years ago, if only she'd refused to send Kitty to the adoption agency, then . . . Then what? Then Clay would have taken his daughter with him that day a few weeks ago. Kitty would be living with her father right now. Would that be better for everybody? Or worse? Jean didn't really know. All she knew was that every time her thoughts flashed onto little Kitty's face, she was filled with a guilt so strong, so caustic, that it burned her insides. She knew she should have done something differently, something . . . If only she knew precisely what.

Jean took a sip of her coffee. It had grown cold. She carried it over to the microwave oven, set the mug inside, and heated the coffee for a minute and fifteen seconds. When the oven's timer beeped, she removed her now-steaming beverage and went back to sit at the table.

Maybe she should have talked to that cop who called last night after all. Maybe she should have told him everything she knew. But what *did* she know, really? The cop—what was his name? Jenson, Jenner, Johnson, something like that—that cop had wanted Jean to tell him where Clay was now, and she honestly had no idea. Still, maybe she should have told him all about that last phone call she'd received from Clay. And Jean did know one thing for certain—she knew that Clay had been looking for Kitty, looking hard, that he'd bragged about how he'd already managed to find his little daughter. Maybe Jean should have told the cop that . . . if it would help keep little Kitty safe.

Jean drained her coffee mug and carried it over to the kitchen sink. As she ran water into the cup to rinse it out, she peered out the window and saw that the sky was beginning to clear in the west, a sign that the sun might break through the persistent cloud cover later today. Maybe a nice, warm, sunny day would make her feel better, Jean thought. Maybe she should try to get outdoors today, breathe a little fresh air, clear her head before the children came home from school. She placed her clean mug upside down on the drainboard to dry and wiped her damp hands on the front of her old pink terry-cloth bathrobe.

The phone rang. Startled, Jean glanced up at the wall clock. It was eight forty-three. Her neighbor, Connie Wilynski, never called her before nine-thirty, so that both women would have time for their morning showers after their children went off to school. Jean's other friends rarely called her at all anymore. It wouldn't be any of her children's friends calling, either; they were all in school at this hour.

Could it be Clay? Jean's slippered feet froze to the kitchen floor. Listening to the second and third rings, she was tempted just to stand there, letting the phone ring until whoever was calling hung up. She absolutely did not want to talk to her brother, not ever again.

But, in the end, Jean didn't have the courage to ignore the telephone's sharp summons. What if something had happened to Ginnie or Stevie or one of the others? What if the children's school was trying to reach her and she didn't even answer the phone? She wasn't *that* bad a mother. Not yet, anyway.

"Hello," Jean said into the receiver, in a timid voice.

"Mrs. Morton," a man said. Jean recognized his voice before he identified himself. "This is Detective Jenrud calling again. We spoke last night."

"Yes?" Jean felt her the tension in her shoulders case slightly. At least it wasn't Clay calling.

"I got to thinking about our conversation last night and I thought I'd call back when your children might be in school, when we could have a little more privacy."

"Yes," Jean said, her mind racing. "The kids are in school now."

"Mrs. Morton," Jenrud said, "I want to be perfectly straight with you. The truth is, I think your young niece is in grave danger, not to mention the woman who adopted her—"

"From Clay, you mean." Maybe this phone call was fated, Jean thought. Maybe this Detective Jenrud had somehow been reading her thoughts.

"That's right, the danger comes from your brother, Clayton Fowler." Jenrud paused a moment, then suggested, "You know all about this, don't you, Mrs. Morton?"

Jean's chin began to quiver. "Not all. No—not *all* about it." He *could* read her mind. Somehow, he knew how guilty she felt about Kitty.

"Why don't you tell what you *do* know?"

The cop's voice was more gentle now, persuasive, and Jean felt herself responding to it despite her gut-wrenching fear. "I'm so afraid, Detective," she told him truthfully. "I'm embarrassed to admit it, but I'm really, truly afraid of my own brother. He . . . Clay beat me up once already over Kitty, broke my wrist. It was in a cast until just recently, still pains me some, and . . . Well, I don't know what he'll do if he finds out I talked to you. I've got five kids, mister, *five*. I've got to think about them, too, not just Kitty."

"Mrs. Morton, if I'm right about what your brother's been planning, and if we can catch him in time, he won't be bothering you or your children for a long, long while. He'll be back in prison. Please, think about your niece for now, tell me what I need to know to protect her."

Jean's mind raced back and forth between her fear of Clay and her desire to relieve her guilt. Could she ever forgive herself if Clay found Kitty and hurt her? On the other hand, what if he came back here, what if he hurt one of her own children?

"Mrs. Morton, please, you're the only one who can help this little girl."

Jean let out a long sigh. Her guilt over Kitty won her mental duel and she began to talk. She told Detective Jenrud all about the newspaper feature she'd saved, the one picturing Jennifer Bennett with baby Kitty on her lap. She told him about Clay's visit to Salem weeks ago, and she confessed that she'd given her brother the newspaper clipping to make him go away, to make him leave her and her children alone. Yes, she said, she'd known Clay would try to find his daughter, try to get her back again. Still, she didn't know where he was now.

"You told me last night that your brother had phoned you recently, Mrs. Morton," the policeman said. "When exactly did you hear from him?"

Jean estimated the date of Clay's last phone call as best she could. "I don't know where he was calling from, though, Detective," she said, "really I don't. But I . . . Well, Clay was bragging about something, really blowing his own horn. I guess I'd better tell you about it."

"What did he say?"

"That he'd found Kitty. He said he was watching her, right then, while he was talking to me on the telephone."

"That's good, Mrs. Morton, you're doing real good here. Now, what did he tell you about what he could see?"

"What do you mean?"

"I mean, did he say he could see Kitty on the school playground, for instance, or maybe she was eating at McDonald's, something like that? Exactly what did your brother tell you?"

"Oh, right, I see. Let me think a minute." Jean entwined her fingers in the telephone's coiled cord as she tried to remember the details of Clay's call. "Yeah, now I remember," she said. "He said Kitty had gotten real tall, and that she was a real good little swimmer. Sounded proud of her, like *he* was the one responsible for teaching her how to swim. I remember thinking it was just more of Clay's self-importance talking. That's nothing new with him. You s'pose maybe they were at the beach?"

"Could be, Mrs. Morton, something like that."

"No, wait! It couldn't be the beach. I remember now. He said something about seeing Kitty dive, a swan dive. You don't go diving at the beach, do you?"

"Not around here, you don't, ma'am."

"So it must have been at some swimming pool." Jean untangled her fingers from the cord. "I'm afraid that's all I can remember, Detective, honest. I—I hope you find Kitty, that she's all right, really I do." Jean's voice dropped to little more than a whisper. "I never meant any harm to come to that little girl, really I didn't." A tear crept from behind her eyelashes.

"I believe you, Mrs. Morton." Detective Jenrud thanked Jean for her help and left a phone number where she could call him, day or night, if she remembered anything else Clay had told her. Anything at all.

After she hung up the phone, Jean Morton crept back to her chair at the kitchen table and sat down again. She leaned forward, propped her elbows on the table, and cradled her head in her hands. In a few seconds, her entire body began to shake with sobs of guilt and regret and bone-deep sadness.

She wept for her damaged young niece and she wept for her battered self as well.

Sitting at his desk in the police station, Mike Jenrud hung up the telephone and stared at it while his thoughts raced wildly. So Clayton Fowler claimed he'd been watching the Bennett girl dive at a swimming pool, supposedly at the same time he was jawboning with his sister on long distance. The ex-con could have been blowing hot air, of course. Mike knew that Fowler was known for his big ego, as well as his acting ability. But he had to take Fowler's statement to his sister seriously, and that gave him a sick feeling in the pit of his stomach.

Mike thought about how Clay might have been able to spy on the kid while she swam. This area didn't have all that many public pools that allowed children. Most of the public pools were part of adults-only health clubs. He knew there was one at the West Los Angeles YMCA that allowed kids to swim during certain specified hours; there were probably a few others like it in the area as well. But a fully-clothed man wouldn't be allowed into the pool area of one of those places to watch the kids swimming, not without first proving he was one of the kids' parents or that he had some other legitimate reason to be there.

Mike seriously doubted that Clay Fowler would risk making himself that conspicuous. From what he'd heard about the ex-con, he was not a stupid man. Mike's guess was that Fowler hadn't been hanging around any public swimming pool.

Where else could a kid go to swim? Mike knew that most either went to Santa Monica Beach when the water was warm enough, or they had access to private swimming pools in their own apartment or condo complexes.

He tried to remember where Jennifer Bennett had said she was living. Opening his file on her case, Mike read from the first report he'd taken from the woman and quickly recognized her address as that of the Edgewater Apartment Hotel, that big temporary executive housing complex over on Centinela Avenue.

Of course, that was it. He smiled mirthlessly to himself as a disconcerting suspicion took hold in his mind. What if Clay Fowler had rented an apartment for himself at the Edgewater? That would allow the wife murderer to watch the little girl in the swimming pool right there, or to spy on her anywhere else on the complex's grounds, virtually any time he wanted to. Without attracting much, if any, attention.

As he developed his theory, a department clerk tossed a stack of mail into Mike's in box. He ignored it and grabbed for the telephone. If he hurried, he might still be able to catch Jennifer Bennett before she left for that Santa Barbara job interview she'd mentioned last night. He dialed her phone number and listened as it rang four times before her answering machine picked up.

Mike left a brief message, asking Jennifer to call him as soon as possible, and adding that he had an extremely important piece of information to pass on to her. Yet if the Bennett woman was already on her way out of town, Mike knew he wasn't likely to hear from her today, not unless she happened to check her calls long distance.

Feeling disappointed, Mike reached for his mail and began to sort through it. The third envelope in the stack bore a Sacramento return address. He ripped it open and dumped its contents out on his desk. Just what he'd been waiting for—Clayton Fowler's mug shots had finally arrived. Mike examined them closely. There he was—Fowler, that mean son of a bitch—in focus, clean-shaven, and looking completely unrepentent. Right now, Mike wanted nothing more than to see this man put back where he belonged—in state prison, where he could no longer torment either his sister or his daughter.

Clayton Fowler had broken his parole by not living where he was supposed to, Mike reassured himself as he slid his arms into the sleeves of his blue plaid suit jacket. That little slip had made the bastard eligible for a spot of police interrogation, at a minimum, and for something far more serious if he actually threatened Jennifer Bennett and her daughter in any way.

Mike decided he could justify spending a couple of tax-payer-financed hours of his time poking around the Edgewater Apartment Hotel, trying to locate Fowler and determining exactly what he was up to. Even if he couldn't justify the time, Mike planned to go there anyway. If anything happened to Amy Bennett or her mother because he hadn't taken Jennifer Bennett's complaint seriously enough, he'd never be able to live with himself.

Mike slipped the mug shots into the inside pocket of his jacket and slid his chair back into place. As he passed the big scheduling board mounted behind the clerk's desk, he chalked himself out until eleven o'clock, then headed toward the parking lot at double speed.

Chapter

48

At KXXT-TV's studios in Santa Barbara, news director Bob Harris was viewing his eleventh audition tape of the morning, searching for someone to fill the soon-to-be-vacant anchorwoman's spot. The dark-haired young woman on this particular tape continually grimaced when she should have smiled, and she'd already mispronounced the name of the Secretary General of the United Nations twice. And this was on her audition tape, Harris thought, rolling his eyes skyward, supposedly a compilation of her very best work. Shuddering as he imagined what the brunette's more typical on-camera performance must be like, he stopped the tape just as his secretary, Gwen, marched into his office carrying a basket of spring flowers.

"Looks like you got yourself a new girlfriend, Bob," she teased.

"Not if my wife finds out, I haven't," Harris quipped in return. He ejected the audition tape and put it on top of the reject pile. "What've you got there?"

"Somebody sent these for you," Gwen told her boss, pushing aside a stack of papers on his desk to make room for the basket of flowers. She plucked off the small white florist's card attached to the flowers and handed it to him. Gwen had never been the least bit shy about her inborn nosiness; she made no move to leave the office before Bob had opened the card and read it, preferably out loud.

He quickly obliged her. "This is really weird," he said, pulling on his chin. "Look what this card says, Gwen: 'Thanks for recommending me to Family Cable News. If I get the job, I'll buy you dinner.' It's signed by somebody named Jennifer Bennett. I don't know any Jennifer Bennett, do I?"

"Jennifer Bennett, Jennifer Bennett," Gwen repeated. "Name sounds familiar. Wait a minute, I think I know who she is. Someone named Jennifer Bennett has called you half a dozen times, about her audition tape and résumé. . . . I guess she must be one of the applicants for Christie's job. I'm certain I gave you her messages. You don't remember her?"

"Oh, that one. Right." Harris searched through the mass of papers littering his desktop until he found the master list he'd made of everyone who'd applied for the job opening. Several names were already crossed out as hopelessly unqualified for the position, a few others because their salary demands were too high for KXXT's budget. About fourteen still remained in the running. But Jennifer Bennett's name was nowhere on the list. "Look at this, Gwen." He held up the sheet of paper. "I never called this woman back because we never got any tape from her. And now she claims I recommended her for a job somewhere I never even heard of. What is this?"

Gwen perched on the corner of the desk. "Got me," she said. "Do you suppose she could have you mixed up with somebody else? Either that, or maybe she's just not playing with a full deck."

"Nice flowers, though." Bob Harris leaned over and sniffed them. "Guess I owe her a thank-you for them, at least. Still got her phone number around somewhere?"

Gwen went back to her own desk and searched until she found the telephone number Jennifer Bennett had left several times with the station receptionist. "Here you go," she said when she returned, handing her boss the small slip of yellow paper on which she'd printed the Santa Monica telephone number.

The news director reached for his phone and dialed it. On the fourth ring, a machine answered. The voice of a woman identifying herself as Jennifer Bennett informed him that she was either out temporarily or could not come to the phone at this time, and asked him to leave a message. Harris felt a wave of relief that he wouldn't have to speak directly with this odd woman who'd sent him a bouquet of flowers but not her audition tape.

"Ms. Bennett," he said to Jennifer's machine, "this is Bob Harris calling, from KXXT in Santa Barbara. Listen, thanks very much for those flowers you sent, but . . . Well, listen, I think there's some kind of mistake here. Truth is, I never received either your tape or your résumé for the job we've got open here at the station, and I didn't recommend you to anybody at this Family Cable News, either. I've never even heard of Family Cable News. Anyway, I hope you get the job there, if it's what you want, but don't worry about owing me any dinner. I'm really not the man who recommended you. Good luck with your job hunt, and, uh, thanks again for the flowers."

As soon as he hung up, Bob Harris slid another audition tape into the VCR and hit the play button on the remote control. Within a few short minutes, as he screened his remaining job candidates, Jennifer Bennett and her flowers had completely vanished from his thoughts.

It was slightly before ten o'clock when Jennifer drove past the sign notifying her that she was entering the Santa Barbara city limits. Traffic on Highway 1 had been light and she'd made good time driving from Santa Monica along the Malibu coastline.

"We've got over an hour to kill before our appointment at Family Cable News," she told Amy. "What would you like to do?"

"I gotta go to the bathroom," the child said, straining against her seat belt. "Can we stop somewhere, real quick?"

"Sure," Jennifer said, responding to the urgency in her daughter's voice. She could do with a rest stop herself. "How about we find a coffee shop? We can both use the bathroom and then sit and relax for a little while."

Jennifer took a left-hand exit off the highway and pushed the speed limit as the road curved toward the beach. When she found a hotel that advertised an open coffee shop, she pulled the station wagon into its parking lot, directly across the street from the seashore.

"Here we go, toots," she said to Amy, shutting off the engine. "This place looks good enough to me."

"Come on, Mom, hurry up," Amy said as she unbuckled her seat belt, threw open her door, and slid off her seat onto the blacktopped parking lot. "I really gotta go bad!" She sprinted toward the door of the coffee shop as her mother locked up the car and hurried after her.

"Nope," said Kent Horowitz, the daytime desk manager of the Edgewater Apartment Hotel, after checking his registration book. "Nobody here named Fowler."

"Fowler probably wouldn't be registered under his real name," Detective Mike Jenrud explained. He took Clayton Fowler's mug shots out of his pocket and held them up for Horowitz to see. "This is him. Take a real good look. He's a big man, six foot one, one ninety." When the desk manager didn't reply immediately, Mike coaxed him further. "Maybe try imagining this guy here with darker hair or possibly a mustache or a beard."

Horowitz picked up the photographs and look at them for a long time, bringing them closer to his eyes, then holding them farther away again. "Could be him," he said, looking up at Mike and then dropping his eyes to the pictures once more. "Looks something like the fellow who was renting three forty-one, 'cept that guy's hair was darker, like you said."

"*Was* renting?" Mike asked. His hopes of intercepting Clayton Fowler here at the Edgewater Apartment Hotel began to sink fast.

"Checked out early this morning. Night desk manager left me a note about it when he went off duty."

"What time would that have been?"

"When the night man's shift ended?"

"Right."

"He goes off at six o'clock."

"Isn't that a little strange, somebody moving out before dawn that way?"

"At a regular apartment complex it would be, I guess," Horowitz said, "but the Edgewater's really more like a hotel. Happens a lot here. You know, somebody's gotta make an early flight out of LAX, something like that. It's not like our tenants are taking furniture with them or anything. And three forty-one's bill was paid up in advance, so there wouldn't be any problem with his leaving . . . whenever."

"This guy who had apartment three forty-one, what was his name?"

Horowitz's eyes dropped to his register. "Carl Farmer," he read.

Carl Farmer. CF. Clay Fowler. Mike began to feel certain he'd found his man. Or more accurately, that he'd narrowly missed his man. He knew it was common for people to use their real initials when they chose an alias. It made their phony name easier to remember, and the identical initials covered them if they had monogrammed luggage or clothing among their belongings. "I'd like to take a look at the apartment this Farmer guy vacated," he told the desk man.

"Sure thing." Horowitz jangled the ring of keys hooked to his belt and emerged from behind the registration counter.

The two men rode the elevator to the third floor. Mike felt his luck changing for the better when Horowitz opened the apartment and he saw that the maids had not yet cleaned the place.

Apartment 341 was furnished in an anonymous hotel-room style and the closets were empty of clothes, but the refrigerator still contained plenty of food, indicating to Mike that Farmer/Fowler either was generally wasteful or that the man was not moving anyplace nearby. But what caught the detective's eye most, giving him fresh hope, was that the wastebaskets in the apartment were still filled with trash.

"I'd like a few minutes to look around, see if I can get a bead on where this guy might've gone," he told the manager.

"Sure thing. Just lock up afterward, will ya? Press that little button on the inside of the doorknob, that'll do it. I'd better get back down to the desk, in case anybody's looking for me."

Mike spent the next half hour sorting through the contents of the wastebaskets—empty beer bottles, grocery receipts, discarded plastic bags from the Lucky Market on Lincoln Boulevard, an empty jar of Skippy peanut butter, a couple of pieces of junk mail. All of the discarded mail was addressed to Occupant or Resident, not to either Farmer or Fowler. If Clay Fowler had received any mail addressed to him here, he'd either have taken it all with him or thrown it out earlier.

The bathroom wastebasket held a soiled and ripped pea green T-shirt, a couple of cardboard collar supports, the kind dry cleaners use to keep freshly laundered shirts neat, a bent wire coat hanger, and an empty bottle of Dye-Out. Mike read the label on the Dye-Out bottle and learned that the product was designed to remove semipermanent hair coloring. If Clay Fowler had tinted his hair dark, it looked like he'd recently attempted to bring it back to its natural lighter color, or else he'd stripped out the old color, then added another new one.

At the very bottom of the wastebasket were two scrunched-up scraps of notepaper. Mike smoothed them out on the fake marble top of the vanity. The first was written in the form of a list and included the words, "Cash, tickets, car, gas, tools." Each item was neatly checked off in blue ink.

Tickets. Assuming this had been Fowler's apartment, Mike concluded, he'd either been planning to attend a show for which tickets had to be picked up in advance, or he was planning to take a trip somewhere—apparently not alone. The policeman's anxiety increased. If the ex-con planned to take that trip with Amy Bennett, Jennifer and her daughter might be in real danger right now.

The second note was simply a phone number in the 805 area code, written in the same blue ink. Mike reached for the bedside telephone. It still had a dial tone; apparently Carl Farmer hadn't bothered notifying the phone company that he was vacating the apartment. Mike dialed the number on the slip of paper and waited while it rang four times.

A machine answered and a male voice announced, "You have reached the offices of Family Cable News." The voice continued with the standard request that callers leave a message after the tone. Mike hung up without doing so.

Family Cable News. An 805 area code, the area code that encompassed Santa Barbara. With a chill, Mike recalled Jennifer Bennett's telling him she was heading for Santa Barbara this morning to interview for a job. Could her interview be with this Family Cable News? Mike had never heard of it, but that didn't count for much. He was hardly a television news buff, except, of course, when reporters got their hooks into some phony story about the police department. That sort of thing really pissed him off. Then he watched the tube religiously, taking mental notes on all the news media's screwups.

He picked up the phone again and dialed Jennifer

Bennett's number once more. When he got her machine a second time, he broke the connection, then dialed the Edgewater manager's number.

"I need your help up here a minute, Mr. Horowitz," he requested, when the manager answered.

In less than three minutes, Kent Horowitz was back on the third floor. "What can I do for you, Detective?" A slim young man with nicotine-stained fingers, he was obviously uneasy about being asked to do any additional favors for the police.

Mike explained that he needed access to Jennifer Bennett's apartment.

"Hey, I don't know—" the manager said, shaking his head. "I mean, it's one thing to let you see an apartment the tenant's already checked out of, but I'm supposed to see a warrant before I let you into one that's occupied."

Mike squared his shoulders and stared directly at the younger man. "I can get a warrant," he said, "but that'll take me an hour or two." He gave Horowitz a brief summary of the complaint Jennifer Bennett had filed with the police. "The woman's worried about her daughter being kidnapped by this man—he's an ex-con with a history of violence—and time could be extremely critical right now," he said. "All I want to look for in Ms. Bennett's apartment is clues to where she and her little girl went this morning. If it's to this Family Cable News outfit, I can try to call up to Santa Barbara and request police protection for her. But, if you make me go get a warrant first, Mr. Horowitz, it might be too late."

Horowitz stared at his shoes for a long moment. "All right," he said, finally, his shoulders slumping. "But I'm going in there with you and you're not to remove anything unless you get a warrant first, agreed? This could cost me my job."

Mike nodded, then followed the manager down the hall

and around a corner to Jennifer's apartment. Horowitz knocked loudly; when his effort drew no response, he used his master key to open the door. Mike barged past the slimmer man into the apartment and began to search it quickly and efficiently.

The phone machine was blinking the number three. Mike hit the play button and listened. The first message was his own. The second was an odd one from some TV news director in Santa Barbara. What caught the cop's attention, in addition to the city, was the mention of Family Cable News. From what he could figure out, this TV guy claimed he had never recommended Jennifer Bennett to any Family Cable News. Said he'd never even heard of the outfit, in fact. But it was obvious that Ms. Bennett thought this news director had done her a big favor; she'd even sent flowers to thank the guy. The third message was from a woman at Channel Three here in L.A., calling to schedule an appointment for Ms. Bennett to interview for a producer's job there. Mike left all three messages on the tape.

He stormed through the apartment, looking for any clue to exactly where Jennifer Bennett was headed this morning. The papers lying on top of the desk in the living room looked promising. Flipping open her desk calendar to the current month, Mike found the confirmation he was looking for. Penciled in under today's date were the words, "FCN, SB, 11 A.M. Homework for A."

The detective glanced at his watch. It was already ten minutes before eleven. He tried to fit all the pieces together in his mind. Clayton Fowler somehow knew that Jennifer Bennett would be interviewing at Family Cable News. The fact that Fowler had checked out of the Edgewater Apartment Hotel indicated that his surveillance of the Bennetts was quickly coming to an end. He probably intended to kidnap Amy Bennett either as she and her mother arrived at the FCN interview, Mike figured, or else on their way out of the building. And if Fowler intended to grab the child in such a public fashion, what plans might he have for the mother?

Mike reached for the telephone.

"Hey, I don't think you ought to use that," Horowitz protested.

The detective silenced him with a look, then dialed information for the 805 area code and requested the number of the Santa Barbara Police Department.

Chapter

51

The address Terry Snyder had given Jennifer was just east of the
freeway, a few blocks north of downtown. She had little trouble finding the compact beige two-story office building—the street number was prominently displayed in large black letters above the entrance. Yet as she drove into the parking lot, she couldn't help feeling that something seemed odd here.

Other than the oversized street number, there was nothing on the outside of this building to identify it as the headquarters of Family Cable News. Perhaps, Jennifer told herself, that information was posted somewhere inside the building, probably on a tenant roster in the foyer. After all, Snyder had said his business was just getting started; this building might not even be its permanent headquarters.

What seemed more strange to her was the fact that there was only one car parked here in the lot, a shiny new burgundy Cadillac that had been backed into a space close to the street. Jennifer glanced at the clock on her dashboard. It was two minutes before eleven o'clock. Could she have gotten the appointment time wrong? Or maybe the street number? If her information was correct, where was everybody?

After parking her station wagon next to the Cadillac and shutting off her engine, Jennifer checked her makeup one last time in the rearview mirror. She looked as good now as she was ever going to, she decided; practically, she knew her appearance would simply have to do the way it was. "I think this is the right place, Amy," she said, unbuckling her seat belt and reaching behind her to grab her shoulder-strap purse off the station wagon's rear seat.

Jennifer felt Amy's hand take hold of hers as they crossed the small parking lot toward the building entrance. "How long're we gonna be here, Mom?" the child asked.

"I don't know, hon. Maybe an hour, maybe longer. Mr. Snyder said you could visit with his secretary while he and I talk business. We'll go get some lunch after that." Jennifer wondered where the secretary's car was parked. It certainly couldn't be that Cadillac, not unless the salaries here were unbelievably generous. More likely, the secretary rode the bus to work.

When she reached the double glass doors at the entrance to the building, Jennifer noticed a neatly lettered card that read "Family Cable News, Room 205" taped to the inside of the left-hand door. Feeling reassured that she was in the right place after all, she pulled open the door to let Amy enter first, then followed her inside.

"Hello there. Ms. Bennett, isn't it?"

Startled by the unexpected voice, Jennifer turned to see a tall, sandy-haired man approaching from her left, just inside the hallway. "Uh, right, Jennifer Bennett. Mr. Snyder?" The man was dressed in an impeccably tailored charcoal pinstripe suit with a burgundy tie and a crisp white shirt.

"Call me Terry, please." The man thrust out his hand. "We're not very well organized around here yet, so I thought I'd better come downstairs and meet you at the door."

The glass door swung shut behind them and Amy darted around in back of her mother, shyly hanging onto the shoulder strap of her purse. As Jennifer shook her host's hand, a chemical odor reached her nostrils; she wrinkled her nose involuntarily. The odor was a little like fresh gasoline. Self-consciously, she wondered whether she'd gotten some gas on her shoes or clothes when she'd filled her car's tank on her way here from the beachside coffee shop. "That was nice of you," she said, hoping that the man didn't notice the odd scent she feared she might now be wearing.

"And this must be Amy." He bent down and smiled broadly at the little girl.

"That's right," Jennifer said. The child held back, half hiding behind her mother. "Say hello, Amy."

Amy peered around her mother, her freckled face solemn. "Hello."

"Well," the man said, his smile freezing in place, "follow me upstairs to my humble office, ladies, and we'll get started, and get to know each other better."

Jennifer and Amy followed the sandy-haired man down the hall toward a carpeted staircase at the center of the building.

"Aren't there any other tenants here?" Jennifer asked, looking around as they walked further inside. None of the main floor offices they were passing had names on their doors.

"Nope," he told her. "FCN's leased this entire building. Don't worry. We won't have any trouble filling it, once we're up and running. The studios will be built here on the first floor, and we'll use the second for offices."

"I see," Jennifer said. Hadn't Snyder indicated that FCN would be at least semioperational, that reporters would be coming to work here, in just a few more weeks? If he could accomplish that with this place, she thought, the man could perform miracles.

As they entered the stairwell, the sharp chemical odor grew stronger. "Mom," Amy whispered. "Something stinks in here."

Jennifer shot the child a warning glance and quickly placed a finger across her lips. But the man who called himself Terry Snyder turned and said, "Sorry about that smell, ladies. Gas truck spilled half its load out back in the alley this morning. Stuff really permeates."

Trying not to let the stench bother them, the mother and daughter followed as their host trudged up the stairs ahead of them. When he reached the second floor, he led the way toward the rear of the building, stopping before a door with the number 205 stenciled on it. When Jennifer and Amy had caught up with him, he pushed open the door and stood aside to let them enter the room ahead of him.

Jennifer looked around quickly. This office was surprisingly spartan, she thought. A large oak desk with a chair behind it, two mismatched chairs opposite the desk. No books, no papers, no computer. Only a telephone and an answering machine on the far corner of the desktop.

"Where is your secretary, Mr. Snyder?" she asked, the crease between her eyebrows deepening. "I—I thought you said she would look after Amy while—"

"Oh, Mary called in sick today." He smiled again. This time his expression seemed more forced. He crossed the floor and pushed open a door at the side, revealing a smaller, adjoining office. "Amy can play here in Mary's office while we talk, though," he said. "She left some children's books and toys in there."

Jennifer and Amy approached the open doorway. The little girl peered reluctantly around the doorjamb into the second room, clinging all the while to her mother's hand. Jennifer looked past Amy and spotted nothing in the room but a small metal desk with a matching chair in the far corner. On the desktop were a small stack of children's books, a huge brown teddy bear, and an elaborate Victorian doll house. No typewriter, no telephone, no appointment book or Rolodex, no paper or pen. If this was Terry Snyder's secretary's office, Jennifer thought, how on earth did the woman manage to do any work?

"I wanna stay here with my mom," Amy announced.

The tall man stiffened. "That's simply not possible," he said. "Your mother and I have important business to discuss, young lady. Private business. There'll be plenty for you to do in here." There was no warmth in his voice now.

Amy's chin jutted upward. She tightened her grip on her mother's hand and stayed precisely where she was.

Her daughter's refusal to cooperate fed fuel to Jennifer's growing apprehension about this place and about Terry Snyder. Something simply was not right here; all her senses told her so. Despite her earlier hopes, her blind optimism that she would have a firm job offer by the end of today, she realized now that she would never work for Family Cable News. "I'm sorry, Mr. Snyder," she said, backing toward the hallway and pulling Amy along with her, "but I'm afraid this just isn't going to work out for us. I—I just . . . Good luck with FCN, but—"

His expression grim, the tall man's left hand darted toward her. He grabbed Jennifer's arm and spun her around until she faced him. Her hand reflexively dropped Amy's and her jaw fell open in astonishment. "Let go of me!" she said angrily. But before Jennifer could pull away from the big man's grip, his right hand arced around and caught her hard across the side of the face. She staggered backward, stunned.

"Bitch!" the man yelled, the purple veins in his temples throbbing. "You fucking bitch! You're all alike."

Jennifer's hip landed hard against the sharp edge of the desk as she raised her hands instinctively to protect her face. But the man was too fast for her. He yanked her wrist away and swung a second time. She swiveled her head in a futile attempt to protect her face; this time, his fist connected with the side of her head. Jennifer toppled to the floor, her ear ringing. As she fell, her purse flew off her shoulder and skidded across the carpet.

Staring in horror at the scene unfolding before her, Amy froze for an instant and watched as the big man's fists landed a sharp blow against her mother's head. From somewhere deep inside her, a terrifying memory swam to the surface. She saw herself vividly, as a baby, standing tiny and helpless, and watching mutely as her father hit Mommy, again and again and again . . . until Mommy lay deathly still on the floor. There was blood all over everything. There was blood all over her. She saw herself running away and hiding so that Daddy wouldn't find her, so that he wouldn't hit her like he hit Mommy. She saw herself burrowing into Mommy's closet, amongst her clothes and shoes, not daring to make the slightest sound.

Amy forced herself back to the present and remembered what she'd been taught. She wasn't a baby anymore. She wasn't tiny and helpless now. She was a big girl. Mommy had told her so. Her new Mommy. This Mommy had taught her what to do if a bad man ever tried to hurt her. What to do if Daddy ever came back to get her.

Yell as loud as you can. "Stop!" Amy shrieked at the top of her lungs. "Stop that!"

Call 9-1-1. The little girl darted across the floor and grabbed the telephone off the desk. Lifting the receiver, she punched in the numbers. "Daddy's hitting Mommy!" she shouted into it when the operator had answered. "Help! Help! Daddy's hitting Mommy! He—"

The big man spun around, enraged, as he saw what the child was doing. "You fucking little traitor!" he yelled, grabbing the telephone out of Amy's hand. He ripped the cord out of the wall, then swatted the little girl away as if she were nothing more than a pesky fly. She stumbled backward, tripped, and fell to the floor.

As Jennifer struggled to her knees and groggily reached a hand out for her purse, she realized with horror exactly who this maniac was. Amy's father. This had to be Clayton Fowler—the vicious man who'd murdered Amy's mother. He had tricked her into coming here, into bringing Amy with her. Pain knifed through her head as she lunged toward the spot where her bag had fallen. Fowler obviously meant to kill her, and he meant to take Amy. She had to stop him. If only she could get that can of mace from her purse—if only—

But as Jennifer's fingers closed around the shoulder bag's leather strap, Clay Fowler kicked it away like a football. The purse's contents scattered across the carpet as he swung his foot again, this time aiming for Jennifer's ribs. She rolled away just as the blow landed against her side, slightly mitigating its strength; still, she shrieked and her vision blurred as pain coursed through her body.

In the corner by the desk, Amy pushed herself to her feet. She screamed when she saw Daddy kick her mother, flying toward him as he stood with his leg arced backward in preparation for another kick. The little girl leapt as high into the air as she could, landing on his back and clinging on for dear life. Her small feet in their hard leather shoes kicked against the backs of his thick thighs. *This can't happen again!* she thought, desperately. She had to save Mommy. She couldn't let Daddy kill Mommy. Not this time.

While Amy's motions momentarily distracted Fowler, Jennifer pushed herself back onto her hands and knees. She forced a deep breath past the pain that ripped through her side. She couldn't give up. She just couldn't. She had to get that mace.

Amy's fingers clung to the man's jacket as he spun around once, then again, trying to fling her off him.

Finally, he stopped abruptly and reached one of his long arms around his side. He grabbed one of the child's ankles as she kicked at him.

Amy tried to wrench her foot free, but the man's grip was too strong. He yanked her leg hard and she lost her hold on his coat. She fell, arms in front of her, to the floor.

Clay Fowler reached down and grabbed one of the little girl's arms, yanking her abruptly upward. His eyes blazed with rage and Amy could smell his breath, hot and rank, as he pressed his face close to hers. "You shouldn't have done that, you little bitch," he said. His voice was calm now, and even more terrifying than when he'd yelled at her. "You're just like your mother." With that, he flung her against the wall. Amy's head hit sharply. Stunned, she slumped to the floor. Her eyes rolled back into their sockets; she could no longer see what was happening around her.

By the time Clay Fowler turned his attention back to Jennifer, her fingers were closing around a small bright yellow metal canister. He kicked out at her hand, but she jerked it away just in time to avoid the blow.

"Thief!" he yelled, bending down to grab her. "Fucking thief!"

As he reached for her, Jennifer rolled onto her back and took quick aim. She waited an instant, choosing the precise moment when Fowler's face was directed straight at her. Then she pressed down hard on the metal lever, releasing a stream of mace directly into his pale blue eyes.

"Aaaaahh!" As Clay Fowler fell back, his hands clawing desperately at his burning eyes, the scream that emerged from his twisted lips was inhuman. He zigzagged across the floor, first one way, then back again, his vision blurred and his face red hot.

Jennifer knew she had to move fast, pain or no pain. There wasn't much time. She had to get Amy out of here before this madman regained his sight and resumed his attack. She pushed herself up off the floor. Panicky, she saw that Amy lay in a heap, completely still. Bending down, she dropped the mace and, gaining strength from that mysterious source of adrenaline that allows desperate mothers to lift cars off their dying children, managed to lift her unconscious daughter into her arms and carry her slowly toward the doorway.

As Jennifer staggered down the hall and toward the stairs under her heavy burden, Clay Fowler blindly ran his hands through his desk drawers. The gun. He knew he'd put it into one of these drawers. He had to have that gun. His eyes still sightless, burning, he pulled open each drawer, feeling around inside, until finally his fingers struck cold, hard metal.

*Police officer Isobel Mendez was driving the squad car with her
partner, Caleb Connors, in the passenger seat when the call
came in on the car radio.* The two had been patrolling
Santa Barbara's sun-drenched beachfront all morning, feeling a little lazy on this unusually warm winter day.

The call was the kind every police officer most dreads, a
domestic disturbance. That this one had been called in by a
child made it that much worse. Still, Isobel decided, at least
it was daylight. This one couldn't be as bad as those wife-
battering calls she frequently answered late on a Saturday
night, when the men got all liquored up and started taking
out their week's frustrations on their women.

"We're only a few blocks from there," Isobel said, recog-
nizing the address the 911 dispatcher was reading off her
computer screen. "Tell 'em we'll catch this one."

Caleb quickly radioed in their acceptance of the assign-
ment while Isobel turned on the squad car's siren, executed
a fast U-turn, and headed toward the office building.

As they sped eastward along the palm-tree-lined streets, a
second radio call came in—a woman and child possibly
being stalked by an ex-con who'd broken parole. A Los

Angeles detective had requested immediate police surveillance of the building the ex-con was suspected of staking out.

"That's the same address as our domestic," Isobel said.

"What the hell?" Caleb gripped the door handle and hung on as the black-and-white screeched around the next corner on two wheels. "This one don't feel right." He reached for the microphone and radioed for backup assistance.

Crashing sounds coming from the office where she'd just left Clayton Fowler spurring her to move faster, Jennifer staggered toward the stairwell with Amy's dead weight in her aching arms. Her right ankle turned painfully and she stumbled, nearly dropping the unconscious child. The medium-heeled dress shoes she'd worn for her job interview were treacherous under these circumstances. Jennifer kicked her shoes off and proceeded along the hallway in her stocking feet.

As she reached the stairwell, she was forced to move slower, to keep from falling under the weight of her unaccustomed burden. Amy stirred slightly in her arms. "Amy, sweetie," Jennifer gasped, trying to catch her breath in the acrid air. A pain shot through her side, where Fowler had kicked her ribs.

She made it down one more step, then two. "Amy, wake up, can you?" she pleaded.

The little girl wiggled a bit and Jennifer stopped for a moment, leaning a shoulder against the wall for support.

"Mommmm." The word emerged as a moan.

"Amy, wake up. Please wake up." Jennifer staggered down another step, terrified that she would lose her balance in her slippery stocking feet, that both she and her daughter would plunge to the bottom of the steep staircase.

But the child did not waken. Jennifer had no choice but to trudge downward, making each painful movement slowly, descending one careful step at a time. Finally she reached the first floor hallway. The chemical stench was stronger than ever here; she had trouble catching her breath as she staggered toward the light flooding through the double glass doors at the front of the building.

"Mommy." Amy's eyelids fluttered open. The child's blue eyes were hazy and unfocused at first, her vision blurred, but soon comprehension began to creep back into her gaze. "Mommy, put me down," she said more clearly. "I can walk by myself."

Her heart beating wildly against her bruised ribcage, Jennifer choked in a lungful of rancid air. "Okay, sweetie." She gently lowered Amy to the floor and held on to her until she was certain the child could stand on her own. "We've got to get out of here as fast as we can. The man's coming after us. Do you understand?"

"Uh-huh." Amy moved slowly forward, the palm of her hand sliding along the wall as she walked to steady her.

"Try to move faster, hon. Just run straight out the front door and get as far away from here as you can. Now!" As the child stumbled forward, Jennifer heard distinct thumping sounds coming from overhead. She pushed forward, her hand pressed against the small of Amy's back. Somewhere in the distance, a siren wailed.

"Stop, you fucking bitches! Stop, damn it!"

Jennifer turned and saw Clay Fowler emerge from the bottom of the stairwell. Tears still streamed down his cheeks, and he continually wiped at his eyes with the backs of his hands. He staggered uncertainly, as though he couldn't quite see where he was going, but to Jennifer the man now looked larger and more threatening than ever.

Now, she saw, he had an added weapon; there was a snub-nosed revolver in his right hand.

"Run, Amy!" she shouted, frantically urging the child forward. "Run!"

As Amy reached the glass doors, a police car skidded to a stop in the parking lot. She turned and saw that her mother was now half a dozen feet behind her. The child pushed against the door handle, then hesitated when she saw two police officers emerging from the black-and-white, their guns drawn and pointed straight at her.

"Mom, they got guns!" she cried. "They got *guns!* I'm too scared!"

"Run, sweetie, run outside, quick, before he shoots us. The police won't hurt you." Jennifer's injured ankle turned and gave way again. She stumbled, landing hard on one knee.

"Mom, come with me." The child stood by the door, tears filling her terrified eyes. "Mom, *please!*"

As Jennifer got back on her feet, she saw Clayton Fowler staggering blindly toward her, waving the gun in the air. He was quickly shortening the distance between them. "Amy, run outside *now!*" she ordered. Her ankle collapsed again and she went down.

Amy pushed open the door and ran out into the sunlight, waving her hands high above her head the way she'd seen people do on TV. "Don't shoot," she cried. "Don't shoot me!"

Officer Isobel Mendez lowered her gun and stepped out from behind her door. "Come over here, honey," she called to the little girl. "Nobody's going to hurt you." She reached out and caught Amy in her arms, then thrust the little girl quickly into the backseat of the squad car. "Stay in there and keep your head down. You'll be okay." The cop resumed her position behind the open car door, her gun pointed in the direction of the low beige building.

"My mom's in there and she's hurt real bad," Amy whimpered. "I want my mommy." She lay face down across the car seat and began to weep as if her heart would never mend.

Up again and staggering toward the glass doors, Jennifer tried to ignore the gun in Clay Fowler's hand as he shortened the distance between them. What difference did it make if he shot her or beat her to death? She'd be just as dead either way. Her only hope now was to make it through that doorway before he—or one of the bullets from his gun—caught up with her.

She tried to ignore the pains that kept shooting through her head, through her side, through her throbbing ankle. She had to get away from here! That's all she could afford to think about. The rectangle of sunlight was closer now. Only a few more feet and she'd reach the double glass doors. Beyond them, she knew, lay freedom.

Clay Fowler wiped at his eyes again. They still burned mercilessly—it felt as though that bitch had taken a hot poker to him—but his vision was slowly beginning to clear up. He fought against rising panic. He'd heard a siren a moment ago, and now another one was shrieking somewhere in the distance, its eerie wail growing louder by the second. That fucking kid! His own daughter! What a double-crosser she turned out to be. She'd managed to bring the police down on him, just like her mother.

But Clay Fowler wasn't going to sit still for it this time. He could still make it to South America. They wouldn't be able to touch him there. He could still escape. All he needed was a hostage . . . for only as long as it took him to lose the cops. Once he became Preston Charles Ames III and boarded that plane heading south, he'd be safe. He gripped his gun more tightly and sprinted toward the light.

There she was, the bitch. The woman was within less than an arm's length now, her hands reaching out to push open the glass door. Clay sprang forward and grabbed her around the waist with his left arm. He was careful not to let go of the gun. It was his ticket to freedom now, along with the woman.

Think, Jennifer ordered herself as Fowler grabbed her from behind. Think! She let her muscles go limp to throw her attacker off balance. When she felt his grip around her waist loosen against her dead weight, she quickly tensed her muscles again. Gritting her teeth, she butted her body upward from the knees, thrusting her head against his chin with all her strength. A pain shot downward from the top of her skull, but she felt Fowler's neck snap backward. He released his grip on her. She spun around quickly, bringing her knee upward into his crotch with all the force she could muster.

"Aaaahh!"

There was that inhuman sound again. Jennifer almost forgot her own pains as she realized her blows had hit home. As Fowler stumbled backward, his left hand clutched tightly over his genitals, she threw herself against the glass door. It opened abruptly and she fell knees down onto the pavement outside.

As she stumbled across the parking lot toward the police car, the unmistakable sound of a gunshot rang out. A chunk of blacktop near Jennifer's foot tore loose and flew into the air. She stumbled, then rolled as a second bullet missed her head by inches.

"Over here, lady," a woman's voice called to her.

A third shot rang out, this time from the vicinity of the squad car. As Jennifer scrambled on hands and knees toward safety and her daughter, a second police car screeched into the parking lot.

As Jennifer crawled into the backseat of the squad car with Amy, Fowler crouched in the open doorway of the office building, his vision still blurry and his aim wild. No way would he surrender. Nobody was sending him back to prison. Not Clay Fowler. He wiped his eyes again and took aim at the police car, then slowly squeezed the trigger. His shot was quickly punctuated by the sound of breaking glass as the bullet hit, shattering the squad car's windshield.

The second police car skidded into the parking lot and stopped. Two more officers emerged with guns drawn. Within seconds, a barrage of bullets streaked toward the office building.

On his knees now, Clay propped open the glass door and got off two more shots before one of the officers' bullets struck the pottery urn next to him. In a flash, the ex-con was at the center of a firestorm. Crimson flames mushroomed skyward as the stored gasoline exploded. Flames from the two urns by the doorway flashed across the floor like a tidal wave, searching out the gas-filled cans spaced throughout the first floor. Half a dozen smaller explosions echoed against the sky, one after the other, like a string of giant firecrackers on the Fourth of July.

Outside, police officers Isobel Mendez and Caleb Connors dove for their squad car. Ignoring the windshield's shattered glass, Isobel backed the police vehicle out of the parking lot at top speed as pieces of the building's low black roof flew off, thrust skyward by a heat so intense it scorched the tops of nearby palm trees. At a safe spot a block away, she braked to a stop while Caleb radioed the fire department.

In the backseat of the squad car, a horrified yet relieved Jennifer Bennett held her daughter's tear-streaked face against her chest. "It's okay, sweetheart," she said quietly, gently stroking Amy's hair. "It's okay. We're both safe now."

Clayton Fowler would never again be a threat to anyone.

Chapter

54

⌒

"*Hand me that last piece of cheese on the bottom shelf, will you, Amy?*" Jennifer asked.

Amy took the wedge of leftover cheddar out of the refrigerator and handed it to her mother, who put it into the Igloo cooler with the other refrigerated foods.

"What're we gonna eat for supper?" Amy asked, looking worried. "All our food's packed."

Jennifer slid the cooler's cover closed. "Mr. Hathaway promised to come over and help us unpack this stuff at our new house, and then he'll take us both out for dinner," she said. She checked the kitchen cupboards one last time, to see if anything else that belonged to them remained unpacked, but she found nothing.

"Can we get a pizza?" Amy rubbed a hand across her tummy. "I'm starved."

"We'll see, hon. It's Forrest's treat, so he gets to decide. But if he asks us where we want to go, we can tell him we want pizza."

"Goody, goody, goody."

Jennifer reached over and gently ran a finger along the edge of Amy's face. The skin beneath her freckles still had a slightly yellow cast to it, but it was almost back to its normal color. Only three weeks ago, the child had had a nasty purple bruise there, the result of Clayton Fowler's throwing her against the wall. To look at her now, though, no one would guess the ordeal she'd been through. The marks on her face and legs had nearly disappeared and the night terrors were slowly diminishing.

Jennifer had immediately put Amy back into psychotherapy after the horrors of Santa Barbara, but this time the little girl's counselor was very optimistic. "As horrible as this whole thing was for both of you," the therapist had explained to Jennifer, "it's given Amy a kind of closure with her tragic background. This time, when her father attacked her mother, she was able to be much, much more than one of his victims. She actually helped save both her own and her mother's lives. Amy's a tough little girl, a real survivor. Now she doesn't have to be scared anymore."

"Does this still hurt?" Jennifer asked Amy as she pulled her finger away from the faint yellow mark.

"Uh-uh, just looks icky. I'm fine, Mom, honest," Amy said, sounding as though she really meant it. "'Cept I'm really starved. When do we get to go to our new house?"

"Right now sounds good enough to me," Jennifer told her, picking up the Igloo. "Got all your stuff?"

"I'll go get it." Amy disappeared into the bedroom she would soon be leaving behind.

The house Jennifer had rented was only about six blocks away from the Edgewater Apartment Hotel, in the Sunset Park district of Santa Monica. It was much smaller than the one they'd had in Pacific Palisades—only two bedrooms and one bathroom, and its only view was of the houses across the street—but it would do nicely for the two of them.

Jennifer found that she could hardly stop smiling these days. She felt truly blessed, as though she'd been through fire and emerged as tempered steel. Of course, her body still suffered random aches and pains—her own bones and muscles were taking far longer to heal than her daughter's much younger ones.

But Jennifer—bruises, sprains, bandages, and all—had managed to land a new job, as one of the producers of Channel Three's new local news magazine show. It paid enough for her and Amy to live reasonably well, although the salary was less than she had been paid at *Only in L.A.* She felt fortunate that the producing job was right here in Los Angeles, so Amy wouldn't have to change schools. And the fact that Forrest Hathaway would be living nearby was a nice added bonus.

Even the IRS was no longer a threat. Jennifer had come through her audit with flying colors, not owing an additional cent in taxes or penalties. She'd been so grateful to have that last albatross removed from around her neck that she hadn't even been angry about all the extra work involved in proving her innocence.

Money simply wasn't all that important to Jennifer anymore. She didn't even resent that the money the police found in the burgandy Cadillac would most likely go to Clayton Fowler's sister in Oregon, and not to Amy, who, after all, was no longer Fowler's legal heir. Jennifer didn't want anything from Amy's early life tainting her future.

Amy emerged from her bedroom clutching Raggedy Ann and her green jacket in her arms.

"Is that everything?" Jennifer asked her.

"Yup." Amy grinned broadly. "Let's go, Mom. I want to see how Annie likes our new bedroom."

Jennifer locked the apartment door behind them for the last time.

"Race you to the elevator," Amy shouted. She streaked down the hall without waiting for her mother to accept her challenge.

Jennifer stood there in the hall for a moment with tears in her eyes as she watched her resilient young daughter speed eagerly toward the rest of her life.

Her heart bursting with love and gratitude, Jennifer Bennett called out, "Wait for me, Amy!" Then, still limping slightly, she hurried after her.

≜ HarperPaperbacks *Mysteries by Mail*

Crimson Green by Bruce Zimmerman

A golfer one shot away from capturing the U.S. Open Championship is dead in a sudden hail of gunfire. His caddy, Quinn Parker enters the sleazy world of golf hustlers and gamblers to hunt down a killer whose devotion to golf is on par with his thirst for violence.

Drift Away by Kerry Tucker

Photojournalist Libby Kincaid learns that her friend Andrea has been murdered by the accused killer she had been defending. Libby goes undercover at Andrea's cutthroat law firm and finds herself in the hot seat as she comes close to a murderer.

Homemade Sin by Kathy Hogan Trocheck

When feisty Callahan Garrity of House Mouse Cleaning Service hears of her cousin's murder, she dons a detective cap and does a job on grease and crime in Atlanta.

Parrot Blues by Judith Van Gieson

A chief suspect in the kidnapping of Neil Hamel's client and her rare macaw has expired. To find out more, Neil enters a dangerous game of bird-smuggling and one-upmanship. So far, the only eyewitnesses are parrots—and they're not talking.

The Weaver's Tale by Kate Sedley

It is the 15th century. A man has been murdered, and the brother of a respected citizen hanged for the crime. Months later, the victim turns up alive—only to be murdered a second time. Who is the killer and how it might this all be connected to a nobleman's fancy?

Death in a Strange Country
by Donna Leon

An American is found dead in a Venice canal. Commissario Guido Brunetti probes the case and lands knee-deep in a toxic waste cover-up controlled by the Italian government, the U.S. Army, and the Mafia. Under their watchful eyes Brunetti must decide how far he can go to right a global wrong.